Lasting Love
Sexy
Stories
Collection

VOLUME 5

7 EROTIC SHORT STORIES

SUSAN STAHLS

Publisher's Note: This is a work of fiction. Names,
characters, places, and incidents are a product of
the author's imagination. Locales and public
names are sometimes used for atmospheric
purposes. Any resemblance to actual people, living
or dead, or to businesses, companies, events,
institutions, or locales is completely coincidental.

Lasting Love/ Susan Stahls. -- 1st ed.
Xplicit Press, an imprint of TLM Media LLC

ISBN-13: 978-1-62327-534-1
ISBN-10: 1-62327-534-2
eISBN: 978-1-62327-586-0

Printed in the United States of America

CONTENTS

1 ONE STEP FURTHER

Jessica was getting ready to turn in, checking the locks and turning off the lights. Another Friday night alone, with a good book brought home from the library where she worked. Since her fiancé, Gregory, had abruptly ended their engagement three months earlier, she'd been reluctant to venture back into any kind of dating scene. Her friends kept setting her up with a series of eager, but always lacking, guys. None of them sparked her interest in the least and she wondered if somehow, something had been broken inside of her. So, the Friday nights alone continued.

Turning off the front porch light, she was startled by a knock at the door. She certainly wasn't expecting anyone and took an involuntary step backward. She thought she heard a muffled voice so she turned the porch light back on. Looking through the peephole, she was surprised to see Jake.

Jake was her best friend, someone she'd known since childhood, but hadn't been able to see him in over a year. As a freelance wildlife photographer and cameraman, he was frequently away on assignments for the top nature documentary TV stations. She always looked for his name in the credits when she watched documentaries he'd talked about. They'd kept in touch though, through phone calls, email and text, and even more so since her broken engagement. Jake had seemed more concerned than usual about her, asking if she'd gotten "back in the saddle" and started dating or if she was seeing anyone special. She'd told him to stop being such a mother hen about her dating life.

Jessica undid the locks and chain and opened the door. Before she could even say a word, Jake grabbed her in a bear hug, lifting her off her feet; a typical greeting from him. Over 6 feet tall, he towered over her and had always called her his pocket princess, joking that he could carry her around in his pocket because she was so petite.

"Jake!! What are you doing here?" She barely managed to squeak out the words. Jake set her down, planting a kiss on the top of her head.

"I am sans employment at the moment. The series for Nature wrapped up yesterday so I decided to take a break for a bit. I grabbed the first flight from Queensland, after trekking out of the rainforest. You know, I've been working almost non-stop for the past two years; I think I'm entitled to a vacation. And I wanted to see you. I haven't seen you in ages." Jake grinned down at her. "And... I need to ask you a favor."

"Sure. Come on in. We can't stand on the porch all night, the neighbors might talk." She grabbed one of Jake's bags and led him into the living room. Jess curled up on the couch, her legs tucked beneath her. "So, what's the favor?"

Jake dumped his gear in the corner and sat down on the other end of the couch. Even in sweats and a T-shirt, her blonde hair pulled back in a loose tail, Jake thought Jess looked beautiful, better than he remembered. Her clear, dark blue eyes caught the soft light from the lamp next to the couch, making them glow like sapphires. It was killing him not to lean over and kiss those gorgeous red lips.

"Well, I need a place to stay for a few days. I'd given up my sublet before the Nature series, so I'm also sans apartment. I wanted to ask if I could stay here - just for a few days - only until I get settled again. I think I'm going to stay in Boston, work locally, settle down for a change."

Jake had considered long and hard how to get back into Jessica's life and stay there. He'd been in love with her since college, but he'd never managed to tell her how he felt. She always seemed to be in a series of lackluster relationships since college and he'd been pursuing his dream of traveling as a nature photographer. A couple years ago, he'd finally gotten the courage to tell her his true feelings, but days later, she had announced her engagement to the latest loser. Still, he kept in touch no matter where he was, because he truly cared about Jess and wanted to stay involved in her life.

When she told him some months ago that her engagement had ended, he'd been genuinely sorry for her pain, but also secretly very pleased. He began planning how to create an opportunity for a real relationship with Jess to blossom. He'd broken the lease on his apartment, losing his security deposit, angering his landlord and probably putting a ding in his credit rating. He'd also turned down a very lucrative new gig because it would have taken him to Southeast Asia and lasted at least six months.

It had taken three long months to wrap up his current assignment and all the while he'd kept in pretty much constant contact with Jess. He knew she wasn't seeing anyone, or even casually dating, and while he didn't want to pressure her, he didn't want this perfect opportunity to slip away. Hence, the little white lie about losing the sublet and not having any job prospects. He did feel a tiny bit bad for it, but reasoned true love could handle a fib or two. Chances are Jess would never even know the truth.

"Of course. You can bunk in the spare room," Jessica said. "The bed's made up and I'll get you fresh towels." As she showed him the way to the bedroom, Jake grabbed his overnight bag and followed her. She turned on the bedside lamp and turned down the quilt and sheets. "There you go. You can use the bathroom across the hall.

Jake decided this was not the moment to

declare his feelings, even though his body ached to hold her. Hugging her earlier had begun a cascade of physical and emotional sensations that had yet to subside. Even the innocent touch of her hand on his gave him shivers. He felt giddy, like a teenager. He knew she had no idea how he felt and he didn't want to rush things. So, rather than the passionate kiss he longed for, he settled for a chaste kiss on the cheek before she left the room, and for a bed he'd be sleeping in alone... but hopefully not for long. His fantasies of his first night with Jessica, exploring every inch of her body, seeing her lying naked beneath him, eyes closed... lips parted... the sounds of pleasure she'd make... thrusting himself inside of her... satisfying her, and himself, over and over... would just have to wait for another time.

Jessica smelled freshly brewing coffee before she was even awake enough to realize why. "Jake," she thought sleepily, "he must be used to getting up at the crack of dawn."

She searched the closet for her one and only robe and pulled it over her silk nightie as she walked barefoot down the hall to the kitchen. She was looking forward to having a good conversation with Jake, learning where he'd been and what adventures he'd had since they'd last had the chance to really catch up. She was expecting good stories and lots of laughs.

What she wasn't expecting was her reaction to seeing Jake standing in her kitchen, wearing nothing but a pair of well-washed gray sweatpants that left little to the imagination. The last time she'd seen Jake without a shirt had been sometime after high school, when they'd gone swimming at the lake. She didn't remember him looking like this. He'd always been sort of a skinny, nerdy kid with a camera. He now looked entirely masculine and not the least bit nerdy.

He was standing at the counter, his back to her, his dark wavy hair still damp from the shower. Her eyes took in the deeply tanned, well-muscled shoulders, traveling down his back to the taper of his narrow waist, which disappeared into the drawstring waist of his sweats where they hung on his narrow hips. The cotton pants also hugged what appeared to be a very muscular and very tight backside. She suddenly wondered if there was a tan line anywhere and had the overwhelming urge to untie the drawstring of his sweats, pull them down and take a peek.

Startled by that rogue thought, she coughed self-consciously. Jake turned, presenting an impressive view of a smoothly muscled chest and perfectly flat stomach. Completely flustered now, and rather weak at the knees, Jessica walked toward the end of the island counter and pulled out a stool. This was not the Jake she remembered, at least physically. And this certainly was not her usual reaction to him. What was wrong with her?

"Hey, kiddo. It's about time you got up. Here, have some coffee, you look like you need it." Jake placed a mug on the counter and leaned over to plant a kiss on the top of her head. She felt his warmth and inhaled his scent, a combination of her shower gel over the top of something deep, rich and very exciting; his own clean masculine scent. Again, she was confused by her own reaction. She felt a warmth in the pit of her stomach she'd never felt before and she busied herself with cream and sugar to cover her confusion.

"Um, yeah. You're an early riser, I guess." She struggled to find words and wished almost desperately Jake would go stand by the sink. But instead he grabbed his coffee mug and sat down directly opposite her, their knees almost touching beneath the narrow peninsula.

She was completely at a loss to explain why being near Jake, whom she had known since almost forever, was suddenly making her stomach do flips and her mind turn to mush. She didn't understand this reaction. He'd always been her friend, her best friend. He'd been her confidant, her sounding-board, her shoulder to cry on more times than she could count. But now the sight of those shoulders was sending shivers down her spine. The hug last night had been his usual greeting, but even that felt charged with sexual energy. Why the change? Who had changed: him or her?

"Yeah, well, I've got a line on an apartment and a short-term assignment, so I wanted to get an early start. I was hoping you'd be up before I left, so I could say good-bye." He took a swallow of coffee and gazed at Jessica across the counter. She could feel his eyes lingering over her face and traveling down her neck; he seemed to be drinking her in. She felt herself blush and practically dove back into her coffee mug as a distraction. But underneath her confusion, she felt a burgeoning sense of confidence; feelings she thought were long-dead were coming back to life. She sensed she held a certain power over Jake. And that sense of power excited her.

Wanting to test her new-found idea, she shifted on the stool, shrugging her shoulders and allowing her robe to slip down, exposing one bare shoulder and the top of her left breast, visible through the peach-colored silk of her nightgown. She felt her nipple becoming hard and that pleasurable feeling triggered a small tremor, starting deep within her, that shook her slightly. She knew Jake would get a glimpse of one breast covered by silk, with the outline of her nipple pushing against the delicate fabric. She wondered what kind of reaction this might bring from him.

As Jake sipped his coffee, he sensed Jessica's confusion and was a bit amused. He'd had no illusions she'd share the depth of his feelings, either romantically or physically, at least not right now. Nor did he expect her to jump into his arms, or into his bed, although he wouldn't have turned her down. But he didn't expect her to be so disarmed by his presence.

She was even lovelier than he remembered; her beauty enhanced by a becoming blush and sexily tousled hair. She apparently wasn't used to having overnight guests; her short nighty was a silky material barely covered by a robe, which had slid from one shoulder, the outline of her full breasts clearly visible through the garment. Her slender, shapely legs were exposed and he could catch an occasional glimpse of dainty painted toenails as she swung her foot back and forth beneath the island counter, occasionally brushing his leg; the effect of those perfectly painted toes was more than he expected.

Jake was rather glad he was sitting down at the moment; certain parts of his anatomy were reacting on their own to her heady scent and the view of one barely concealed breast, which had escaped the confines of her robe. Although the swell of her skin remained partially covered by a swath of thin material, he could make out the outline of one nipple, erect and hard either from the cool air or from excitement pushing against the silk. Jake mused that there was nothing sexier than a luscious breast and perky nipple playing peek-a-boo through silk. It was so tempting to just reach across the counter and rub his thumb across that nipple, cup that perfect breast in his hand. He shifted on the kitchen stool as he felt himself stiffen even more. He'd have to wear something a little more substantial than his old sweatpants, if this was going to be his reaction every time he was in the same room with Jess.

"So, a job? And an apartment? That was fast," Jess said. Jake thought he sensed a hint of disappointment in her voice. He tore his eyes reluctantly from that perfect breast and answered Jess.

"I've got contacts and made some calls this morning. Besides, I can't take advantage of your hospitality forever, can I?" He swallowed the last of his coffee. "I've got to get going, my first appointment is in 30 minutes."

As he got off the stool, Jess saw an unmistakable bulge through the thin material of Jake's sweatpants. Her theory was right; it was suddenly apparent to her that she was not the only one feeling something out of the ordinary. The realization that she could elicit that kind of reaction from Jake and that maybe he did desire her made her almost giddy with feminine power.

As Jake went to the spare room to change, Jess rinsed her cup in the sink. She wanted time to think about how she suddenly felt, what this could mean, the possibilities it presented. As she walked past the spare room, lost in thought, the door popped open and Jake collided with her in the hall. Jess stumbled and suddenly found herself pressed against Jake, who was still wearing only his sweatpants. His arms automatically went around her waist and her hands instinctively went to his bare chest. She found her balance in Jake's arms.

"Whoa, sorry," Jake said. "Didn't mean to run you down." He looked down at Jess, who had gone completely still in his arms. Her lips were parted as she looked up at him. Jake could feel the warmth of her skin, the weight of her breasts pressing against him, her still-firm nipples brushing against his chest through the silk of her gown. He inhaled her intoxicating scent and the perfume of her hair.

Without conscious thought, he pulled her closer, his hands spread across her back, aching to cup her sweet round ass in his hands and pull her against his cock, which stiffened again as it pressed against her warmth. Jess could feel his heat, feel him pressing the increasing hardness of himself against her belly. She slid her arms around his neck and tipped her head back, closing her eyes, another tremor shaking her body. Jake bent his head to her lips and kissed her, a kiss he'd longed for more times than he could remember. One hand slid up to cup that perfect breast, its weight and size filling his hand. Jess moaned as his thumb slid across the hard nipple, his earlier wish fulfilled. He felt an involuntary shiver run through her.

A long moment passed with no sound except the sound of their breathing and the pounding of their hearts.

"I'm going to be late." Jake broke the kiss and the embrace, his voice husky. Reluctantly he let go of Jess, setting his hands on her shoulders. "Now isn't the time for this." Before he could change his mind, he walked back to his room and closed the door behind him. He leaned back against the door, his thoughts a tangled mess of desire and longing, love, hesitation – and a healthy dose of plain old lust. More than anything, he wanted to open the door, find Jess and take her wherever she was: in the hall, in her room, the shower, even bend her over the kitchen counter if need be. Instead, he grabbed a towel and went to take another shower, a cold one this time.

Jess made her way to her room, her lips still hot from Jake's kiss, feeling the warmth and promised passion that kiss had held, her body still trembling from his heat and power. She had an almost overwhelming desire to run her hands over her own body, to feel her own breasts and nipples, as Jake had, to recreate the feeling of his hands on her flesh. Instead, she headed to the master bathroom, thinking a cold shower might be more appropriate.

The phone rang as Jessica was cleaning up the last of her lunch dishes and puttering around the kitchen. It was Jake.

"Hey, Jessie, I got the job." Jess could hear the excitement in his voice.

"Great," she said. "And the apartment?"

"Well, not so great on that," Jake said. "Someone beat me to it by 20 minutes. Guess you're stuck with me for a little longer. And to pay you back, I'm bringing home dinner. I don't want you cooking for me. I'll pick up something from Chinatown, okay? You still like lemon chicken and yang chow rice, right?"

"Yes, but..." she started to protest. "No argument, Jess. I'm serious," Jake said with mock sternness. "I'll see you about 5:30."

A while later, Jessica heard Jake at the front door and went to meet him. He had his hands full of Chinese take-out containers and the aroma was amazing. They both shared a love of Chinese and had enjoyed many good conversations over lots of Chinese food.

Jake followed Jess into the dining room, where she had set the table and lit candles. "I said you didn't need to do anything special, Jess, really. I feel like I'm taking advantage of you enough."

"Dishes and candles aren't special, they're just nice." Jess blushed and hoped Jake didn't notice. Candles and china were far from the norm in her life; paper plates and eating in front of the TV had been her habit of late. But she had felt the need to make this a special meal. "Let's eat, I'm starving."

During the meal, they had the conversation Jess was expecting. Jake entertained her with tales of adventure, exotic locations, and all the exciting details that she craved. Eventually, they moved from the dining room to the living room, bringing along a bottle of wine and two of the candles for the coffee table. Everything seemed normal, like the way she remembered. No one brought up that morning's steamy encounter in the hall or the seemingly shared feelings they had experienced. Jess wondered if she'd imagined the whole thing.

As they drank wine and the candles burned down, the conversation slowed. Jake sat back on the couch, his head on the backrest, closing his eyes. Jess looked over and realized he must be exhausted from his long flight, his early day out scouting jobs and apartments, and from the effects of the wine. He looked like he was asleep.

Jess reached over to take the wine glass from his hand. As she touched him, without opening his eyes, he said, "I'm not asleep. I'm enjoying the sensation of sitting still, full of good food and wine, and in the company of a beautiful woman." He leaned forward and set the glass on the coffee table. He turned to face her, moving closer on the couch.

Jess sensed that same electricity between them again. She felt a deep sense of heat start low in her stomach, spreading outward, and she didn't think it was the wine or the spicy Chinese food. Jake reached out and tucked a strand of hair behind Jessica's ear, then cradled her cheek in his hand. Jess again felt confusion at her feelings; this was her best friend, but somehow he'd become this incredibly sexy man, exciting her in ways she didn't think she could feel about him, or it had seemed, anyone. But she also felt powerful, confident and in control of herself. And she liked feeling that way.

This should be all wrong, except that it all felt completely right.

Jess leaned into his hand, turning her head and kissing his palm. Jake pulled her to him and kissed her gently on the lips. Jess shifted on the couch, moving closer to Jake. As they came together, their kiss deepened. Jake gently probed Jessica's lips with his tongue and she opened her mouth to him. She made a small noise deep in her throat; she felt like she was melting inside.

Jake sensed she was becoming aroused and that excited him. But he wasn't sure if it was all due to being kissed or the effects of the wine. He knew she'd had her heart broken and her confidence shattered by the failed engagement. He didn't want to push her, but he also knew once he started, he'd have a hard time holding back. His desire for her had been the driving force bringing him back to Boston. Now that she was here, in his arms, all smooth skin and luscious curves, he wasn't sure he could remain in control of his own body. The last thing he wanted was to jeopardize any part of his plan at starting a relationship by coming on too strong.

Jake was brought back from his thoughts by Jess's more insistent kisses. His body was reacting on its own again, his jeans pulling tight across his stiffening cock, his breathing faster. Every physical part of him was telling him to press on, but his mind was telling him to back off.

As hard as it was to do, Jake gently pushed Jess away. The puzzled look on her face almost made him rethink his decision, but he knew this was not the time to give in to his lust. More than anything, he did not want to scare her off by this sudden change in their relationship. He didn't want to give his plans away too soon. He needed her to catch up with his desire.

"Jess, I think we need to slow down. We've both had a lot to drink and like you said, I'm tired. We're not thinking clearly."

"Okay... but..." Jess really was confused now. Had she misread all of Jake's signals? Was she more drunk than she realized? Or was she really just desperate for sex and willing to seduce her best friend for a night in bed.

"I think we should call it a night and talk in

the morning, okay?"

Jake stood, pulling Jess up by her hands. She stood uncertainly. "Well, goodnight," she said softly. She stretched up and kissed Jake on the cheek. "See you in the morning."

Jake watched her walk down the hall. His mind was spinning, but he thought he was doing the right thing. Except that it felt all wrong.

Jess closed her bedroom door and wondered again if she was making all this up. She got undressed for bed, slipping on a fresh silk nightie. She crawled in bed, punching the pillows and pulling up the blankets, then pushing them down, tossing and turning. Her mind was whirling; her body still craved contact with Jake.

Jake closed his door, leaned his forehead against it and wondered if he'd really managed to screw up this whole plan. He'd thought he had it all figured out, but it seemed to be a big mess. He stripped off his shirt and jeans, kicking them in the corner, and crawled naked between the sheets. I'm going to spend my whole life sleeping alone, he thought. Might as well start tonight. He turned over, rearranged the pillows, punching them with a little more aggression than he intended. He was still hard, still aching for Jess. Aside from jacking off, which seemed unappealing and not satisfying in the least, there wasn't much he could do at the moment to satisfy that particular need. He wasn't in the mood for another cold shower.

He must have dozed off; he didn't remember hearing his door open, but abruptly he realized Jess was sitting on the edge of his bed.

"Hey," he said sleepily, "I'm..." He started to sit up, framing an apology, but she put a hand on his chest and pushed him flat.

"You listen for a change and let me do the talking," she said, in a much more assertive voice than he ever remembered hearing from her. He smiled in the semi-darkness, lacing his hands behind his head and settling back on the pillow. "Yes, ma'am," he said playfully.

"I'm being serious. Something is happening here. I know you feel it and I know I'm not making this up. And I'm not drunk. I'm not quite sure what or why, but I know that whatever it is, I like it," Jess said, her words spilling out in a rush.

"For a long time, I've thought that something... that some part of me was broken, that I couldn't feel love... or lust... or whatever other women felt. And it made me sad. Every relationship was the same; nice guys but no spark. When I got engaged to Greg, I thought it would make that part of our relationship come to life, fix my broken parts, but it didn't. Maybe that's why he broke our engagement, I don't know. But with you, now, it's all come alive... I've come alive. I feel things I've never felt before, or knew I could feel, and not just the physical part. And I want to keep feeling like this. I think you feel the same way, or at least some parts of you feel the same way, because I've noticed they seem to work just fine. Your cock isn't broken, from what I've seen." A teasing tone had come into her voice as she trailed her hand down his chest, resting her palm on the flat plane of his stomach, below his navel, sending a thrill through him.

Jake wasn't quite sure how to react to this new version of Jessica. She'd never told him any of this; this was a far more personal revelation than she'd ever made. He'd also never heard her use the word 'cock.' Somehow, hearing that word come from Jessica's lips, and used to describe him, was almost as exciting as her warm hand just inches away from his cock. He pushed himself up on his elbows. He knew his idea of returning to her had been the right plan. Things seemed to be falling into place.

"Jess," he said, "This is all new to me too. I mean, how I'm feeling. You know I love you; I've always loved you as my best friend. But seeing you now, this time, something is different. You're right. Maybe we've grown up, maybe it's fate finally opening our eyes to what our relationship could be, or really is. And yes, I want this to continue just as much as you do."

Jess leaned over Jake, lightly running her tongue over his lips. "I want this... and you too." She continued exploring his lips with her tongue; he opened his mouth and she met his searching tongue with hers. Tongue play quickly turned to deep kissing, their tongues continuing to explore and probe. Jake tried sitting up again, and again, Jess pushed him back. She traced her way back up his chest with her hand, stopping to circle one nipple with a forefinger, and then leaned down to trace the same circle on his now-erect nipple with the tip of her tongue.

Jake gave up and gave in, he stopped trying to sit up and let the new assertive Jessica have her way. His last conscious thought, before his mind gave in to the sheer pleasure her tongue was creating at the moment, was that if he let her take the lead, maybe it would make it easier for him to become a part of her life.

Jess had started kissing a trail down his chest. Her tongue circled his navel, darting in and out. Jake had never felt such amazing sensations; apparently Jessica had a hidden talent. He ran his hand through her hair, pulling it back from her face, then reached over and turned on the bedside lamp. Jess looked up, startled. "I want to watch you," he said, his voice rough with passion. "I want to see what you look like when we make love."

During Jessica's explorations of his body with her tongue, Jake's cock had taken on a life of its own. Jess could feel it pressing against her through the sheet. She raised her head and placed her hand on top of the sheet, Jake raising his hips in response, pressing himself against her hand. She gently rubbed his cock through the material, sending waves of pleasure through him. He reached out and cupped her breasts, again rubbing his thumbs across the nipples, the areolas puckering and the nipples growing harder. He pinched her nipples, rolling them gently between his thumb and index finger. Jess caught her breath, arching her back, pressing against his hands, the sensation taking her by surprise; an exquisite mixture of pain and pleasure. She felt what seemed like a small explosion go off low in her stomach, sending warmth flooding her body, making her whole body shiver.

Jess pulled the sheet back, looking down at Jake's cock in the soft light of the bedside lamp. Watching Jess looking at him made Jake's cock swell even more. He was almost completely hard; the touch of her hand on his flesh would bring him fully erect, something he'd like to beg for at this moment. But he let her stay in control, not wanting to break the spell.

Jess leaned forward, hands on either side of him, shifting her weight on the bed and straddling him with her legs. He longed for to feel her body against his, feel those silky thighs against his hips, but she teased him by keeping her body above his, only her breasts lightly brushing his chest. The sensation of the silk fabric between them, rubbing against her sensitive nipples was making her wet, making her pussy throb with pleasure and anticipation.

"Jess..." Jake's voice was husky with passion. She sensed he wanted—needed—physical contact. She shifted her weight and sat up. Jake grabbed the edge of her nightie and tugged it up; Jess pulled it over her head and dropped it on the floor. She reached down to his cock, taking the shaft in her soft, warm hand, gently stroking it, circling the tip with her thumb. Jake closed his eyes and a deep moan escaped his lips. "Jess... please..." he begged roughly.

He grabbed Jessica's hips, pushing her down toward his now throbbing cock, wanting nothing more than to bury the whole length of his shaft in her warm, wet pussy with one thrust. Jess, however, had a different idea.

She spread her legs more, lowering herself just enough to allow the crown of his cock to touch the softness of her pussy, to feel the warmth and wetness. And she was very wet now. She rubbed the tip of his cock slowly back and forth against her wet and swollen slit, then circled it around her clit, teasing herself as much as she teased Jake, his hands now finding her naked breasts, kneading them, crushing them, still moaning her name. They both caught their breath, twin moans of pleasure escaping them. Jess increased the pressure of Jake's cock against her clit, rocking her hips as she masturbated herself with the sensitive skin of the tip of his penis. He continued fondling her breasts, pinching the tight pink nipples, squeezing and stroking the firm globes in his hands.

Finally Jake forced Jessica's hips down again, and she willingly let him. She was ready to feel him inside her. She was slick and hot and suddenly wanted all of him, all at once. "Now, Jake," she gasped. "Now, and hard. Fuck me hard."

Jake was more than ready to give her all of his throbbing shaft, her words again exciting him almost as much as the prospect of

21

actually fucking her. As Jess spread her legs even more and brought her body down, Jake thrust his rock hard cock up, meeting her with a force that took both of their breaths away. They held still for a moment. Jake was groaning with pleasure at the sudden feeling of his cock surrounded by her wetness and heat in that velvety pussy. She was fully aware of every inch of Jake's cock buried to the hilt in her, filling her completely. "God, Jess, I never thought you would feel like this, you're amazing."

Jess looked down at Jake and saw in his eyes the mirror of her own feelings. They both knew this was the right thing, at the right time. There was no going back, and neither wanted to. They had crossed the line, taken their relationship one step further.

Jess worked her hips in a circle for a moment, grinding her sensitive clit against Jake, feeling his hard length move inside her, watching him watch her. Jake rocked his hips back, sliding his cock out of Jess, then slowly sliding it back into that delicious dark honey hole, loving the feeling of her slick juices on him, catching the musk of her, of them together.

They continued fucking each other, finding that perfect rhythm that kept them on the edge but not pushing them over, wanting this new sensation to last. Jake reached down and rubbed a thumb across Jessica's swollen clit, causing her to shiver with increased pleasure, to rock her hips forward to meet his touch. He continued rubbing her wet clit, sliding his fingers back and forth. He could feel the shaft of his cock with his fingers, stretching her pussy; he watched it slide in and out of her, covered in her juices. He could see her clit in the soft glow of the lamp and could feel it growing harder beneath his wet fingers. He pinched it softly between is fingers, pulling it gently, eliciting a sharp cry from Jess. He continued to knead and roll her clit, sensing this was a new sensation for Jess, but something she clearly enjoyed.

Her rhythm changed then, became faster, harder, her breath now coming in ragged gasps. Jake responded by grabbing her hips, digging his heels into the bed for leverage and thrusting his cock more deeply into her, matching her rhythm, letting her set the pace. He sensed she was close to orgasm and he longed to watch her, to see the whole experience play out across her body, if he could hold back long enough to let her come first. He could feel his balls tensing but concentrated instead on watching her face, head thrown back, eyes closed, and mouth open, breath coming in short gasps. With one hand she found her own clit, pinching it and rubbing it in time with Jake's thrusts; the other hand pinched the nipple of her left breast.

Jess was lost in a world of sensations. Jake's cock filled her inside, stretching her and pushing further into her than she thought possible. His fingers had done magical things to her clit, giving her intense sensations she had never felt before. She needed to recreate that sensation when he grabbed her hips and she replaced his fingers with her own, rolling and rubbing her own clit, just as Jake had done, feeling it hard beneath her fingers, wet with her own juices. She kneaded and rolled the nipple of her breast with the other hand; both her swollen clit and rigid nipples sending waves of sensations through her body.

Jake held himself back, mesmerized by what he was seeing, watching Jess take control of her body, of this experience. He felt her pussy tighten, felt her body begin to fall slightly out of rhythm and knew she was on the verge of her orgasm. He tilted his hips, looking for the perfect angle to get her off, and found it. She suddenly called out his name, arched her back, her body racked by a series of increasingly intense spasms. Jake could feel her orgasm ripping through her, feel her pussy contracting around his aching cock, could see the rush of pleasure on her face. He wanted nothing more than to join her, to shoot his load in her but watching her come was more than he had ever imagined. He did not want to take his pleasure until she was almost spent.

Jake felt Jessica's orgasm release a hot rush of juice, flooding over his cock and onto his balls. That sent him over the edge. With a grunt and a final deep thrust, he began to shoot his load into Jessica, mixing the first spurt of his own hot juices with hers. He felt her respond to his orgasm, settling her weight on his body, forcing his cock even further into her wetness, his balls rubbing against her sweet ass. His body took over then, his hips rapidly thrusting his spurting cock into Jessica's wet pussy, pumping his cum deep into her.

Jake looked up at Jess, her eyes watching his face. His balls were still contracting, his cock pulsing inside her, moving on its own, pumping out the last of his hot cum, still anchored deep in Jess's pussy.

"Don't move," he said, as Jess shifted her weight off of him. "Come here." He reached for her, hugging her to his chest, his cock still inside her warmth. "Let me hold you."

She leaned forward, resting her head on his shoulder, his arms around her back. They were both slick with sweat, both spent and satisfied. Eventually they grew cold in the night air. Jake eased Jess off of his now relaxed cock, turned off the lamp, pulled up the blankets and snuggled her against him. He realized she had drifted off to sleep. He gently kissed her forehead, brushing a strand of hair from her face. He lay back, marvelling at the change that had come over her, and him, tonight. He hoped this was to be the beginning of their new relationship.

Jake woke slowly, not quite sure of his surroundings. Jess was lying next to him, and it all came back in a rush. He was aware of the musky smell of their lovemaking and also became aware he was sporting a semi-erect morning hard-on.

Jess lay curled with her back to him. He reached down and stroked his cock, feeling it come to life. He leaned forward and kissed Jessica's bare shoulder, softly using his tongue to trail a path up to her neck. She stirred in her sleep. Jake continued to kiss her neck and nibble her earlobe.

Jess woke to movement in the bed. She sensed more than felt that Jake was awake. Her suspicions were confirmed when she felt him kissing her shoulder and nibbling her ear. She took a deep breath and reached a hand up to fondle his cheek, smiling with her eyes closed. She was drowsy but awake, the memory of last night coming back to her. She lay quietly as Jake moved closer to her.

His cock was now fully hard. He slid one arm beneath Jess's shoulders and one over her hips, pulling her to him, cradling her against his chest and stomach. She was pliant in his arms, content to let him take the lead this morning. He rolled his hips forward, his cock sliding into the warm space between Jess's upper thighs, the skin almost as soft as he remembered her pussy being the night before.

Jess pushed her hips back into Jake, causing him to feel a delicious friction as his cock rubbed against the soft skin of Jess's legs. He pulled back, gently pushing his cock back and forth between her legs, slowly increasing the speed.

Jess rocked her hips back and forth in time to Jake's thrusts. His cock rode higher on her leg, sliding between the lips of her slit, which had become increasingly wet. She reached her hand between her legs, feeling the head of Jake's cock as he thrust forward. She placed her palm over his penis, forcing it further between the lips of her cunt, causing the shaft to rub over her clit.

Jake felt her hand pressing him closer to her musky warmth. The combination of her hand and her wet slickness made him moan. "Oh, yeah Jess. You're so hot, so wet and so soft. I want to fuck you hard. I want you now."

Jess tried to turn toward Jake but he held her firm. "No, stay like this. Hold still." He pulled his cock from between her legs, tilted his hips and with his hand, guided himself into her hot, wet slit. As he thrust forward, Jess shifted her hips back, raising her leg and using her hand to help guide Jake's cock home.

"Jake, oh, my God, yes. Fuck me, fuck me hard." Jess's breath was coming in short gasps. Jake ran his hand up Jess's flat stomach, over the mound of her breasts, finding her erect nipples, rolling them beneath the palm of his hand. Jess rolled back against Jake's chest, allowing him to thrust deeper into her, feel his balls against the round curve of her ass. He curved his back, putting more of his cock into her, her pussy taking all of him. "Feel me in you, feel how hard I am. It's all for you Jess."

Jake held Jess against his chest, his hand cupping one breast, his other hand moving down her smooth stomach to her slit, his fingers sliding between them. He found her clit, drawing her wetness from her cunt up over that little button, rubbing it with his fingers, feeling it grow harder beneath his touch and occasionally feeling the shaft of his cock against his own fingers, sliding in and out of Jess.

Jess moaned deep in her throat, turning her head to receive Jake's kiss, his tongue finding hers. She was totally in Jake's control, literally in his hands. She began moving her hips in time to his thrusts, feeling his heat and taking all of him with each thrust. She enjoyed the sensation of him behind her, his cock filling her from a different angle. And she was content to let him take the lead after dominating him last night.

Jake was lost in the amazing feeling of his cock in Jessica's hot, tight pussy. The swell of her sweet ass against his stomach was incredible, all soft, warm skin. Jess raised her leg a little higher; there was a momentary tangle of limbs as she reached down between her legs and found Jake's balls. At her touch, he broke their kiss with a moan, burying his head in her neck, his breath coming in ragged gasps. Her hand on his balls, his cock in her pussy was pure heaven. He felt his balls tighten in anticipation of his orgasm.

His thrusts became faster, his back curving more, his cock taking over and acting on its own. He hugged Jess to him harder, felt her tense beneath him and realized she must be close to her own orgasm as well. He pulled on her clit, rubbing it harder between his fingers. She cried out, her head back.

"Too hard?" he asked, alarmed. "Am I hurting you?"

"No. Harder... do that harder," was Jess's reply. Jake again was pleasantly shocked by Jess and he complied with her request. He stroked and rubbed Jess's hard clit in time with his own thrusts, feeling her pussy begin to contract, and felt her breathing coming faster. He could hold back no longer, and his cock exploded inside Jess, his hot load filling her. At the same moment, Jess arched back against him, her own orgasm ripping through her. Both of them let out sounds of pleasure; Jake a deep grunt as his cock pumped into her, Jess almost a scream. Jake held her, feeling her body tremble in his arms, feeling the walls of her pussy contract against him, the last of his load pumping into her.

Thcy lay spent in each other's arms, slowing recovering and eventually moving slightly apart. Jess turned to look at· Jake, reached up to stroke his face. "That was amazing."

Jake kissed her forehead. "No, you're amazing. And, not to completely kill the afterglow, I'm starving. We need breakfast. I'll meet you in the kitchen."

Jessica punched him lightly in the arm. "You're such a romantic. I'm going to take a quick shower."

When Jess came into the kitchen after her shower, Jake was making coffee, again in his gray sweats. This time Jess knew there was no tan line and if she felt the urge, she could undo the drawstring and tug them down.

"Hey, babe. Coffee will be done in a minute.

I think there's a message on your answering machine. I left this number yesterday on one of the applications. The manager wanted a local contact number. I hope you don't mind."

"No, that's fine. I'll check the machine." Jess hit play on the answering machine. The message was brief: "This message is for Jake Wheeler. Your application for the apartment on Newbury is on hold until we receive an explanation why the lease was broken at your last listed residence. Please return the call within 24 hours. Thank you."

Jake stood on the other side of the counter, sliding a mug of coffee toward her.

"Wait. I thought you lost your sublet, not that you broke the lease? Which is it?" Jess frowned up at Jake.

"Well, I—I broke the lease."

"I'm confused. Why would you break the lease on a perfectly good apartment, and lose money too, just to come here, to tell me you have no place to stay, when you didn't even have a job lined up yet?"

"Jess, you're making more of this than there really is. I left my old apartment to come to Boston, and why isn't important. I have no place to stay, and I thought of you. I'm not trying to hide anything from you. There is no plan behind this."

"Who said anything about a plan? Are you telling me you planned this, planned to show up here pretending to need a place to stay, just to seduce me? Is what you said last night true, or just a part of the 'plan?'"

"Jess, you're overreacting. It's just a misunderstanding of terms, that's all."

"Jake, you've never been a good liar, so don't start now. I don't know what game you're playing, but I don't find it amusing." She turned and stalked down the hall.

Jess slammed the door. She sensed Jake moving about in the rest of the apartment. She contemplated asking him to leave but in her heart she couldn't bring herself to do that, no matter how mad she was or how used she felt at the moment. Jake had done things in the past that hurt her, but never with malicious intent. He'd taken Chelsea Granger to the prom, even though he knew Jess had wanted him to take her. But that was high school; they were adults now. Maybe she was overreacting. Could he really care about her that much, to give up basically everything and come to her? Or did he really have a big plan that was about nothing more than getting her into bed?

She didn't know what to think, and to make matters worse, now she didn't even have her best friend to talk to about it, and it was her best friend she wanted. It was making her head hurt. In frustration, she flung herself down on her bed.

Jake didn't know where to go. He wanted to talk to his best friend, except his best friend was what he wanted to talk about, and now she was mad at him, with good reason. He'd screwed up the whole thing. He paced back and forth in the kitchen, running his hands through his hair. Then he tried pacing in the living room, and then paced up and down the hall. Finally, in frustration, he decided to go for a walk. He went to his room and pulled on more appropriate clothes for a stomp around the block.

Jess heard the front door close. She went to the kitchen and got a glass of water. She sat down on the couch, pulling the afghan off the back and wrapping it around her. She was chilly. She felt cold on the inside. It felt like she was hollow and a wind was blowing through her. As much as she felt in some way used or taken advantage of, in her heart of hearts, she didn't think Jake meant to hurt her.

Jake walked along the sidewalk, hands in the pockets of his jacket, his mind in turmoil. He thought everything was going according to his plan, a plan which never included hurting Jess in any way. He only wanted the best for both of them. He believed they belonged to each other.

He eventually made his way back, hoping Jess had calmed down and was willing to listen to him. He found her sitting at the kitchen counter, sipping a fresh cup of coffee. He walked over and poured himself a cup.

"Are you still mad at me?" he asked. He sat down across from her at the counter, in the same spot they were in just yesterday morning. So much had changed between them since then.

"No." Jessica sipped on her coffee.

"You're not? What changed? I thought you were ready to kick me out not long ago." Jake took a sip of coffee, thinking this may work out yet.

"Well, you had another phone call. The Natural History channel called. They wanted to see if you would reconsider that Southeast Asia job. I told them you had reconsidered and now decided to accept their offer. Oh, and they offered you a larger salary as well. Seems like things worked out quite well for you." Jess slipped off the stool and put her coffee cup in the sink.

"Wait, you did what? You told them I'd take the job? I don't want that job; I want to stay here in Boston, with you." Jess eyed him from across the room, her arms folded across her chest. "I love you, Jess." There was nothing else he could think to say. "I've loved you longer than I can remember, not only as a friend, but I really love you. I am in love with you, Jess." He moved toward her, stood before her. "Jess, you mean more to me than anything, including any job. I was offered that job, but turned it down to be here with you. I want a relationship with you."

Jess didn't know what to say. She wanted to believe Jake; she wanted what happened over the past days to be real. Maybe she had misunderstood Jake, maybe she was overreacting. She knew she was confused but she also knew she did want something close to what Jake was talking about.

"Jake. This has been the best weekend of my life. I've felt things, both physically and emotionally, that I thought I could never feel. And I loved that. But I've also been very confused. If you're looking to take our relationship to another level, I'm willing to try that. But I don't think it was fair to either of us or our futures to try and jump start a relationship by telling little white lies or trying to force the situation on me."

Jake had been holding his breath, convinced Jess was going to toss him from her apartment, and from her life. But her words made sense. She continued.

"How about this: you take the job and we try this relationship. They said there was also a short-term assignment in the Maldives. Although a long-distance relationship would present some challenges, I also think facing those challenges in a beautiful tropical setting could make all the difference in the world. I'm willing to give that a try if you are."

Jake pulled Jessica into his arms. "I think you're right. I pushed this on you. And that wasn't fair. I'll take the short-term assignment, you can come along and we can start this over the right way, in a tropical setting. I'll make long, slow love to you under a beautiful full moon on a white sand beach, the warm ocean lapping your toes...."

Jess smiled up at Jake, a smile playing about her mouth. "That, Jake, I will take you up on." She wrapped her arms around his neck, turning her face to his. "But first, let's go make up. One of the benefits of a relationship is make-up sex."

Jake grinned down at Jessica. "You, my dear, have a completely dirty side I never knew about. I think I like this side of you." Jake picked Jess up and carried her down the hall to her room.

Jake laid Jess gently on the bed. He felt as if they were starting over, as if this was the beginning of their relationship. He looked down at her and thought again of how beautiful she was.

Jess was still wearing only her robe; she had never bothered to get dressed. Jake reached down and pulled the robe away from her body; her breasts were firm and upright, the nipples tightening as the cool air hit them. Jessica reached for the waistband of his sweats. Jake gently removed her hand.

"This is all for you, babe. You just lay back and enjoy. If this is make-up sex, then I'm making it up to you, for making you feel like I tricked you. Just let me do all the work."

Jake sat on the bed, leaned over and kissed Jess deeply, his tongue playing with hers, his hands on her breasts, gently squeezing them together. He moved down and began kissing Jessica's right breast, licking the nipple, and felt her gasp. He looked up at Jess, her eyes dark, watching him. He bent back to his task, licking and kissing a trail between the globes, licking the other nipple, drawing circles around it with his tongue. He took the rosebud nipple into his mouth, sucking on it gently, and then increasing his efforts. His other hand moved down her stomach, over her thighs, between them to that hot place between her legs. Jess spread her legs, knees falling open. Jake gently rubbed the swollen lips of her pussy, feeling how wet she already was. He continued working her breast with his mouth, sucking and kissing the nipple. He slid one finger into her warm wet pussy, slowly sliding it into that velvet tunnel. He then slid two fingers into Jess, working them back and forth in that wetness, his thumb circling her clit, which was growing hard beneath his touch.

Jess began moving her hips in time with Jake's exploring fingers, rocking up and down, seeking more penetration. She was making small noises in her throat, her eyes closed, head thrown back. Jake moved down her body with his tongue, kissing her flat stomach, licking her navel. He changed position on the bed, settling himself between Jessica's legs, kissing her inner thighs, the skin so soft and warm. His fingers found her pussy again, gently spreading her open. He began gently kissing her clit, circling that wet flesh with his tongue. Jess gasped and he felt her sit up. "I want to watch," she said in a husky voice.

Jake began rhythmically licking her clit, flicking it with the tip of his tongue, feeling Jess shudder beneath him, arching her back. He took her clit into his mouth, sucking on it, feeling it harden in his mouth. Jess made a sound, halfway between a groan and a cry. "Harder... do that harder." Jake sucked her clit harder, sliding three fingers into her pussy, feeling her wetness, working them back and forth as he had done earlier. Jess soon bucked against him, thrusting against his hand. "Oh, God, Jake... I'm so close, bring me off, please... bring me off. Fuck me, Jake, fuck me now."

Jake sat up, pulled his sweats down and thrust his cock into her, pumping into that wet pussy. Jake was instantly close to his own orgasm, as was Jess. He thrust into her hard, watching her, seeing her body start to shudder, arching against him, losing herself in her orgasm. The sight and feel of Jess coming beneath him sent him over the edge. He thrust into her hard, feeling his own hot cum shoot into her hot juiciness. He threw his head back; eyes closed, and felt his cock pumping out more of his seed into Jess's receptive pussy.

Jake opened his eyes, looking down at Jess, who was watching him. He leaned down and kissed her. "And that," he said, "is make-up sex."

2 AS A LAST RESORT

Anna loved her job at Regency Travel. She enjoyed planning all types of exotic honeymoons for newlyweds and sincerely wanted them to have extraordinary experiences. However, even though she loved planning all the details for those happy couples, each trip she planned was tinged with a tiny bit of sadness and, possibly, a bit of jealousy, although Anna never begrudged any of her couples their happiness. Anna felt she would never be able to experience what those couples had: being whisked off to an exotic destination to start a new life together, being deeply in love, and having a wonderfully romantic experience. That made her sad.

Her latest in a series of disappointing relationships had fizzled out and left her with an empty feeling that was becoming all too familiar. It also left her determined, this time not to start up with anyone else until she'd had some time for herself.

It seemed the universe heard her. Anna's boss came to her with a proposition, and this was a proposition she actually liked.

"Anna, I've got a project for you. You're familiar with Island Resort, right?" Was she familiar with Island Resort? Anyone who had followed the recent wedding and subsequent honeymoon of the royal couple knew about the Island and the private resort.

"The corporation who owns the Island and several smaller islands in that chain has decided to open them up to selected agencies, ours being one. They came to the realization that the publicity from the recent high-profile honeymoon was a good thing, even though, at the time, they were bothered by the paparazzi. It may be that many of their private clients have decamped for even more private enclaves. Nevertheless, we have a golden opportunity, or rather, you do. They've given us one all-inclusive "honeymoon special" package, and I'd like you to go. You're free to take a guest, if you like." Apparently her boss had not sensed her love life was less than spectacular. She didn't want to explain that particular failing to her boss.

"I think I'll go solo," Anna said. "I'd like to be as objective as I can and evaluate all the services without any, um, distractions." She'd hoped she bluffed her way out of that potentially embarrassing discussion.

"Very well, Anna. I'll forward you the details. I believe the travel dates are early next week."

Anna's 18-hour flight deposited her at the islands' nearest international airport. From there, a small charter jet carried guests to the resort. The pilot was waiting for her, holding a small placard with her name. For this trip, she had the jet to herself, alone, with one very courteous and discreet flight attendant. The plane was quite luxurious, with beige leather seats, inlaid wood paneling, and an abundant selection of refreshments, served in cut crystal glasses.

The jet landed smoothly at the private airstrip on the Island. A car was waiting to carry her to the resort, a luxurious and extremely comfortable vehicle. The drive was through a stunning tropical landscape. While the effect was lush and untamed, she realized the plantings were carefully groomed to maximize views of sandy beaches and sapphire blue waters. The effect seemed effortless, but she knew the expense must have been great.

The car glided up to the main resort building. With polished and seemingly effortless efficiency, doors were held open, and she was greeted, by name, by every employee. She was escorted to a private check-in desk, given her room key, and assigned a personal resort liaison, who would be available to assist her with anything she desired. All this information was delivered in a very professional but completely personal manner.

Anna felt as if she'd been welcomed into a very exclusive new family.

As she started to leave the building, she noticed a tall, dark-haired man passing through the public reception area. As she walked by, he caught her eye and smiled. She assumed he was one half of a honeymooning couple, but there was an overt sexuality radiating from him that definitely did not seem like that of a newly married man on his honeymoon, unless he was trolling for a new wife already. She felt his frank gaze traveling from her face down her body, apparently taking in every detail and liking what he saw. Normally, she would be offended by such a blatantly lascivious look, but she felt something different, some immediate and visceral attraction. She boldly returned his smile, slid her gaze down his body, and continued on her way out of the lobby.

Anna was taken to her villa, her bags already there. Her day had been very long, but she wasn't as tired as she thought she would be. Her mind went back to the brief encounter with the mysterious stranger in the lobby. The sexual energy she felt was still coursing through her body. It was as if he hadn't only looked her up and down but had run his hands up and down her body as well.

There were several things Anna knew she needed to do, such as unpack and take some notes. She decided to start enjoying the amenities provided, so she ran a bath, sniffing the various bath products arrayed on the marble vanity. She decided on something that smelled deep and rich, with a hint of vanilla.

She added a generous amount to the warm water and watched the bubbles accumulate. She returned to the bedroom, stripped off her clothes, grabbed her robe, and padded barefoot back to the bathroom.

The bath was wonderful, and the water was soft and warm, silky against her skin from the bath product and the scent, which was luxurious and intoxicating. She relaxed in the warm water, any tension remaining from the flight ebbing out of her body. Her thoughts returned to the stranger in the lobby and his smoldering sexuality. Remembering the way he had looked at her, seeming to appraise her body yet almost worshiping what he saw, brought a flood of heat rushing through her.

She ran her hands over her breasts, cupping them and running her thumbs over her nipples. She continued to massage her firm breasts, pinching and rubbing her nipples, feeling the heat coalesce deep within, her stomach muscles contracting and her hips moving slowly in the warm water. She moved one hand down her stomach, spreading her legs and rubbing her hand over her clit, shivering slightly. She slid a finger into her pussy, drawing it back over her clit, feeling the warmth of the water against that sensitive spot, amazed at how aroused she was at just the memory of that man, of an encounter that lasted only seconds.

Her fingers continued playing over her now-throbbing clit, the other hand rubbing and kneading her breast, still pinching the erect nipple. The twin sensations sent waves of pleasure washing over her. She tipped her head back and closed her eyes. Her mind conjured up the mysterious man. Her imagination removed the finely tailored suit he wore to reveal a hard and muscular body, strong and capable and very well endowed.

She imagined feeling the weight of that body on hers, feeling the strong hands parting her legs to lay between them, then caressing her breasts, showering them with kisses, licking the nipples, sucking on them as he moved to enter her, sliding himself into her warmth, both of them thrusting against each other, bringing pleasure to the other and to themselves.

Anna rubbed her clit faster, seeking release from the building sensation she was creating. In her imagination, the stranger reached his climax, his head back, eyes closed, and her name on his lips. In her imagination, she climaxed with the stranger, in a flood of passion, triggering her own orgasm in the warm bath. She arched her back as the sensations tore through her, feeling her muscles contract, releasing a gush of warm liquid as her orgasm peaked. Her fingers slowed their motions over her tender clit. She relaxed the hand on her breast. Anna floated in the warmth of the bath and the afterglow of her orgasm, wondering how a brief encounter with one stranger could have such a profound impact. She thought, maybe, it was just a combination of the surroundings and jetlag, but whatever it was, she had enjoyed every second.

Anna finished her bath, slowly toweling off with one of the most luxurious towels she had ever encountered. She idly wondered if she could stash one away in her luggage, or if the resort counted their towels after the guests left. Pondering that larcenous thought, she pulled her silk robe over her naked body. Walking into the sitting area of the villa, the warm breeze from the open windows briefly played over her, the friction of the fabric causing her nipples to contract and tighten, an involuntary shiver coursing through her. The breeze carried the scent of exotic tropical flowers, and once again, Anna thought any honeymoon couple would have a truly magical, sensual experience at this resort. Even by herself, she could sense the latent sensuality of the setting. Every detail was carefully planned to cater to and enhance the mood, to set the perfect stage for romance, she thought, and mind-blowing sex. The resort was certainly getting her recommendation, and she'd only been there a few hours.

A discreet knocking at the door brought Anna back from her musings. Thinking it might be a resort employee with a welcome gift, she opened the door, slightly. Much to her surprise, the dark-haired stranger from the lobby was standing there, the soft glow of the villa lights casting shadows over his features, revealing high cheekbones and a straight nose. Anna took an involuntary step back, pulling her robe around her.

It was not Devlin MacGregor's normal custom to interact with guests directly. However, this guest was a representative of one of the travel agencies MacGregor Corporation had invited to the resort. It was in his best interests to get to know these people. He had not expected a representative who was so lovely, nor was he expecting to be greeted by one so fetchingly clad in just a silk robe, which did very little to cover what appeared to be a very alluring figure. He had a brief glimpse of full breasts caught in the soft light of the door lamps before she pulled her robe tighter. Contrary to her intention, pulling the robe tighter had not provided more concealment. Instead it only served to show her narrow waist and full hips and to pull the silk taut across those breasts, revealing two erect nipples pushing against the delicate fabric. Devlin was momentarily at a loss for words, but not for physical sensations. He felt a subtle stiffening of his penis, a sensation he seemed powerless to control. Devlin was not used to losing control, even to beautiful and scantily clad women.

"I am sorry to disturb you, Miss....?" The man looked at her with one eyebrow raised.

"Ah, Miss Deveraux, Anna Deveraux." She managed to stammer out her own name, amazed, she could remember it. The man was standing no more than an arm's length away from her, the same man who had just made love to her in her imagination. She wondered if she was blushing and hoped he could not read minds.

"Miss Deveraux, then. May I call you

Anna?" She nodded. "I will make this brief, as I have, obviously, caught you at an inopportune moment. I am Devlin MacGregor, the resort's owner. I have come to ask you, provided you do not already have dinner plans, if you would be so kind as to join me."

Devlin was used to taking control of situations; it was the nature of his business. He'd not gotten where he was by being passive. He was also used to having people follow his commands. But there was a moment of hesitation before Miss Deveraux replied. At that moment, he feared she may turn down his invitation, and he felt a tug of disappointment. He'd not felt that in a long time, and it puzzled him. Women were usually falling at his feet, or, at least, the most recent ones he had met had fallen all over themselves in his company.

Although she was being asked a question, Anna didn't feel she had the option to say no. For one thing, this was the owner of the resort, and she should get to know him for business reasons. Besides, she had a stronger sense that this man was used to giving orders and having them followed. It probably came with the territory.

"Yes, Mr. MacGregor. I would be happy to join you for dinner." Anna, again, felt something change in Mr. MacGregor's manner, a certain tension leaving his body. He seemed to relax, as if he had been afraid she would say decline and was relieved she had agreed.

"Very well. I will send a car for you at seven-thirty. I trust that will be acceptable."

Again, his words were not framed as a question, but more of a demand. Anna was not certain how to take this, but she nodded her agreement. "I shall see you, then." With that, he turned and walked down the path, the tropical darkness swallowing him. She heard a car drive away.

Anna dressed for dinner with more care than she normally would. She had anticipated eating alone or in her room, since she was at a honeymoon resort with couples, who were probably not planning on sharing dinner with a single woman. She decided on a green silk halter dress, appropriate for the tropics, and draped a lace shawl over her bare shoulders.

There was a knock at her door promptly at 7:30. The driver escorted her to a waiting car, and they drove away from her villa. She was surprised when they turned down a gated driveway; the gates swung open automatically. The car glided silently down the lane, into a circular drive before a two-story home, obviously not one of the resort buildings. The driver opened the door for Anna, and she looked up at the beautiful facade of the building. The front door opened, revealing Devlin MacGregor, waiting for her.

"Please, Miss Deveraux— Anna. Welcome to my home." He ushered her inside, gently removing the delicate shawl from her shoulders and placing it over a chair. "Would you care for a drink? I believe we have time before dinner is served. The view from the balcony is quite lovely this time of night, especially with the full moon."

"Yes, please. Something light. I'm still a bit jet-lagged." Anna stepped out onto the balcony. The view was stunning: a broad sweep of pristine sand, the rising moon casting a soft glow over the lush tropical foliage, a shimmering trail of moonlight catching the crests of the waves as they gently lapped along the beach. The scent of tropical flowers filled the air, a heady scent that made her inhale deeply.

As Devlin took their drinks to the balcony, he was again struck by Anna's beauty. The dress she wore was backless, showing an expanse of creamy skin, partly covered by a cascade of ebony hair. Her narrow waist set off full hips. Her dress blew in the breeze, molding to her, outlining shapely legs and the sweet curve of her backside. Devlin stopped for a moment, again, overcome by physical sensations he could not control. He had the strongest urge to drop the drinks, grab her hips, and pull her against him, to feel the curves of her against his body, to rub his now awakening cock against that flesh, to plant kisses along the curve of her neck, and to bury his face in that mane of hair. He shook his head and, instead, walked to her side and offered her the drink he held.

"I trust your villa is to your liking?" She felt MacGregor's presence at her side, his arm brushing hers, holding her drink. Their fingers touched briefly as she took her drink, an electric current running up her arm. How could one man she'd spent only minutes with have such an effect on her? Or, was it the setting? Jet lag? She wasn't sure, but the sensation was amazing.

"Yes, it is. It's very luxurious and quite well suited for honeymooning couples. It seems every last detail has been thought through. You must have a very experienced staff working for you, Mr. MacGregor."

"Please, call me Devlin, or Dev if you prefer. My employees call me Mr. MacGregor. You are not an employee. As far as the details here, many of them are my ideas. The whole concept of this resort sprang from my own desires, from what I would want to experience if I were looking for a tropical paradise in which to fulfill my deepest desires with the woman I was now sharing the rest of my life with, and she, to fulfill hers, with me; a sacred space and time to allow fantasy, desire, romance, and discovery to be indulged and explored. And, most of all, a place for love to deepen."

Devlin's words took her by surprise. His look had grown distant as he spoke, and she was aware that his voice had changed, grown softer, as if he were describing a past experience, or speaking of something he wished for the future. She wondered if there would be a Mrs. MacGregor joining them for dinner and was momentarily dismayed at the thought.

"I see. Well, you've accomplished that." Anna disliked the curt, business-like tone of her voice, but she didn't trust herself to say anything else. Devlin turned, looking at her, his eyes soft in the moonlight, his look unreadable, apparently searching her face for something. She felt a liquid heat curl deep in her core, and shivered in the warm air.

They were interrupted by a male voice announcing that dinner was served. Devlin hesitated a moment longer and then gently took her elbow, guiding her toward the dining room.

"We have a chef's tasting menu for this evening's meal. I hope you don't mind. I thought it would give you a sampling of what the resort has to offer and my chef could show us his best work. Will that suit you?" Devlin's voice had returned to its former business tones.

"Yes, that's fine." Anna wondered if she was imagining the sexual tension she felt, if the moonlight was playing tricks, or if the overtly romantic location was making her read things into conversations that weren't there. She resolved to treat this as what it really was, a business dinner.

Devlin held a chair out for Anna. As she sat, he caught the scent of that beautiful black hair and her perfume, along with the underlying scent of her body, warm and feminine. He hesitated, feeling almost intoxicated. He had grown used to the scents of the island. The flowers no longer held his attention. Yet her scent filled his head, and again, he felt an electrical current between them. He briefly brushed her shoulder with his hand as he walked past, the skin as soft as he had imagined, and he could almost hear the crackle of sexual electricity in the air.

Dinner was delicious. Anna realized she was famished. She lost herself in the meal, each course offering some Island specialty, or the one of the chef's favorite techniques. Dinner conversation flowed smoothly, each growing more comfortable as they discussed common subjects. Both had traveled for business. Devlin owned other resorts, and Anna had traveled extensively for the agency. She had never stayed at any of Devlin's other resorts, but he did admit all were private, this resort being his first venture into the public, albeit exclusive, domain.

Devlin turned the conversation to a subject he wanted more information about and began formulating a plan: how to get Anna Deveraux into his bed. He was used to getting what he wanted, and this, he decided, was something he wanted, very badly. He'd prefer she go willingly, but if not...

"Is Deveraux a family name, Anna?" Devlin asked.

Anna was a bit startled by the shift in topics. "Yes, on my father's side. The original family settled in New Orleans, but we've managed to spread ourselves all over the country. I'm living in Maryland, now. It's close enough to the agency, but not in D.C. proper."

The answer seemed to please him. Deveraux was her maiden name, not her married name. One of the first things he had noticed was a lack of a wedding ring on Anna's delicate finger, but at this point, a ring would not have been a block to his plan, just a pesky obstacle.

"And you? MacGregor is your family name?"

Devlin laughed. "Actually, both my first and last names are family names. I am the result of two headstrong Irish families coming together, neither of whom wanted to give up their family names. There's also a fair bit of Gypsy blood in my veins. Apparently, there was a wandering ancestor or two who enjoyed sampling the local delicacies, as it were. I believe I inherited my wanderlust from them. I find it hard to remain in one place very long. Owning resorts gives me a reason, or excuse, to move about frequently."

"That must be difficult for your family, moving all the time, although it would be an exciting life." Anna was doing her own detective work.

"There is no immediate family." The answer was abrupt, and Anna mentally kicked herself for treading on what appeared to be, sensitive territory. "There is, of course, family back in Ireland, and my parents currently live in Greece, the country of my birth." Devlin fell silent, apparently lost in his thoughts for a moment.

Anna broke the silence. "Thank you for dinner, Devlin. It was truly delicious. Please, give my compliments to the chef."

Devlin looked up at her. "Please, excuse me, Anna, for being distracted. It certainly was not due to your company. Perhaps you would enjoy a walk on the beach. There is a view of the resort from there. At night, it is particularly beautiful."

Again, Anna felt she could not refuse, but she found she did want to walk on the beach.

"Yes, Devlin, that sounds lovely."

They walked down a short flight of stairs from the balcony. Devlin held Anna's elbow. "Careful," he murmured, as they reached the path. Anna shivered at his touch.

They continued to the beach, the moon now higher in the sky, lighting the path and making the sand appear to be lit from beneath.

"It's beautiful," Anna breathed. "Oh, Dev, it's stunning." The main resort building was visible, across a small bay, along with several of the individual villas. The lights from the buildings cast yellow trails across the bay, flickering on the waves.

"When I bought the island, this area was undeveloped. I had a small tract cleared for the main house and drive, and left the surrounding jungle untouched. You may have noticed much of the area around the main building and villas is manicured, an accurate recreation of the native landscape, but made more aesthetically pleasing. The undergrowth is kept down, and views are framed and enhanced by floral groupings, subtly enhancing every aspect of the resort property, but still remaining true to the Island's original foliage. It's not overly manicured, but enough to leave a positive psychological effect. It also affords me this stunning view, as you so accurately describe it. But here, step off the path, and the jungle will swallow you whole."

Anna laughed. "This is a beautiful spot for your home, even with the deepest, darkest jungle at your door." They had reached the beach, Anna's shoes sinking in the soft grains.

"Wait, I need to take off my shoes."

"Here, allow me." Devlin knelt down, at Anna's feet. "Foot, please." Anna placed one hand on Devlin's shoulder, and balanced on one foot. With infinite care, Devlin slipped the sandal from Anna's foot. The feel of his hands on her skin was amazing. She felt a deep heat forming in her. "Other, please." The process was repeated. Devlin stood, Anna's shoes in his hands. "We'll just leave these by the path. No sense in taking them along. I think I'll leave mine here, as well." Devlin slipped his shoes off and set them beside Anna's.

They continued walking, the sand working its way through their tocs. Anna gingerly stuck a toe in the water, discovering it was quite warm. Devlin was aware of the scent of her hair and her skin. He wanted nothing more than to take her in his arms. Anna's effect on his body was intoxicating. His penis was semi-erect, every sense attuned to her. But his emotional reaction was totally unexpected. He hesitated, where normally he would be the aggressor. He felt the need to treat Anna as more than one of his conquests. He wanted something more to develop. He wasn't sure what, but he didn't want Anna to be just a one night stand. He wanted more than just sex.

Anna turned, and found Devlin looking at her in a way that made her knees weak. She lost her train of thought. Devlin ran his hand up Anna's arm, feeling the warm silk of her skin. He felt her shiver under his touch. Devlin took a step toward Anna, expecting her to resist. To his surprise and great pleasure, she stepped into his embrace. Devlin ran his hands across her bare back, feeling the smooth skin. Her body pressed against him, and he realized she was not wearing a bra. He was unexpectedly disarmed by this. He had held many braless women, but with Anna, feeling those breasts pressed against him covered only by the thin fabric of her dress, excited him more than he could have imagined.

Devlin bent his lips to Anna's, kissing her passionately, feeling her respond beneath his touch. She opened her mouth to him, her tongue meeting his. She wrapped her arms around his neck, pulling herself against his body, feeling his erection against her stomach. She realized she was moving against him, sliding her hips back and forth, enjoying the feeling of his cock pressing against her.

Devlin was almost overwhelmed by the warm contact of Anna's body against him. She was soft, but firm, and obviously interested in pursuing this encounter. He ran his hands up her sides, cupping her breasts, feeling her arch against him. She responded to his touch with a soft cry.

Hearing her, Devlin could hold back no longer. "I want you, Anna, more than anything. I want you, all of you, now." He looked at her eyes, dark with passion, and realized she was ready.

Anna reached down and unzipped Devlin's pants, rubbing her hand over him, over his very large erection. The size of it gave her a thrill deep in the pit of her stomach. He responded with a groan, pushing himself against her. He tried to find some way of removing Anna's dress. He felt a sense of urgency to possess her, and was momentarily confused by her clothing. Anna felt him fumbling and stepped back, giggling.

"Allow me." She undid a simple closure at the neck of her dress, and it seemed to magically fall away from her body, pooling in the sand at her feet. Gracefully, she slipped out of her panties. She stood naked before him.

"So beautiful," Devlin smiled, looking at her with something like awe. She was bathed in moonlight, looking like a goddess, and he devoured her with his eyes. Anna felt his gaze almost burning her with intensity. She moved back into his arms, fingers working the buttons of his shirt, as he pushed down his pants and stepped out of them. Devlin practically tore the shirt from his body the minute she was finished unbuttoning it.

He pulled Anna's naked body against his, feeling her softness and heat. She could feel the strength of his erection, his cock moving against her stomach. Devlin cupped her ass in his hands, increasing the pressure between them, rubbing himself against her, a delicious taste of what to expect.

Anna was overtaken by an animal passion, the desire to have Devlin inside her, almost unbearable. She tugged him down with her, lying back on the cool, firm sand, watching him above her, his face lit by the moonlight. She saw an almost wild look in his eyes, and she felt a thrill at the thought: her earlier fantasy was coming true and she'd have him inside her shortly.

Devlin held himself over Anna, feeling her spread her legs, her silky thighs moving up and over his hips and sides, pulling him toward her. He reached down and ran his fingers lightly over her slit, feeling the heat and wetness of her arousal. He took his cock in his hand, guiding himself to her, rubbing his cock over her, feeling her pushing against him.

Anna looked up, at Devlin. "Now, Dev. Please." He responded to her words by thrusting himself into her in one stroke, feeling her accept his cock, feeling himself surrounded by her heat and wetness. He felt her inhale, sharply, a small cry coming from her. He looked down, afraid he'd hurt her but saw only a look of pure pleasure on her face.

"Oh, my God, Dev." He smiled down, at Anna. "Do that again!" He pulled back, holding himself with just the head of his cock inside Anna, moving slightly, teasing her. He could feel her squirming beneath him, seeking more contact.

"Do you like that?" Devlin rarely talked to women during sex, or more accurately, he'd never had sex with a woman who talked. He found it quite arousing to hear Anna's words, hear the rough edge of passion in her voice. "Do you like my cock inside of you? Does that feel good?"

"Please, yes, Dev. I want you inside me. I want to feel your cock inside me, all of it. Now, please. Fuck me, now!" He could hold back no longer, the sound of her voice and her rough language arousing some part of him that had been dormant for a long time.

With an animalistic noise, Devlin began thrusting into Anna hard, feeling her lift her hips to meet him. He held himself above her on extended arms, wanting to watch every nuance of emotion on her face. She was crying out in time to his thrusts, her noises growing louder with each stroke.

Anna grabbed her breasts with both hands, crushing them together. Devlin saw her lick the first two fingers of each hand, then rub the wet fingers over her nipples, seeing them grow hard as she pulled and rubbed them. That simple movement, watching her giving herself pleasure, sent a thrill through his body. That started an intense heat building in his stomach, and he felt his orgasm start to build.

Anna's own orgasm was swelling, fueled by Devlin's expert thrusts into her, surprising her with its intensity. She wanted to keep making love to Dev, but her body was already headed toward its climax. She looked up, watching his face, trying to gauge his arousal.

"I'm so close, Dev," she whispered. "Make me cum. Push me over the edge." Dev looked down at her. He changed their position, spreading his legs for leverage, grabbing her hips and pulling her up his hard thighs. He slipped his arms beneath her thighs, pulling her legs up, over his shoulders, opening her up to him even more. He drove himself into her, watching his cock slide in and out of her pussy.

With a shout, Devlin's cock seemed to explode, pumping his hot load into her. Anna felt the first flood of his heat inside her, and responded with her own cry, pushing against Devlin, coming against him in a flood of liquid. Devlin thrust into her in short quick strokes, his cock working to shoot the last spurts into Anna's accepting pussy. He watched as her orgasm ripped through her, muscles straining, her body quivering beneath him. He watched her face, her pleasure playing across her features. Eyes closed, she smiled. He hadn't experienced such an intense orgasm in a long time, nor watched one so intense happen to any woman.

He felt he'd been allowed to witness something private and intimate. He hadn't felt this way with a woman in a long time. Sex had always been just sex, even if it was great sex. But this was different. He felt he was seeing something deeper than the basic physical act, a world he thought he'd abandoned being reopened. He wasn't sure how he felt about it.

Anna watched Devlin's face as his orgasm subsided. She wasn't sure what exactly he was feeling. She obviously didn't know him that well. Yet, she sensed there were conflicting emotions raging behind those eyes. She knew she couldn't ask how he felt. She didn't think now was the time or the place, even though she was very curious to know what was going on in that mind.

Devlin relaxed, gently lowering Anna's legs, and reluctantly sliding his semi-erect penis from her warmth. He sat back, looking down at her body, at her beauty. She looked back at him, admiring his body, as well. He was totally disarmed by her frank and unembarrassed gaze. He leaned down and kissed her gently, then stood.

"I think a swim would be nice, don't you? The water's quite warm." Devlin held out his hand, pulling Anna up. They walked into the ocean, the warm waves lapping about their heated bodies. Devlin dove, surfacing a short distance away. Anna was content to wade out until the water was over her hips, splashing her face and arms. Devlin swam back and stood before her, taking her in his arms. They kissed, a slow, gentle embrace. As the ocean waves gently rocked them, none of the animal urgency they felt before was evident. Each was content, sated for the moment; nothing more was needed than to just enjoy the warmth of the ocean and to be held by the other.

"Dev, this is beautiful. I could stay here forever." She leaned against him, looking at the moonlight playing over the water.

"As could I, except eventually, I think we'd get hungry." He smiled down, at her. "Let's go up to the house."

They retrieved their clothes, Anna slipping into her dress and Devlin pulling on his pants. He draped his shirt over Anna's shoulders, as they walked up the path, their shoes left behind.

They walked back to Devlin's villa in silence, Devlin trying to untangle his emotions and Anna trying to decide what was in

Devlin's mind. She was extremely attracted to him sexually, and had decided to take advantage of finding this available man to abandon her normal reserve, throwing caution to the wind. In Devlin, she'd found the perfect excuse to relax and let go, to indulge in a no-strings affair, and so far, with the benefit of fantastic sex.

Devlin was confused by his emotions. He had started the evening with the intent of seducing Anna. Yet, he'd found her more than willing to engage with him. While that was refreshing, he also found he wanted more than just a sexual conquest in Anna. He wanted to move beyond just sex. He wanted, and was feeling, a deeper connection, to learn what made her tick, how she felt and what excited her intellectually. In essence, he found her fascinating, on many levels.

"Stay the night, Anna." Devlin turned to her, as they walked up the steps to the house. He paused, rephrasing his request. "Would you like to stay the night?" Devlin had bedded many women, but he'd never asked them to stay the night. With Anna, it was different.

She reached up to kiss him, intrigued that he'd actually asked her, rather than demanded she stay. "Are you sure? It's no trouble?"

Devlin wrapped her in his arms. "It would be no trouble at all. It would be an honor and a pleasure to have you as a guest."

They continued into the house. Devlin asked if Anna wanted a drink, but she declined. They realized they were on their way to continuing what they'd started at the beach. While they were both eagerly anticipating what might come next, there was a relaxed quality to their movements, as if they had all the time in the world.

They walked up the wide staircase to the second floor, Anna looking over the artwork on the walls and the small statues on pedestals in the hallway. She was quite impressed with the caliber of the collection. Many of the pieces were quite rare and very valuable.

"You have some really exquisite pieces here, Devlin. It must have taken some time to collect them." She was looking at a small painting she thought looked like an original Degas. "This is very beautiful." She turned to Devlin, who was looking down, at the painting, with a sad, distant, look in his eyes.

"I am not the collector here. It was someone else who collected all these pieces." He reached out and gently touched the gilded frame of the painting. "This is... was, a particular favorite." He hesitated a moment longer, lost in thought. With a shake of his head, he pulled his thoughts back and turned to Anna. "I'm glad you are enjoying them."

Devlin led Anna to the master suite, closing the door behind them, the room lit by soft lamps. The room was simple, but luxurious. Anna was drawn to the view from the windows. It was the same from downstairs, of the ocean and the moon, which was now riding high in the sky, casting its silver light over everything.

Devlin watched Anna, struck by her beauty. He reached over and turned off the room's lights, leaving Anna lit only by the moonlight.

She turned to him in surprise, but was silent. He crossed the room to her, taking her in his arms, both of them sensing a new dimension to their lovemaking, of being able to take their time. Their first coming together had been primal and immediate. They, now, felt they had all the time they needed to explore and satisfy each other.

They kissed, gently and slowly, taking the time to play, sensually exploring each other's mouths with their tongues. Devlin's hands made a slow circuit of Anna's body, running from her shoulders down her arms, back up her sides, caressing her breasts. He ran his hands over her belly, down her flat stomach, before cupping the mound between her legs with his palm. Anna rubbed against him, every place he touched brought to life, her nerve endings tingling.

Anna's hands did their own exploring over his bare arms and chest, running her hands lightly down his sides to the waistband of his pants. Devlin jumped at her touch, grabbing her hands with his, laughing softly.

"Ticklish," he murmured. He guided her hands back to his chest, returning his own to their exploration of her body and resuming their kiss. Anna found his nipples with her fingers and broke their kiss long enough to lick the tips of two fingers of one hand. She ran her wet fingers in circles over Devlin's nipples, feeling them harden. She felt him inhale sharply at her touch, deepening their kiss.

They stood in the moonlight, savoring the touch and feel of each other's hands. Devlin wanted to feel Anna's breasts in his hands, kiss the pale skin, lick her nipples, and see the reaction he could cause with his mouth and hands. Now, knowing the secret to Anna's dress, he undid the clasp and the dress obeyed, falling to the floor.

"We seem to have forgotten some articles of clothing," Devlin said. "You're missing your shoes and your panties."

Anna smiled up at him. "That's fine with me."

He looked down at Anna's breasts, cupping them in his hands. They were beautiful: full, round, and the nipples darker against her skin. He bent his head, running his tongue over her skin, down the rounded top of her breast, kissing a trail to her nipple. He licked her, making her nipple hard, flicking his tongue over it. He felt Anna shudder beneath his touch.

He could feel his cock tightening, but was content for now to just pleasure Anna. She reached for him, once or twice, but he deftly evaded her grasp. "Not yet," he murmured against her skin. She gently cradled his head against her, thoroughly enjoying the sensations he was creating with his tongue and mouth.

Devlin worked his way to her other breast, taking the nipple in his mouth, running his tongue over it, sucking it further into his mouth. He grabbed the hard nipple gently with his teeth, tugging softly, teasing Anna. He heard her moan, as much pain as pleasure in the sound.

"Too hard?" He lifted his head, looking at

her face.

"No. Perfect. Just perfect."

Devlin smiled and bent back to her breasts. He alternated sucking and kissing her nipples, occasionally tugging them with his teeth, enjoying every moment of giving Anna this sensual pleasure, of feeling her respond beneath his mouth and hands.

He stood, moving to kiss her luscious mouth. His attention to her breasts had started a slow burn deep in Anna's center. She wanted to ignite the same heat in Devlin, and she pulled him against her. She reached down and slowly rubbed her hand against his erection, feeling how aroused he was. He groaned as her hand fondled him, running up the length of his cock.

Anna gently pulled down the zipper on Dev's pants, releasing his cock into her hand. "I see you're missing your underwear too, Devlin." She smiled a wicked little grin. "I rather like this." Devlin smiled back, tugging his pants down and kicking them away. He pulled Anna against him, reveling in the feel of her naked skin against his, the warm, tropical breeze caressing both of them. It occurred to him that he'd never brought a woman into this bedroom. There was, obviously, no single women at the resort for him to seduce. While he had bedded a few married women, he did draw the line at sleeping with women on their honeymoons, even if they made advances. Plus, it would have been very bad for business.

Yet, he found he wanted to have Anna here, in his bed, in his private space. He gently steered her toward the bed, lowering her down as he covered her body with his. She kissed him deeply, passionately, and he could feel his arousal increasing. His cock was pressing into the soft skin of her leg, caught between their bodies. He felt it growing harder at the touch of her skin as she shifted beneath him.

Anna felt his cock pressing against her and rolled on her side, facing Dev, reaching down and taking him in her hand. She felt him shudder as she began stroking him slowly, still locked in a kiss. His hands had found her breasts again, softly running his fingers over them, tickling the nipples with his fingertips, the feeling exquisite.

They continued to caress each other, bathed in moonlight, touched by soft breezes, no hurry to move any further, each working to give pleasure while enjoying the touch of the other. Devlin felt time was standing still, that they could continue in this erotic play for hours, slowly building to the point where they'd come together, when he could make love to Anna again.

Devlin slid one hand down Anna's stomach to her slit, running his hand over her mound and between her legs. He felt her warmth, how smooth she was to his touch. He delicately slid one finger inside the lips of her pussy, slowly rubbing the edges of her, feeling how wet she already was. He worked his finger further into her as she gently pushed against him, slowly moving her hips, guiding him into a rhythm of thrusting his fingers into her pussy. She increased the speed of her stroke on his cock to match the play of his fingers inside her, pressing her body closer to his, her hard nipples against his chest.

Dev's hand worked its way over her clit, rubbing it, circling it with his finger, feeling it already hard beneath his touch. Anna responded instantly, with a shudder and thrusting forward of her hips. Her clit was exquisitely sensitive from their prolonged foreplay, and the touch of Dev's hand had brought her to the point of no return. She wanted his cock inside her now, needed to feel him thrusting into her.

She pushed him over onto his back, rolling on top of him, his fingers still buried in her and his cock in her hand. She looked in his face and saw that he was ready as well. She raised herself up on her knees, straddling Devlin's hips, guiding his cock toward her waiting slit. Dev grabbed her by the hips, suddenly ready to plunge inside of Anna, to mate with her again.

She held him in her hand, held herself above his body, watching his face. She was still stroking him slowly with her hand and the continued pressure, combined with the nearness of her waiting pussy, was almost too much for him. He pressed down on her hips, willing her to lower her body.

"Please, Anna, please, oh God, let me make love to you." Devlin had never begged a woman for sex. This was totally unexpected for him. It shocked him, but at the same time, he was amazed at the power Anna had over him. "Please, Anna, I want you so badly, now."

Anna heard Devlin, looked in his eyes and saw the naked emotions playing on his face.

She felt his body tensing beneath her in anticipation. She settled herself on him, sliding him into her warmth, feeling him exhale as he entered her. He seemed to fill her completely. She hadn't realized on the beach just how large his cock was.

They began moving together, Anna rising up, as Devlin pulled back, settling on him as he thrust up into her. He relaxed the hold on her hips, allowing her to set the pace. Now that he was buried to the hilt inside of her, where he wanted to be, he felt back in control.

There was no holding back, though, for Anna now that Devlin's cock was inside her. She felt an orgasm start to build deep within her and felt powerless to control it. She began losing control, her rhythm faltering.

Devlin sensed she was building to her orgasm. He reached down between her legs and found her clit, rubbing his finger over that nub of flesh, feeling the tremors start in Anna's body. Her speed increased as she worked Devlin's cock in and out of herself. He massaged her clit in time to his thrusts, occasionally feeling his cock with the tips of his fingers.

Anna grabbed one breast with her hand, rubbing the nipple, pulling it between her fingers. Devlin reached up and grabbed the other, repeating her actions with his own hand. The combined feeling of his hand on her clit while he fondled her breast was enough to send Anna over the edge. She bucked up against Devlin once, twice and then her orgasm erupted.

With a sharp cry, she thrust her hips

forward, a gush of orgasmic juice spurting onto Devlin's cock. She still held one breast in her hand, crushing it while Devlin held the other. His fingers still worked to rub her clit, but he sensed she was overstimulated by that, and gently slowed his movements. She continued to shudder as her orgasm tore through her body. Devlin could feel her muscles contract around his cock, then slowly begin to fade as her orgasm slowed. She was breathing heavily as she finally opened her eyes and looked down at Devlin, who had been mesmerized by what he'd seen.

"That was amazing, Dev. I have no words to describe that." She leaned down and kissed him. "Thank you." Devlin kissed her back, wrapping his arms around her back. He held her for a moment, as her breathing slowed. He began slowly moving into her, testing to see if she was ready to continue. She broke their kiss, looking into his eyes, still holding him close. He saw she was ready, and he increased his thrusts, feeling her juices running over his balls and inner thighs. The feeling of that warm wetness excited him tremendously, and he was instantly ready to cum.

Anna sensed this and tried to sit up, but Devlin held her tightly. "No, stay here." His voice was rough. "Let me hold you." He planted his feet on the bed, spreading his legs for leverage, and began thrusting up into Anna. She was powerless to thrust back, held in the grip of his strong arms. She could only receive his pounding, riding along on his journey to his own orgasm. Being this out of control normally would have bothered her, but with Devlin, she felt safe and realized she was being driven to another orgasm as well. She relaxed against Devlin, letting the feeling of his cock thrusting into her wash over her.

Devlin ran his hands down Anna's back, pushing her down on his cock, cupping her ass as he drove himself into her body. He wanted at this moment to control, to take pleasure as much as he gave it. He sensed Anna was willing to allow this, and her acquiescence to his silent request fueled his passion. He drove into her hard, feeling heat moving from his core to his balls, moving up the base of his cock, and finally bursting into her, pumping his hot load.

His thrusts grew increasingly frantic for a moment as his hips and cock seemed to take on a life of their own, jerking and thrusting, seeking more release. He continued to cry out with almost every thrust, unable to stop the sounds, not wanting to stop. He was briefly aware of Anna steadying herself on the bed, with her hands, but he couldn't have stopped the waves of his orgasm even if he'd wanted.

Anna was amazed at the intensity of Devlin's orgasm. She braced herself on the bed to keep from being tossed off. She felt a brief, second orgasm of her own race through her, as she heard his sounds of pleasure. It was more than she had ever experienced with any man.

They lay spent in each other's arms for a long time. So long, Anna thought Devlin had fallen asleep. She worked her way under the sheet, trying to pull it up over both of them, without waking him. Devlin surprised her by sitting up and straightening out the bed linens, covering both of their bodies, trapping the scent of their lovemaking beneath the sheets.

Devlin pulled her close, tucking her against his shoulder. She reached up to kiss him and was very surprised to find tears on his cheek. She sat up.

"What's wrong? Are you all right?"

Devlin pulled her back down, against him. "There is nothing wrong. Everything, right now, is perfect."

"But, you're crying. Why?" She tried to sit up, again. He held her tight.

"If you listen, I'll tell you a story. I've never told this to anyone, you're the first. It's not something I thought I'd ever want to share. But you've brought it close to the surface, and I think it's time to say the words." Devlin took a deep breath.

"I was married once, to the love of my life. We'd known each other for a long time, since childhood. I'd watched her grow up, into a beautiful woman, the woman I knew I would someday marry." Devlin grew silent, lost for a moment, in his memories.

"We were very happy, very content. We had a home, wanted to start a family. But she died suddenly. Then, I was alone and angry at the universe for taking the one thing that mattered the most to me." Anna heard the sadness in his voice.

"The artwork you see here, the Degas, those are her things. She loved that little Degas painting. It hurts me more than I can say, to see it in the hall every day, but it would tear my heart out to sell it, or any of her collections. They're in various homes I own, but this had been a favorite spot of hers. So, her favorite items are kept here." Devlin shifted, looking down, at Anna. She was totally silent, completely still, afraid to break the spell.

"I have had many, many women, since my wife. I'm not sure why, and I'm not interested in the psychology of why I feel the need to seduce women and take them to my bed, then discard them." Anna raised an eyebrow at this information. Devlin gave her half a smile and a shrug.

"Yes, I'll admit you were to be another conquest, another seduction. You came willingly into the arrangement, though, so I sensed you had some of that same intent running through your veins." He kissed the tip of Anna's nose.

"But, you're not like any other woman I've known, or bedded. There is something more to you that I want to possess, more than just your body. You've awakened something deep inside me that has been dead to me for a long time. I don't know why, or why you, but this is different, you're different."

"Do I remind you of your wife?" Anna asked, thinking she must resemble the woman in some way.

"No, you don't. That's not it. You're not like her at all. I'm not looking at you as the reincarnation of my wife, or as a replacement. I'm looking at you as Anna, this beautiful and amazing woman who has fallen into my life." Devlin kissed Anna. "The tears? Joy, happiness, something along those lines. Again, I don't analyze my feelings. I usually tend to ignore them."

Anna was silent for a long time. "And now what? That's a lot for me to take in. I'm only here for a few days. What are you suggesting we do?"

"I hadn't thought that far; or rather, I did start thinking about it and decided to stop." Devlin laughed. Anna gave him a puzzled look.

"Anna, I am a wealthy man. There is a great deal of resources available to me. I've never really thought about my money as a means to secure my happiness. I'd resigned myself to not having any happiness. I've always just used it to accumulate more wealth. But now, I think that all that money may come to a good use."

Anna looked up at him. "Are you going to kidnap me and lock me away somewhere? Build me a palace and keep me prisoner?" She smiled at him.

"Well, if you insist." Devlin was amused by the shocked look that briefly crossed Anna's face. "But more seriously, I can afford for us, if you're interested and willing—and I hope and pray, to any and all deities that are listening, that you are—to try to find out where this relationship can go. My money can create opportunities for us to be together, to get to know each other on many different levels, besides the sexual. Of course, if you're interested in sex, we can continue to make wild, passionate love together. There are parts of your body I still need to explore." Devlin leaned down and kissed her gently.

"It's a great deal to take in. I don't really know what to say."

"Say nothing, now. Think it over and give me some kind of answer." Devlin looked at his watch. "Say, in 20 minutes?" He smiled. Anna made a face at him.

Anna had already come to a decision. She knew this was a risk, and she could be making a huge mistake, but in looking back over her fizzled and failed love life, and at the possibility now being offered, she decided to take a chance. Worst-case scenario, she'd go back to D.C. and pick up where she left off. Best case, who knew? The sky was the limit.

"I don't need 20 minutes. I've already decided." Devlin found he was holding his breath, waiting for the rest of her answer. "I have decided, Devlin MacGregor, that I accept your offer." It was Devlin's turn to look shocked.

"You do? You will?" Devlin drew Anna into his arms. "Oh, my God, Anna, you don't know how happy you've made me. I can promise you this, from this moment forward, you are the center of my life, as grandiose as that sounds." He looked down, at her smiling up at him. "You've made me a very happy man." He leaned down and kissed her, wrapping her in his arms, the light of the rising sun coming through the bedroom window, bathing both of them in the light of a new day.

3 LOVE FOR ALL THE WRONG REASONS

Lara Lawton was lonely. Even though she was married, she'd never felt so alone in her life. Her husband, Greg Lawton, was a very successful businessman and the owner of his own company—a company that was actually doing well, despite the challenging economy. While she was grateful for all that he provided, she was constantly frustrated at being left alone for long stretches of time.

They had staff for the house, of course. They could afford it and Greg didn't feel it was appropriate for his wife to be cleaning the bathrooms. Yet, even when Jennie, the personal chef who came in three times a week to make meals, or one of the other staff was in the house, it wasn't the same. For one thing, they were busy. For another, she was looking for more than just someone to pass an afternoon with. She was looking for a friend, a lover. In essence, she was looking for her husband, and she was not finding him.

When they were dating, Lara had been an art major at the local university. Greg had thought it was charming having a bohemian girlfriend. He did not, however, think it was charming to have a bohemian wife. So she had dropped out of college in her senior year, when they got married.

She had been happy for the first couple of years when Greg was just starting his business. Even though he'd been putting in twelve-hour days, he'd been attentive and passionate with her. She remembered staying up late in the tiny apartment they first lived in, waiting for him to come home, knowing he'd come to her full of desire, and they'd spend several precious hours making delicious love.

She still got aroused remembering those wild nights. He'd take her in the shower. Take her in the kitchen, wherever she happened to be. He'd ravage her, both of them pulling at each other's clothes, Greg, already with an erection, ready to pound into her waiting pussy the minute she was semi-naked. She'd had rug burns on her knees and elbows from one night of incredible sex, she on her knees on the cheap living room carpet, him holding her by the hips as he took her from behind, thrusting into her with such force, he ended up pushing her across the carpet. He'd come with such an animal yell that she was afraid the neighbors would call the police. Her orgasm had been just as intense, if not just as loud.

He had confided in her as well, sharing his insecurities about his business, his failures and his successes. Yet, the more successful the business became, the less he seemed to need her emotional support, or her physical presence. She wondered sometimes, if he'd outgrown the need for a wife.

She tried, for a time, to reconnect with Greg, to at least rekindle the passion they felt back then. She kept in shape to keep the figure Greg had said he worshiped. Her breasts were still high, her legs slender but curvy, and her ass was as round and firm as it had been when they were first married. Yet she knew it wasn't her body Greg didn't like anymore. He'd become obsessed with his work and she had been pushed down the line of his priorities. She didn't know what else to do to get back to the way they were. She wasn't sure it was possible.

She had decided to stop trying to change Greg and make some changes in her own life. The first was to get out of the house, so she had signed up for an art class at the local college. She craved some kind of human contact and wanted to get back into the arts. Jewelry making was one of the things she had just gotten interested in. The local college in her town had a great teacher, a man who was an award-winning glassblower. She looked forward to having somewhere to go every day, to have some structure in her life.

Lara was early for her first day of class, a hands-on jewelry making lesson. She was settling into her workspace, watching the other people taking their places. She was looking forward to meeting the rest of the class and actually creating something beautiful. She also entertained the thought of having a little romantic fling, if the opportunity presented itself, with one of her classmates. The idea of having an affair excited her. She was only in her late twenties, ripe for the picking. If Greg didn't appreciate her, she was sure there was some other man who would. However, she really didn't know how to go about starting an affair. Did she just walk up and ask a guy for sex? She suddenly felt far older than her years.

The instructor walked in, talking to a few other class members. He caught Lara's eye, smiling at her. Lara was immediately struck by his physical presence. He was tall with sexily messy, blonde hair and brown eyes. Lara gave a little gasp. Then, she laughed self-consciously at herself. She was acting like a love-struck high school girl, she thought, already getting a crush on her teacher.

Mark Wolfgang looked over his new class of students. This class was open to the public, so he expected to see a range of students, old, young, male, and female. He enjoyed teaching and interacting with the diverse types of people who took his classes. As his eyes moved around the room, his attention was caught by a woman sitting near the front. He wasn't quite sure what about her made him stop. She was a petite redhead, with a pixie face and sparkling green eyes. Although very pretty, her looks alone weren't what caught his attention. There was something about her, the way she looked up at him, her lips parted, as if she were just on the verge of saying something. He walked over to her.

"Hi, I'm Mark Wolfgang." He held out his hand. "Nice to see a new face in class."

Lara was momentarily flustered. She was out of practice talking to men. She shook his hand. "Hi, I'm Lara Sanders." She'd registered under Sanders on a whim. Greg had laughed at her for taking the class, and she wanted to keep this part of her life as separate from home as possible. Going by her maiden name seemed like a start.

She realized Mark was still holding her hand. She had that sensation that time was standing still. He was watching her, as if he was waiting for something. She felt a tingle of energy running between them, amazed that something as simple as a handshake could feel so good. Mark felt it as well, something he'd not felt in a long time. He released her hand slowly, her fingers trailing across his palm. Both of them were a little flustered.

"It's nice to meet you, Mark. I'm looking forward to class." Even to Lara's ears, she sounded lame.

Mark smiled down at her. "Feel free to let me know if you have any questions, and don't hesitate to catch me after class if there's something you need to have explained in more detail." He briefly touched her hand again and walked to the front of the room, starting the class.

Lara spent the next few hours both mesmerized by Mark and enthralled with what he was teaching. It had been a long time since she'd been in any kind of studio environment, the chance to get her hands on materials and creation was exactly what she craved. They'd gotten right down to work, Mark giving them a simple project to work on in class, and granting them open access to the studio anytime it was unoccupied in the future.

Lara decided to stay when class was over, the only one left after Mark dismissed class. She was pleased with her creation, a small metal pendant, two contrasting pieces of metal cut and folded together, almost woven, creating a three dimensional piece that looked far more complex than it really was.

Mark stopped by her bench to take a look. "Hey, that's really good. You have a real talent there." He examined the little pendant. "Nice cuts, good proportion. Your cold connections are really solid and neat." He pulled a chair over and sat next to her, startling Lara and making her heart flutter. "Here, let me show you a trick for working with this type of material." They spent the next few minutes, heads together, as Mark worked with a piece of scrap metal, manipulating it.

Mark moved his chair closer to Lara as they worked, and she realized that he was sitting so close his leg was pressed against hers. Mark was very conscious of her body next to his, and created little reasons to touch her as they worked, brushing her hand with his, touching her arm. Her reactions were subtle and unexpected. Lara realized she was growing flushed, and a bit embarrassed at acting like a schoolgirl. Yet there was something undeniably sexy about Mark, and her body was responding to him.

They'd worked together for almost an hour. When they finally sat back, looking at the second pendant she'd made, Lara was amazed at what she had done. It was the same basic design as her original, but with Mark's help, it was far more detailed and refined.

"Wow, this one is so much better than my original." Lara looked at the two lying side by side on the table.

"No, not better, just enhanced. You had a great design and were headed in the right direction. You just needed a little more knowledge on how to take it to the next level. Look, if you already knew how to turn out really high level stuff, you wouldn't need me to teach you." He grinned at her. "I'd be out of a job."

She laughed. "Got it. Okay. What's next?" She wanted to keep going, to make more.

"What's next is a break and a cup of coffee, if you're interested. You've been working most of the day on this." Mark looked at her expectantly. "It's my treat." Lara's heart skipped a beat as she realized he'd asked her out for coffee.

"Okay. Sounds like a good idea. Where do we go for coffee?" Lara wasn't familiar with the college layout.

"Well, I was thinking of leaving here and heading over to a little place I know, on Porter Street. It's a nice little bohemian place with some great coffee, or tea if you prefer, and some interesting ethnic sandwiches. I don't know about you, but I'm hungry." Mark stood, stretching the kinks out of his back. "What do you say?"

"I say that sounds great." Lara was feeling far more relaxed with Mark and was looking forward to talking with him. He held out his hand, pulling her up from her chair, that little current running between them again. They stood still for a moment, just looking into each other's eyes. Lara thought he was going to kiss her.

Mark had never seen eyes quite so vibrant and was lost in the different colors of blue and green swirling in her irises. His instinct was to kiss her and, before he had time to change his mind, he leaned down and gently captured her lips with his. The heat between them was instant and searing. Lara couldn't remember being kissed like that, certainly not in many years. Mark was equally astonished by the arousal he felt at such a brief touch. They both deepened the kiss, Mark pulling her toward him. Lara responded with a little shiver and allowed herself to be wrapped in his arms. They held this kiss for a moment longer, neither really understanding what was happening, and neither of them really wanting to. Both were just enjoying the sensations their exploring lips and tongues were creating.

Mark finally broke away. "Wow. That's never happened before. I usually don't kiss my students on their first day. I usually don't kiss my students at all." He grinned, his face a mix of emotions. "You're quite an attractive woman."

Lara took in his words with amazement. She had wanted to have an affair, and the ideal man seemed to have presented himself, with no work on her part. A tiny voice in her mind said she might regret this, but a louder voice, and all of her body, said go for it. "I find you quite attractive too, Mark."

"What do we do about that?" Mark asked, a glint in his eyes.

"I think we skip coffee and find out just how attracted we really are to each other." Lara wasn't good at flirting and decided a direct approach would get her what she wanted the fastest. "I think we should find some place a little more private and see how things go." She looked up at Mark's brown eyes, now wide with surprise.

"Well, I'm never one to disappoint a lady, especially one as pretty as you. My apartment is right around the corner. It's fairly clean and, if we're in the mood, I can make you some coffee and a sandwich." Lara grabbed her purse and Mark led them to his battered VW in the parking lot. "Sorry for the state of the chariot, but she's been mine longer than I can remember, and she's always reliable. I have a soft spot for her."

He opened the door and Lara slid in. Mark glanced down and caught a glimpse down the front of Lara's sweater. He felt a sudden heat bloom in his stomach, and laughed at himself. I'm like a teenager on a first date, he thought. He'd seen plenty of women's breasts before, but for some reason, the glimpse of Lara's, all tawny golden skin and round curves disappearing into the lacy edge of her bra, had a profound effect on him. He quickly closed the car door and got in, before she realized he was blatantly staring at her.

The ride to Mark's apartment was short. They made easy conversation, realizing they shared interests in art and literature. Lara enjoyed the conversation, relishing having someone intelligent to talk to that shared some of the same loves she did. They were still talking as Mark let them into his apartment. She was struck by the amount of artwork on the walls and the shelves of books. Mark showed her a few pieces, giving her a quick tour of the place, pointing out certain books and artwork. They ended up in the kitchen.

"Would you like a glass of wine?"

"Yes, I think that would be great." Lara sat at the table in the kitchen, watching him move about the small space. She noticed, not for the first time, how broad his shoulders were, tapering down to a narrow waist and hips. She caught her breath at the thought of seeing him shirtless, of running her hands across his chest, feeling the muscles in his arms as he held her. She realized she was staring, and practically drooling.

Mark grabbed some wine glasses and opened a bottle for them. As he poured the wine, he noticed Lara watching him, her face a bit flushed and her pupils dilated. As he handed her the wine, their fingers brushed and they both felt that same electric charge they'd felt before. Only this time, it was magnified. They both knew they could continue down this path without hesitation. Lara broke contact, taking a sip of her wine. Mark moved around the table, taking a swallow of wine and setting the glass down.

He reached for her then, gently cradling her face in his hands and tilting her face up, to his. He leaned down and kissed her, gently rubbing his lips along hers, his tongue softly flicking out to tease her lower lip. Lara managed to put her wine glass down without spilling it, and reached up, wrapping her arms around his neck, pulling him closer to her. They kissed, tongues exploring gently at first, then with more urgency.

Lara pulled Mark closer so he was standing between her legs, her light skirt riding up on her thighs. He could feel himself growing erect at the contact between them, feeling Lara respond to his kisses. He suddenly wanted to feel all of her against him and he pulled her off the chair, standing her on her feet and pulling her hard against him, tightening his hold on her. She came to him willingly, rubbing her body against him like a cat, her breasts against his chest, her stomach rubbing against his hardening cock. He groaned softly at the pressure of her body against him, against his penis.

Lara hadn't been held like this in a long time and she wanted to keep this feeling going as long as possible. But the nearness of Mark's body, the strong arms around her, and his growing erection pressing against her made her hotter than she could have thought possible in such a short time. She couldn't stand still. Her body took on a mind of its own, twisting against him, feeling her breasts crushed against him, her nipples hard and sensitive in the lacy fabric of her bra.

Mark wanted her naked right then. He wanted to take her where she stood. Lara felt his urgency and it fueled her own. She found the zipper on his jeans and tugged it down, sliding her hand in to massage his cock through the cotton fabric of his boxers. Mark pushed himself against her hand, loving the contact, wanting more and more of Lara.

He slid his hands into the waist of her skirt, pulling the soft fabric down over her hips, the garment sliding to the floor. Lara released her hold on his cock to slip her sweater over her head, revealing two tawny breasts, barely concealed in a sheer lacy bra. Mark looked down at her, marveling at the beauty of the woman who stood before him. He pushed his jeans and boxers down, kicking them away, and pulled his T-shirt over his head.

He ran his hands down her back, sliding his hands beneath her panties, pulling them tight against her mound, capturing her sweet ass in his hands. He pulled her to him then, his cock rubbing against the thin fabric, the friction of the material over the heat of her body making him moan softly. Lara responded by twisting her hips against his cock, the fabric pulling tighter as Mark ran his hands further down over her ass. She could feel the material sliding into the wetness of her pussy, rubbing against her clit, and the feeling was intense.

Mark watched as Lara continued rubbing against his erection, pulling back from her to watch her fabric covered mound sliding over him, the tip of his penis visible as his cock slid against her soft skin. Lara looked down, her lips parted as she took in a sharp breath. She tipped her hips forward, increasing the pressure on his cock, continuing to move side to side, pulling the fabric of her panties tighter still against her throbbing clit. Mark had begun thrusting his hips back and forth, pumping his cock slowly up and down against her. They both watched as drops of pre-cum began to form on the tip of his cock as it slid against her body.

Lara rubbed her thumb across the tip of his penis, coating it with liquid, his cock jerking in her hand, Mark groaning with pleasure. She spent a moment gently rubbing the crown of his penis, watching it grow harder at her touch. Mark watched, lips parted, as she moved her hand over him, increasing the pressure on the sensitive crown of his cock.

She knelt down in front of Mark, stroking his cock with her hand. She looked up, at him, her eyes dark with passion.

"I want to put you in my mouth. Do you want me to suck your cock, Mark? Would you like that?" Lara had rarely taken the initiative with Greg. He'd always been the aggressor. She wanted to take the lead with Mark, to be able to take control if she wanted. She also found she wanted to talk dirty. Oddly enough, Greg had never spoken much during sex. She decided, if she was going to be brazen enough to have an affair, she was going to do all the things she'd wanted to do for years.

"Oh, God, yes. Hell, yes. I'd love it if you'd suck me." Mark could hardly believe this gorgeous woman was offering to give him head. He watched with mounting excitement as she delicately licked the tip of his cock, her tongue working the slit in his penis. He groaned out loud, reaching out and caressing her face, running his fingers through her mane of hair. She looked up at him with large eyes, eyes that silently asked if he'd like more.

Mark was lost to her then, letting her take complete control of this experience. Lara began slowly circling the crown of his cock with her tongue, licking the underside, running her lips down the shaft of his penis. She kept up this delicious routine for several minutes before sliding him completely into her mouth, her hand wrapped around the base of his cock.

She held him there a moment, swirling her tongue around the head of his cock. Then, she slowly drew him out of her warm mouth, increasing the pressure with her lips, her tongue still working the crown of his cock. He watched as she took him back into her mouth, watched as his cock disappeared between her lips. He began slowly moving his hips back and forth, his ass tightening and relaxing in time to her ministrations.

Lara had never experienced this kind of power before. She felt a rush of heat, waves of pleasure rolling over her as she sucked and licked Mark's cock. She slid her free hand down the front of her panties, finding them soaking wet. She ran one finger over her clit, jerking as she hit that sensitive mound of flesh, then rubbing her finger in a circle around it, feeling it grow hard at her touch.

Mark looked down, watching Lara sucking his cock as she fingered herself. He was starting to feel his orgasm building and, as much as he might want to grab Lara by the hair and pump himself into her mouth until he was spent, more than that he wanted to feel her pussy around him, to bring her to orgasm with his cock.

He could hold back no longer. He made a noise deep in his throat and pulled away from Lara, grabbing her by the shoulders and pulling her up to him, making her cry out in surprise. He spun them around and lifted her up, setting her ass on the kitchen table, pulling her to the edge and grabbing the waistband of her panties. He tugged them down and off of her, tossing them to the floor and spreading her legs with his hands. Her eyes had grown large and, for a split second, he thought he'd gone too far, but he saw a wild look of passion in her eyes.

"Yes! Fuck me, Mark, pound me with your cock—pound me hard." Lara almost growled out the words, surprised at hearing them coming from her mouth. Yet, saying them had an instant effect on both of them. As Mark grabbed her by the hips, she leaned back, steadying herself on the table, pulling her legs up and further apart. Mark stepped into the space between her legs, looking down at her. Her breasts were still covered by her lacy bra, the nipples hard and pressing against the fabric. He grabbed one luscious breast, crushing it with his hand, making Lara cry out with pleasure.

He drove himself home into her, then thrust his cock into her pussy, feeling the wetness and warmth, the tightness of her around his cock. He held himself there a moment, watching her face, and saw pure pleasure. He pulled back, tensing for the next thrust, eyes locked with hers. He waited. Then, she made the softest whimper. That sound sent him over the edge.

He thrust into her, then, hard and fast, pounding repeatedly into that warm, tight pussy, moving her back on the table. To keep her balance, Lara moved one leg up and over Mark's shoulder, opening her up and giving him a different angle of penetration, letting him push even further into her pussy. Mark reached up and ran his index finger along her lower lip. Lara opened her mouth and he slipped the finger inside. She slowly sucked his finger, Mark sliding it in and out of her mouth in time to his thrusts.

Lara began crying out with each thrust, softly at first, but growing louder, her cries sharper. She could feel her orgasm building, starting in the pit of her stomach, swelling through her body. Mark watched her face, her head tilted back, eyes closed, lips parted. He trailed his finger down her neck, grabbing her breast, rubbing the nipple with his thumb. Lara jerked beneath his touch. He felt her muscles start to tense beneath him.

Mark felt his own body responding, heat starting to build low in his belly, filling his balls, and moving up the shaft of his cock. He wanted to hold back and let Lara come first, to watch her come. He continued rubbing her nipple, thrusting hard into her pussy. She opened her eyes, looking at Mark. The heat and passion in her eyes was tremendous, but there was also hesitation.

Lara was close to the edge, trembling, on the verge of her orgasm. She was looking for that one trigger that would send her over the edge. She looked at Mark, looked into his eyes, wanting him to say something that would bring her off, but not knowing how to ask. Mark sensed she was on the verge, but needing something to push her over.

"I want to watch you cum, Lara, I want to feel you cum," he breathed the words against her ear, running his tongue along the edge of her ear, taking the lobe in his teeth, tugging on it, while he kept thrusting into her. "Cum for me, Lara. Cum for me, now."

His words and breath in her ear were enough to send her over the edge. She convulsed against him, her back arching, an animal sound starting deep inside her, growing louder as her orgasm peaked, finally coming out as a scream. Mark could feel her cumming, contracting around his cock, wetness flooding over him. He watched her face, saw her totally lost in her pleasure. It was enough for him.

With an animal grunt of his own, he felt his balls contract and his cock explode in Lara. He thrust into her quickly, his hips driving several short, sharp thrusts that began pumping his load into her contracting pussy.

He held, pulling Lara against him, her body still shivering from the force of her orgasm, as his peaked and he drove into her one last time, his cock shooting the last of his cum deep into Lara.

He held her in his arms as both their orgasms slowly subsided. Reluctantly, Mark pulled his cock from Lara's slit, sliding her off the table, guiding her until her feet hit the floor and she was steady in his arms. He kissed her deeply, feeling the warmth of her body against his. They stood in the fading afternoon sunlight, holding each other.

Mark drove Lara back to her car at the college. They sat in his car for a moment, talking quietly. Lara kissed Mark and let herself out of his car. She pulled out of the parking lot, heading home. She felt amazing, like some empty space deep inside her had been filled. She laughed at that image. Mark had filled her pretty full with his orgasm. But some missing emotional space had been filled as well, something more than just an afternoon of sex could take care of.

As she turned the corner to her street, she was horrified to see Greg's car in the driveway. She hadn't expected him home. He was never home this early. She pulled in and parked next to his car, walking in through the garage.

Greg was sitting at the kitchen counter, a glass of whiskey on the rocks in front of him.

He looked up as she came in. Lara automatically ran a hand through her hair.

"Hi, hon, you're home early." Lara tried to move past Greg. She really wanted to clean up, before he got too close. Greg looked up from his drink. He reached out an arm and caught her as she walked past, pulling her to him.

"Where've you been? I've been waiting for you for hours."

"I had school, remember?" She moved out of his grasp, setting her purse on the counter and walking into the living room. "It was my first day."

"Ah, yes. School. I forgot." He took another drink. "I thought your class was in the morning, though. It's almost four-thirty." He frowned at her. "Where've you been, Lara?" His voice had grown cold. He stood, covering the distance between them, placing a hand on her arm. He could feel her trembling.

"Lara." He took another step closer. "Fuck, Lara, you had sex. I can smell it on you. You're having an affair. There is no school, is there? You've just been fucking around with someone." Greg had grown angry, his voice rising.

"Greg, I'm not in the mood for an argument." Lara started to walk away, but Greg tightened the hold on her arm.

"No, you're not leaving. We're going to talk about this. I want to know how long you've been fucking this guy. Who is he?"

"I'm not having this conversation with you, Greg. You have no right to accuse me of anything. You're not around enough to even notice what I do, and you certainly don't have any control over my life."

"I do too. I'm your husband. Doesn't that mean anything to you?" Greg pulled her toward him, breathing heavily, his look intense. Lara glared back at him. She looked him straight in the eye.

"No. It hasn't meant anything to you for a very long time. I never see you, you're never here. I wanted to do one thing, to go to school, and you laughed at me. You laughed, Greg. You don't take me seriously. You ignore me. Then, you get upset when you think I've been unfaithful." Lara was furious, breathing just as heavily as Greg. They stared at each other like animals for a moment.

Suddenly, Greg pulled her against his body, crushing her mouth with his kiss. Lara stiffened in his embrace, resisting his kiss. He persisted, holding her to him, forcing her mouth open with his tongue. As much as she tried to resist, Lara felt herself melting against Greg. Her body automatically responded to his touch, remembering what it was like to be held in his arms, something she'd wanted for so long. She stopped struggling, wrapping her arms around his neck, pressing her body against him. She could feel his erection, feel how hard he was.

Greg ran his hand beneath Lara's sweater, groping for her breast, grabbing her bra and pulling it, tearing the strap. He crushed one breast in his hand, rubbing and pulling at the nipple. Lara felt an incredible sense of heat run through her, a primal urge she could not control. She grabbed Greg's belt and zipper, hearing the button pop off his pants as she tore at his clothes. She tugged them down, Greg's cock springing out at her, throbbing and fully erect.

"Here, Greg. Take me here, on the floor." She didn't need to say it again. Greg lowered her down, pulling up her skirt, tugging her panties off, exposing her to him. Greg spread her legs with his knees, kneeling between them, grabbing her by the hips and pulling her up his thighs, toward him, toward his hard cock.

He grabbed himself, roughly rubbing the head of his cock against the lips of her pussy, covering himself with her wetness. He slipped the tip of his cock into her, watching her pussy take him. Lara gasped; she'd forgotten how big his cock was. He looked up into her eyes, saw she was almost begging him to fuck her. He held himself still another moment, feeling heat grow in his stomach, as much as he felt Lara's growing passion. Finally, he could hold back no longer.

With an animal growl, he thrust himself fully into her waiting pussy, holding her by her hips, pulling back and pumping into her again and again. She took him each time, pushing herself up against him as best she could, feeling him stretching her with his cock. He felt the heat moving to his balls, to the base of his cock, moving upward, filling him, and making him hot.

Lara felt her orgasm building, amazed at how quickly she was ready to cum. She felt the warmth moving from her limbs, into her stomach, filling her with heat. Greg was thrusting into her faster, pounding her hard, driving with his hips, grunting with each stroke. She knew he was close, recognizing the noises he made.

Greg felt himself cumming, and his cock exploded into Lara, pumping his hot load into her, letting go with an animal yell. As his cock pulsed into her, he felt Lara arch against him and her orgasm broke. She bucked up as he shot the last of his hot liquid into her. He felt the waves of her orgasm move through her body, watching her quiver as the last of it subsided.

Greg collapsed on top of Lara, then, both of them spent. Lara eventually worked her way out from under Greg, pulling her sweater and skirt down, combing her hair with her fingers. Greg rolled on his back, watching Lara.

"I guess this shows you who you're meant to be with, Lara." She looked down, at him, heard the smug tone in his voice.

"No, Greg, this shows me that you know how to push my buttons and that we fuck really well together." Lara saw the look of shock in Greg's eyes at her language. "But it doesn't change the basic fact that you've been ignoring me for years. And that I've finally decided to make some changes."

"So you're moving out? Leaving me for someone else?" Greg sat up, resting on his elbows. "You've found someone that fast?"

"No, I'm not leaving you for someone else. I'm leaving you for myself, to find my own way." Lara was shocked to hear herself admit she was leaving Greg.

"You leave and there's nothing of mine that

comes with you, you know that." Greg spoke quietly and steadily. "Nothing, Lara. I think you should take some time to think about what you're doing."

Lara was glad for the distraction of class and the chance to see Mark again. She had no illusions that he was the answer to any of her problems, but she was still looking forward to seeing him. She was also happy to be doing something creative, something that was only for her own enjoyment.

Mark walked in, taking her breath away with his handsome presence. He smiled and winked at her, wanting nothing more than to go kiss her, to hold her against him. He decided, though, that wouldn't be a very professional thing to do. The rest of the class period was spent with Mark teaching and Lara totally involved in creating. Both were in their element.

After class, Mark asked Lara if she was interested in learning to make glass lamp-work beads. They went to the glassblowing studio on campus. Mark gave her a quick tour of the area and they watched one of the other artists working. Lara was fascinated with the whole process.

The other artist left the studio, leaving Mark and Lara alone. They'd managed to keep everything on a professional level, but as soon as they were alone, they were wrapped in each other's arms, kissing passionately. Mark managed to flip the lock on the door, before they got too carried away.

There was a couch in one corner of the studio and they stumbled to it, Mark pulling Lara onto his lap, sliding her panties down and pulling her skirt up around her waist. Lara moved to straddle Mark's legs as she worked the zipper down on his jeans. He lifted his hips, sliding his jeans down, his cock already erect. Lara sat back on his legs, taking his cock in her hand and stroking it for a moment, as Mark unbuttoned her blouse and unhooked the clasp on her bra, exposing her breasts. He reached up to hold them, making Lara moan as he tweaked her hard nipples.

As she sat up, Mark slid one hand between her legs, rubbing his fingers over her wet slit, feeling her heat, watching her eyes darken with passion as he stroked her. She looked down at him, a smile playing about her lips.

"That feels so good, Mark. But I want your cock in me. I want you to fuck me, right here, right now." Lara guided Mark's hard penis into her slit, feeling it pushing her open. She lowered herself onto him, hearing his moan. She rubbed herself back and forth, feeling her clit rubbing against the base of his cock, making a delicious friction. Mark continued rubbing her nipples, making them hard and very sensitive.

As she began to ride his cock, Mark leaned toward Lara, licking one hard nipple, flicking his tongue across it, then moving to the other, making Lara shudder. She placed her hands on the back of the couch, pulling her breasts closer to Mark as he took the nipple of one breast in his mouth, sucking on it, pushing his face against the soft flesh, almost suffocating on that luscious globe. Her breasts were perfect, firm but giving, allowing him to take a mouthful of nipple, areola, and soft skin into his mouth, fueling his arousal and sending a jolt of electricity through Lara, right to the very center of her body.

He ran his hands down Lara's back, cupping her, running his fingers down the cleft of her ass, feeling her pussy stretched by his cock. Lara began moving up and down on Mark's shaft. He could feel himself, with the tips of his fingers. He'd reluctantly released Lara's breast from his mouth, his lips parted, moans escaping him. He kept his face between those soft globes, though, her movement rubbing them against his face. He felt totally surrounded by her, his cock buried in her pussy, his face buried in her breasts.

Lara could feel Mark's cock filling her completely, as she moved up and down on him, feeling his hands spreading her ass further apart. She increased her speed, feeling Mark respond by pushing his hips up, thrusting his cock into her. He resumed suckling her, moving between her breasts, which were aching with pleasure from the prolonged attention.

Her position on Mark was causing her clit to be in almost constant contact with the shaft of rigid penis, the friction making a delicious heat start to grow, spreading outward from her clit, building toward her orgasm. She began making little noises in time to Mark's thrusts into her. Mark had spread his legs further apart, sliding down on the couch, changing the angle that he thrust into her, bringing him closer to his own orgasm.

Mark now wrapped his arms around Lara's body, hugging her to him, his head tipped back, almost frantic in his thrusts into her, seeking release. Lara looked down at him, wondering what would tip him over the edge. She leaned down and licked his ear, nibbling his earlobe, breathing into his ear. She rode Mark's cock with more speed and force, bringing herself down on him with each stroke. The change in speed was enough to trigger Mark's orgasm.

With a hoarse groan that was a mix of pain and pleasure, Mark's orgasm hit, his cock exploding into Lara, shooting his first load of hot cum into her warm pussy. She felt the heat of him, his cock spurting inside her. He stopped thrusting upward, grabbing Lara by the hips and forcing her down onto him, moving his hips back and forth as his cock continued pumping into her, almost growling as he ground against her.

The increased contact against her clit, coupled with watching and feeling Mark cum, sent Lara over the edge. As her own orgasm tore through her, she threw her head back with a sharp cry. She spread herself even further over Mark, pushing forward and grinding her pussy against him, rotating her hips as Mark held her against him, both of them locked together as their orgasms flooded through them.

Lara dropped her head to Mark's shoulder

as he held her, the last waves of her orgasm washing through her body. She could feel his cock still twitching inside of her wet pussy, the aftershocks of his orgasm slowly fading. Her blouse had slid off her shoulders and Mark was gently running his hands up and down her back. Lara was struck by this simple gesture, the tenderness it exhibited, something Greg had never shown. There was never any tenderness, or cuddling after sex, with Greg.

She sat up, looking down at Mark. He looked up into her flushed face, pushing a strand of hair from her forehead. "Well, now to make a really horrible joke: there's more than glass that's been blown in this studio."

Lara made a face. "Yes, I agree. That is a really horrible joke."

He continued to hold her for a moment longer, reluctant to remove his cock from her warmth. "This has really been a special couple days, Lara. I know that sounds ridiculous, since we just met, but I haven't had feelings like this, for any woman, for a long time." He pulled her toward him, softly kissing her lips.

"It's been special for me, too, Mark, on many levels." Lara realized she was actually content at the moment, obviously sexually sated, but also satisfied on some emotional level, a feeling she hadn't experienced with anyone, since she was first married to Greg. "You make me feel very special, Mark."

She moved from Mark's lap, sliding down next to him on the couch. He pulled her legs up, so her silky thighs were across his lap. He held one foot in his hand, absently rubbing the arch. Lara pillowed her head on his chest, one hand tracing circles around one of Mark's nipples, which had grown hard beneath her touch, just as hers had been. Mark watched her for a moment, then suddenly grabbed her hand, stopping her.

She looked up in alarm. "What is it?"

"Your arm, you have bruises, like fingerprint bruises. Did I do that to you?" He looked at the purpling marks on her upper arm, a look of horror on his face at the thought he could have hurt her.

"No, Mark, it wasn't you." Lara sat up on the couch, tucking her legs underneath her. "That was my husband, last night."

Mark frowned at her. "You're married? That was not what I expected to hear. But, he hurt you? That's not good, Lara."

"No, it's not." Lara wasn't sure how to explain her life to Mark. She hadn't really thought much about what an affair would entail, and, in this case, it was complicated by the feelings she was experiencing for Mark, and apparently, the feelings he had for her. She decided to just tell Mark the whole sordid story and let him make of it what he would.

"Mark, you don't know me very well. I'm sorry for not telling you sooner, but I really didn't think this was going to be anything other than a one night stand. I didn't think you'd get this involved, or that I'd get this involved, emotionally, that is."

Mark didn't respond. His initial reaction to hearing Lara was married was to run from the room, but he cared about her, and was worried about her being hurt. It was enough to keep him there, holding her.

"Well, the condensed version is this: I've been married for some time. My husband's a businessman, a very successful businessman, one who is never home. I decided to take this class for something to do during the day. Also, because I miss creating things with my hands, I was an art major in college. As far as you and I are concerned, I had been toying with the idea of having an affair. You happened to be in the right place, at the right time. Or, wrong time, I guess." She smiled up at Mark, who didn't return her smile. "You were supposed to be something light and frivolous, something to engage the body, but not, necessarily, the mind. That isn't exactly what happened, though." Mark was still silent. She plowed on with her story.

"My husband has always been very passionate about his business, but never about our marriage. He was always passionate about sex, but I think, for him, it was just the sex, the mastering, or conquering, or something like that. He'd come home from a long day at work, trying to establish himself, fighting his way to the top, doing whatever he did there, and when he got home, he could be the one in control of me. The only way he could really do that was through sex." She stopped, then, amazed she'd never seen her marriage in these terms. She realized it was an emotionally abusive relationship.

"I guess, after a time, he was successful enough in his job, that he felt he'd become lord and master there, and whatever he had with me paled in comparison. Whatever passion he invested in our marriage just faded away. He'd invested it all in his business."

"So, you're a bored and lonely housewife looking for a diversion, and I'm it?" Mark's voice was cold. Lara sat up, looking in his eyes, which were not cold at all. They were filled with pain.

"In a sense, yes. I guess I'm that cliché. But, you've made things different for me. The class was a way to reconnect with the self I was before I got married, someone who was creative, who was artistic, who felt vital and alive. As far as our affair, I admit I thought I wanted something frivolous. But you turned out to be anything but that. Now, it's gotten complicated, and I've hurt you." Lara sat up, moving away from Mark.

"I'll understand if you don't want to see me, if you want me to take a different class, or not come back. I realize this must be painful for you. That was never my intent." Lara looked at Mark. She could see the conflicting emotions in his face.

"Lara, I need to think about this. I've had my heart broken in the past. I've broken them, as well. I'm not sure if I'm ready for this. Hell, I'm not even sure what this is." He realized, they were still half undressed, his penis lying on his thigh and Lara's blouse off her shoulders, still unbuttoned. Her breasts were still visible, faintly damp, from his earlier attentions.

"We need to get dressed. Someone's bound to show up here, eventually." He pulled her blouse up, over her shoulders, letting her button it herself. He zipped his pants and pulled his shirt down, from where it had gotten wrinkled up in the back. Mark reached out and absently straightened Lara's hair.

"Let's go. I'll see you tomorrow. I need to think about what happened." Mark walked her out to her car and watched her drive away.

Lara drove home, not really caring if Greg was there or not. She'd moved into the guest room and went there to take a nap. She was emotionally drained. She lay down on the bed, pulling a light blanket over her shoulders, and dozed off quickly.

She woke in the dark, momentarily disoriented. She lay for a time, listening to the sounds of the house, trying to sense if Greg was home. She wasn't sure, but she didn't think he was. She thought about going downstairs, to get something to eat, but decided she'd rather take a hot bath.

As the tub filled, she added some scented oils to the water and lit a few candles. She poured a glass of wine and brought it to the bath, along with the most recent paperback she'd been reading.

She stripped off her clothes, dropping them on the bathroom floor. She turned off the water, swirling the bubbles around in the tub. She got in and settled back, sipping wine and reading her book. She was relaxing, enjoying the bath, when she heard the garage door open. Greg was home.

Lara heard him calling her name. She sighed. She really wasn't in the mood to deal with him, but she supposed as long as she was still in this house, she'd have to at least talk to him. She got out of the tub, dried off and slipped on her clothes. She took her wine and walked out, onto the upstairs landing. She could see down into the living room. Greg was sitting on the couch with a glass of whiskey. She walked down the stairs, carrying her wine.

"Where have you been? School again?" He asked. He didn't seem as angry as the last time she saw him, but she knew he could control his outward emotional appearance easily. He could be very hard to read sometimes.

"I was taking a bath. I didn't hear you come in." She sat down in the chair across from him.

"So what do we do now, Lara? Are you leaving me for someone else, or for yourself, as you put it? You're giving up on us completely?" Greg took a swallow of alcohol. "Don't I have a say in any of this?"

"Greg, listen to me. For a long time now, I've been trying to tell you how I feel about our marriage, what I'm missing in my life, what I think we could do to make things better. So far, you've ignored me, or laughed at me. You act like being married takes no work, that once you said, I do, and paid for everything, that the hard part was done. But, there's more to it than that." Greg was watching her and she went on.

"You've never shied away from a fight in

your business. You know that each day is a challenge to keep what you have, what you've worked hard for. A marriage is the same thing, but you've given up the fight and you've lost our marriage, and lost me. Now, I'm fighting to get back my life." Lara took a drink of wine. "I'm the one who's trying to fight for my life."

At that, Greg snorted with derisive laughter. "Fighting for my life. Hell, Lara, it's not a war zone here. It's not that big of a deal. You want to go to school, play artist, that's fine. But that's not the same as fucking around on me, behind my back. That is unacceptable." He drained his glass, walking to the kitchen for a refill. He continued talking over his shoulder.

"You think your life is so hard. You've had everything handed to you, Lara. You haven't had to work a day, the entire time we've been together." She could hear the clink of the ice as he filled his glass. "You think my life is easy? I've had to fight, fight for everything, we— you— have here: staff, a big house, traveling, all of it! Some fantastic sex, also, if I do say so myself. And you want to throw all that away, because you can't find something to do in the afternoon. I don't understand you."

Greg sat back down on the couch. Lara looked at him, a frown creasing her forehead. She had no idea where to start with Greg, how to make him see how she felt. They'd had this conversation, minus the references to an affair, many times. It always ended with her in tears and him not changing, or, more precisely, not thinking he needed to change, but not this time.

"Screw you, Greg." Lara spat the words at him, taking a moment to savor the look of utter shock on his face. "If you think all I want from you is a big clean house and the occasional fuck, then you're sadly mistaken. You haven't even held up that part of your agreement. The only fuck I've had with you lately was yesterday. And, that was only because you wanted to claim me as your territory, like a dog pissing on a tree. I'm no tree, Greg. And you can't piss on me, anymore." Lara knew she sounded grandiose, but she was past caring. She stood up, eyes blazing, and walked out of the living room.

Greg caught her before she reached the kitchen. He grabbed her arm, spinning her around to him. He tried to kiss her, but Lara slapped Greg across the cheek, surprising them both. Greg let go of her arm, hand to his face.

"Don't ever lay a hand on me again, Greg," she said, with cold intensity. "You have crossed the line. I am leaving you, and I'm leaving tonight." She went past Greg, heading up the stairs. At the landing, she looked down. He was still standing there, watching her with an unreadable expression on his face. She wasn't quite sure if he was angry enough to follow her, but she didn't want to wait to find out.

She went to their room, threw an overnight bag on the bed, and tossed in whatever clothes she could grab. She got dressed in jeans and a T-shirt, pulling on a leather jacket.

She went down the back stairs, through the

kitchen, and grabbed her keys and purse. Greg was sitting on the couch, the whiskey bottle and ice bucket, now, on the coffee table, in front of him. He looked up when he heard her keys jingle.

"So, this is really it, huh?" Greg looked her over. "Like I said, nothing of mine goes with you. That includes any part of the business. You're shit out of luck, financially. I give you a month before you're back, looking to get back in here." He waved his glass around, indicating the living room. Whiskey sloshed on his arm. She realized he was really drunk. She wanted to leave before anything else happened. Greg was still talking.

"There are lots of women who'd kill for what you have. I've met some, you know, who are impressed by what I am, what I've done. They appreciate a man who's self-made, with money and a nice house, and gives them things, shows them a good time, gives them a good time in bed." Suddenly Greg fell quiet, appearing very interested in the facets of his glass.

"You've met women who appreciate a good time in bed? With you?" As much as Lara wanted to bolt, she walked toward him. "Who have you given a good time to recently, Greg? Is that why you're never home? Have you been fucking around, Greg?" She stood next to the couch. He was slouched down, his tie loosened, his shirt untucked, legs spread. He smelled, now, of whiskey. In a word, he looked like hell.

"Yeah, so you think you're original? You never even knew, Lara. At least I was discreet.

You're not even good at having affairs." She was appalled at him, for his admission and at herself, for not realizing what was happening. In an instant of anger, she picked up the ice bucket and dumped it over his head, threw the bucket on the floor, and stormed out. A cascade of ice and melted water ran down his chest, into his lap. He jumped, spilling more of his drink, trying to brush the cubes from his lap. "You bitch!" he cried after her.

Lara got in the car, her hands shaking. She started the car, backed out into the street, and had no idea where to go. Her parents were too far away, she didn't have any real friends in town, and a hotel seemed too cold and alone. Mark flashed into her mind, and, before she really gave it too much more thought, she drove to his apartment.

She rang his buzzer, suddenly apprehensive. He opened the door, a shocked look on his face. "Lara. What's wrong? You're shaking. Did he hurt you again? Did he hit you?" Mark searched her face, concerned.

"No, not tonight. But I have left him, for good. I just don't have any place to go to. You're the only person I really know, other than my personal chef, and I don't think that's where I want to go. I'm not asking for anything, other than a place to stay for tonight, until I can make some plans. I'll sleep on the couch." She heard her words come out in a rush and realized she sounded desperate.

"Come in. Drop your stuff there." She did as she was told, then promptly burst into tears. Mark held her a moment, then led her to the couch. She cried quietly against his shoulder for a little while, eventually sitting up and wiping her eyes.

"I'm sorry." She looked up at him. "This is probably the wrong place to be and the wrong thing to do."

Mark looked down, at her. "Yes, it probably is. But, here's the thing. After you left, I did some thinking. I thought of all the reasons this was wrong, all the reasons I shouldn't continue this, with you. Then, I stopped thinking and started feeling. I felt empty, like something was missing. I can't really explain it, other than I missed you. I was angry with you. I am still angry, and hurt, but the overwhelming feeling I had was loss."

Lara was watching him, intently, almost holding her breath. She felt some of the weight lifting from her heart.

"Don't look quite so relieved," Mark cautioned her, seeing the look of hope on her face. He smiled for the first time since she'd arrived. He spoke gently. "I can't tell you what's going to happen next, other than I don't want you to be out of my life. I can't make you any promises, but if you're willing to see where this goes, I'm willing to give us a chance. I may be making a big mistake. We may both end up with our hearts broken. But, that's where I am with this. With us."

Mark took Lara's face in his hands, kissing her, gently. "You can stay here, until you figure out what you need, and where you want to stay. I'm thinking you're going to need some kind of job. If you're interested, the college is looking for some part-time help in the art department. It's not anything glamorous. I think it's a basic administrative position. But it would be a foot in the door and some income, which I think you're going to need."

Lara looked up at him, relief and gratitude in her eyes. "Thank you. I know this is hard for you and I've put you through a lot in a really short time. I appreciate you letting me stay and really appreciate the lead on a job. You're right, it is something I need." She hugged him and he wrapped his arms around her. She felt his heart beating through his shirt.

She looked up at Mark, tears in her eyes. "I don't know how I can make up for hurting you. And I don't want to hurt you anymore." Mark leaned down and kissed her, gently running his lips over hers. She was hesitant, not sure of his intent, and Mark sensed this.

"I may be angry with you and I may be hurt, but I still find you incredibly attractive, and very much want to make love to you, as illogical as that may sound. Hormones overruling common sense, I guess." He shrugged his shoulders, giving her a small smile. "We're going to have to take this one day at a time, Lara. Right now, on this day, I want to take you to bed." He pulled her up off the couch, wrapping her in his arms.

Lara felt Mark's attraction to her and felt her body respond. He pulled her against him, kissing her deeply. She could feel his growing erection as he held her. They managed to stumble the few steps to his bedroom, still locked in an embrace.

The only light was from a low lamp in the bedroom. Mark's face was in shadow, but she could read the passion in his eyes as he pulled her shirt up and over her head. Lara worked at the buttons of his shirt, sliding it off his shoulders and down his arms, running her hand over his broad chest.

Mark looked down at Lara, the light catching the round tops of her breasts, pushing up from a simple white bra. He ran his hands up her sides, holding her breasts, pushing them together, his thumbs skating across the nipples, pressing against the fabric of the bra. He leaned down and kissed the top of one breast, then the other, rubbing his cheek against her, nuzzling her silky skin. Lara twined her fingers in his hair, enjoying the attention he lavished on her breasts, feeling a jolt of heat run through her. She reached behind her and undid the hooks of her bra, letting it fall to the floor.

He continued kissing her breasts, licking the nipples, taking one into his mouth to suck for a moment. He flicked his tongue across the other hard nipple, teasing it, feeling a shiver run through Lara. His body responded, both to her arousal and to the sensation of sucking on her breast. He felt his cock grow harder, pushing against his sweats, making him moan softly.

Lara heard him and reached down to touch him, running her hand over the bulge in his sweatpants. Mark abruptly straightened, pulling his sweats down to release his erection, huge and hard.

"Touch me, Lara. Rub my cock while I suck on your tits." Lara looked down at his cock, and took him in her hand, slowly stroking him. Mark watched her work his cock for a moment, one hand still on her breast. "Oh, yes. Just like that, nice and slow." He bent his head again to her breasts, licking one nipple, until it was hard. He pulled that nipple into his mouth, holding her breast in his hand, sucking it slowly, taking as much of her breast in his mouth as he could.

Lara looked down at Mark sucking her breast, and felt a searing heat low in her stomach, and what felt like a small orgasm run through her body. She'd never had any man make her feel that hot, just from having her breasts sucked. It was incredible.

Mark was rocking his hips, slowly, back and forth in time to her strokes. He wanted to stay here forever, sucking and kissing Lara's breasts, but his cock had different ideas. Reluctantly, he lifted his head, releasing Lara's breast, standing straight and looking down at her. He reached down and gently tugged at the zipper on her jeans, pulling them down with her panties. Lara stepped out of them and kicked them to the side. They stood naked for a moment, looking at each other's bodies in the soft light.

"Make love to me, Mark. I want to feel you inside of me." Lara lay down on the bed, pulling Mark on top of her. She could feel his cock rubbing against her thigh as he reached between her legs, stroking her pussy. He could feel how wet, how ready she was, thrusting against his hand. He moved between her legs, holding his cock, rubbing the tip over her lips and clit.

Lara was whimpering, ready to have him

enter her. He looked up at her, the passion in her eyes intense. He could hold back no longer, thrusting hard into her, feeling her take all of him. Lara cried out, pushing against him, her hips lifting to meet his cock.

Mark stroked in and out of Lara at a steady pace, watching her face, keeping her on the edge for as long as he could. He could sense she was building to an orgasm. Her thrusts against him became more forceful, and she started whimpering, crying out with each thrust.

Lara's increased arousal triggered a response in Mark. He began thrusting into her with more force, pumping faster into her pussy. He felt heat building in his stomach, flowing into his balls, as his orgasm started to build. He closed his eyes, head back, as he felt himself close to peaking.

A sharp cry from Lara as her orgasm broke, sent him over the edge. They climaxed together, hips thrusting, waves of passion washing over them, Mark shooting his load into her, his cock pumping over and over as his hot cum exploded from him.

The waves of the climax slowly subsided, leaving them both spent. Mark lay beside Lara, pulling her against him, covering them with the sheet. They lay in each other's arms until Mark started falling asleep. Lara gently nudged him.

"Are you sure you want me in your bed? I can sleep in the guest room, or on the couch, if this is going to be awkward." Lara propped herself up on one elbow.

Mark didn't open his eyes as he spoke.

"There is no guest room and the couch is lumpy. I wouldn't make you sleep on that, and I'm not enough of a gentleman to offer to sleep on it and let you have the bed. So, this is the best you'll get here, even though it's entirely the wrong thing for us to do."

Lara leaned down and kissed him. "In this case, I think the wrong thing is entirely right."

4 LOVE'S MASQUERADE

Greg Finch stood uncomfortably in the corner, tugging at the too-tight collar of his shirt. He was attending a charity ball—a masked ball—of all things. His cousin Beth arranged these events and had begged him to attend, dressed in costume. He looked like the Phantom of the Opera, complete with the mask over his face. Beth said these things were always short of good looking men who were willing to wear costumes. He could see why.

His mask itched. As Greg fidgeted and glanced at his watch, he caught the scent of exotic perfume. When he turned, he found himself looking into a stunning pair of emerald eyes visible behind a bejeweled and feathered black mask. The rest of the woman was dressed in a black velvet gown, cut very low, displaying bare shoulders, porcelain skin and the tops of two rounded breasts. Her long arms were covered in black velvet gloves that extended up over her elbows. As he was taking in this costume, he noticed with a bit of a start that she was wearing a spiked dog collar, instead of the ornate costume jewelry the other women were wearing. His eyes traveled back up to hers and he found her smiling at him.

"Enjoying the view?" She had a low pitched voice, soft but strong, tinged with something dark and mysterious.

"Um, oh, well, sorry." Greg stammered.

"Don't be. I didn't wear this to be a wallflower. And speaking of wallflowers, why is a handsome man like you standing in the darkest corner of the room? We need to get you out and in circulation. You're wasted here." With that she took his arm and propelled him onto the dance floor. The music for the evening was an eclectic mix modern music with a few waltzes mixed in. The orchestra was currently warming up for a waltz, something Greg had never attempted before.

"I don't know—" he started.

"Yes, I know, you don't know how to waltz." The woman expertly turned him to face her, arranged his arms in the proper position and looked him in the eye. "Just follow my lead, you'll be fine."

The music started and she began expertly moving him on the dance floor. His initial clumsy trips soon gave way to something resembling a waltz. They made several circuits of the dance floor and Greg found he was actually enjoying himself. The woman in his arms was lithe and graceful. The parts of her face he could see were stunning and the body beneath his hands was firm but still held luscious curves. Her hair, done in an upsweep of curls with tendrils trailing down her long neck, was a fiery red that caught the light, practically sending sparks into the air. Greg realized he was mesmerized by this whole experience.

The waltz stopped and the band began a slow number. Without missing a beat, the masked woman pulled Greg to him, her sensual movements overwhelming his senses. He pulled her closer still, feeling no resistance from her. In fact, she adjusted their embrace so that one long leg rested between his, her hip not so subtly rubbing against him. He felt himself stiffen at her touch and attempted to put some distance between them. "Don't move, this is perfect," the silky whisper in his ear said. "Hold me tighter."

Not knowing what was really happening, and not really caring, Greg ran his hand down her back, to that sweet spot in the small of the woman's back, just above the curve of her ass, where the waist narrows before her hips began their gentle flair. He really longed now to reach down and cup her ass with his hand, to increase the pressure between them, but that didn't seem quite right. But what they were doing was incredibly arousing for Greg. He had never done anything like this, nor known any woman who would act this way. The touch of her, moving slowly back and forth across his growing erection, was sending shivers up his spine. The fact they were in public made this even more exciting. He could feel her breasts pressing against the starched front of his shirt, feel the warmth of her along the length of his body. He hoped the orchestra would play a long set of slow dances.

But, as luck would have it, the next song picked up the tempo. "Let's find some place to continue this," she whispered in Greg's ear.

She led him to a side door, both of them slipping through and down a short hallway. She opened another door near the end of the hall to what appeared to be a small office. The woman locked the door behind her and turned to Greg. In the light from the window at his back, he could see her eyes on him, eyes that almost glowed in the dark. Before he could speak, she walked forward and put her gloved hands on his shoulders, drew him close and kissed him. He stumbled back against the desk in the middle of the room.

Greg's hands found themselves now giving way to his earlier fantasy, cupping what proved to be a very sweet ass, round and firm. She made no move to stop him and allowed him to pull her against his erection. She wrapped her arms around his neck and deepened their kiss, her tongue flicking over his lips. He opened to her, their tongues meeting and exploring each other's mouths.

They continued kissing, Greg pressed against her, as she slowly moved her hips back and forth, rubbing herself against him and apparently enjoying the feel of his hardening cock against her stomach. Greg was aching to release that cock from the confines of his pants. The woman apparently read his mind. She backed away from Greg, slowing removing her gloves and dropping them on the floor. She worked the zipper down on his pants, reaching in with one warm hand to fondle his penis.

Surprised by her actions, Greg groaned and his hips involuntarily thrust against her hand. This seemed to be a reaction she anticipated and she began a slow massage of his erect cock, moving her palm up and down over the fabric of his boxers, stroking the length of him, cupping his balls on the down stroke.

Greg found her breasts and ran his hands over the globes, which were spilling out of the top of her dress. She arched her back, pushing them into his hands, obviously seeking more contact and Greg obliged. His cock was almost completely hard, her hand continuing to stroke him slowly. He wanted more and he wanted it now.

A primal urge came over him and he spun the woman around, turning her so she faced the desk, bending her over its top. He grabbed her hips and ground his cock against that round ass. She bent over further for him and in a surprising move, pulled up the skirt of her dress, exposing her perfect ass to Greg, who realized she was not wearing any panties. He yanked down his pants and boxers in one motion, reaching between her legs with one hand, eagerly fingering her hot opening, the other stroking his now rock hard cock. To his amazement, she was quite aroused and very wet.

As he watched his fingers sliding back and forth over her pussy, she arched her back and tilted her hips, exposing more of her wet slit and swollen pussy to him. Greg couldn't hold himself back; he plunged his cock into her in one thrust, burying himself completely in that warm wetness. He felt her shudder beneath him, briefly losing her balance. He pulled back and thrust into her again, this time feeling her rock back against him, gaining control. Greg continued to pound into her and she matched him, stroke for stroke. He leaned over her, changing the angle of his thrust and sliding one hand into the bodice of her dress, freeing one breast. He fondled the firm globe, feeling the nipple grow hard beneath his fingers. He caught a glimpse of the dog collar around her neck and had a brief but highly erotic and rather startling image of her on all fours wearing nothing but the collar and a leash, at his beck and call.

He felt her touching herself then, fingering her own clit, occasionally brushing his cock with her fingers. She was so very wet now, rubbing herself harder, small cries coming from her throat. Her knees bent slightly and her hips tilted forward. Her breath was coming in short gasps.

He sensed she was close to coming and that brought him nearer to his own orgasm. He began thrusting harder, spreading his legs for leverage. He had the sense of losing control of his body and he grabbed her by her luscious hips. His own hips tilted forward, his knees bending, his cock seeming to take on a life of its own, driving into her faster and faster. He felt his orgasm starting, that familiar heat building in him, beginning in his center, gathering and moving down into the base of his cock. His balls began to contract and he felt the hot liquid of his imminent orgasm filling his shaft, bringing him closer to his peak with each thrust.

The woman beneath him now shuddered violently, letting out a hoarse cry as he felt her orgasm rip through her body. She threw her head back, her hand still rubbing her swollen clit as her body shook with the waves of her orgasm.

Feeling her contract around his hard cock sent Greg over the edge. He thrust into her twice, hard and quick. Then one final thrust buried him to the hilt in her, as his hot cum exploded from his cock into her wet pussy. His head fell back and a cry escaped his lips as his cock continued pumping his juices into her. He made several more short thrusts into her, amazed his cock could still be pushing out more hot cum. This was the most intense orgasm he'd had in a long time.

The woman braced herself against the edge of the desk, letting him thrust into her as he finished his orgasm. They were both breathing hard, both momentarily lost in the aftershocks that shook their bodies.

Greg pulled back from her, his penis still semi-erect, and watched his cum continue to dribble from its tip. The woman turned around, dropping her dress back in place and adjusting her bodice to cover her breasts. She looked down at Greg's glistening wet penis covered with their hot juices and before he could register what she was doing, she dropped to her knees and began delicately licking the slit of his penis, catching the pearly drops of his cum with her tongue. Her eyes met his, her face still covered by her mask, a smile playing around the corners of her mouth. He watched in amazement as she worked the head of his cock with her tongue, the sensations almost overwhelming after such a huge orgasm. But he didn't want to stop the delicious torture she was inflicting. He felt his cock twitch, becoming harder again. He wanted to set her on the desk, to thrust into that pussy again, to tear the mask from her and watch her face this time, to see the passion in those emerald green eyes as he brought her to another climax.

She seemed to sense this all and stood. "I'm afraid our time is up for tonight. We should return to the dance." She stood on her tiptoes and leaned in to kiss him, flicking her tongue into his mouth. "Can you taste yourself? Can you taste how you taste, how good we taste together?" Greg was dumbstruck; no woman he'd ever known had ever said or done anything like that to him. He was entirely at her command at that moment. If she had asked him to go naked back to the ball, he would have done so.

"You shouldn't leave here with me. Stay here a moment and then go back to the dance." She walked to the door, unlocked it and slipped through. Before closing it, she blew him a kiss and dropped a demure curtsy. "Thank you, sir, for a most wonderful ball... in more ways than one." And with that, she was gone.

Greg realized he was standing in the middle

of a strange office, with several hundred party-goers in the room next door, his pants around his ankles and half of a hard-on sticking out in front of him. He should have felt embarrassed, he thought, but instead he felt like he could rule the world.

Greg returned to the ball, searching for the woman, looking for the distinctive mask, carrying her discarded gloves. He had made a brief stop at the men's room, quickly but regretfully washing away the rich musk of their encounter. He thought he saw her at one point and made his way toward the woman, only to discover it was not her. He made several rounds of the floor, but could not find her. He eventually found his cousin Beth, deep in conversation with one of the event's sponsors.

"Hey, Greg, where have you been?" Beth looked up at him. "And what have you been doing? You look like the cat who swallowed the canary."

Greg smiled. "I met someone. But now I can't find her. Do you know who the woman in the black dress with the mask is?"

"Geez, Greg, be a little vaguer, please. There are a couple dozen women here in black dresses and they're all wearing masks. Anything else you can tell me besides that?"

"Um... well, she has green eyes and red hair. And she was wearing a dog collar."

Beth laughed. "That's Cassandra Holland. I don't know her, but she was invited through her employer. Wait, I have that list here somewhere." She turned back with a clipboard, running a finger down the list. "Here, she's from Erskine, Backer and Galang. I'm not sure if she's a lawyer or not, but that's who's listed as her employer." Beth looked at him with a puzzled expression on her face. "Are you planning to track her down?"

"Yes." Greg spoke with a little more force than he anticipated. They were both taken back by the conviction in his voice. Beth shot him a warning glance.

"Greg, what exactly happened here that you want to track down someone you don't even know?" she asked, planting her hands on her hips.

He leaned over, planting a kiss on Beth's cheek. "Beth, it's been a fantastic event, thanks for inviting me. But I need to go now." Leaving her with more questions than answers, he strode out of the ballroom and into the cool night air. His senses were still alive from his encounter with the woman, with Cassandra. He said her name softly to himself, imagined whispering it in her ear, feeling her body again beneath his hands. The image of her in the dog collar and leash rose up in his mind again, raising his still-sensitive cock to a semi-erect state. He'd need to put a leash on his own mind pretty soon, or he'd be spending his days with a perpetual erection.

Greg did a few internet searches at work the next day on the Erskine, Backer and Galang website and quickly discovered Cassandra Holland was an attorney in the intellectual property area of the firm. He had no idea what intellectual property was, nor did he really care. What he did care about was that her contact information was listed on the site: her email and phone number were right there.

Suddenly he didn't know how to take the next step. Should he call? Email? Just go there? What if she didn't remember him? How could she not remember him? How could she forget? Before his courage left him, he picked up the phone and dialed her number. Almost wishing for her voicemail, he was momentarily lost in thought when she answered.

"Cassandra Holland." The voice was the same, but the efficiency in which she answered threw him off. He hesitated. "This is Cassandra Holland. How may I help you?"

"Ah, yes. Um, well, you don't know me..." Greg wished he'd at least planned something to say before he decided to call. "I... we, well, you and I... we met last night at the charity ball." He heard a muffled sound on the line. "Hello? Are you still there?"

"Yes, I am. And can you tell me your name?" The voice had taken on a teasing quality, although still professional.

"Oh, yeah. I'm Greg Finch."

"And Mr. Finch, how can I help you today?"

"Um... Well, I was wondering... I thought, since we... would you..." This was not going well. Greg had the overwhelming urge to hang up the phone.

"Mr. Finch, I appreciate your interest. I am otherwise occupied at the moment, but would be happy to call you back in 20 minutes. Can you give me a number where I can reach you?"

Greg felt like a complete fool. He gave her his office number and they ended the call. She'd never call and there was no way now he could call her back. He dropped his head in his hands and spent a miserable few minutes contemplating this depressing development. He opened up his spreadsheet program and started entering numbers, creating charts and doing other mindless tasks to take his mind off the epic failure that had just occurred. He was just finishing up the monthly production numbers when his phone rang.

"Greg Finch here."

"And Cassandra Holland here. Now we know where everyone is. I believe you have a question for me?"

Greg almost dropped the phone. "Oh, hey... thanks for calling back. Um, yeah, I was wondering if you'd like to get together for drinks sometime. I... we, well, last night you... and I have your gloves." Again Greg's mind went blank.

"Are you saying you're interested in getting to know me better, after our encounter last night at the charity ball, and would like to pursue that goal over drinks? And return my gloves?"

"Um, yeah... I mean, yes." Greg's mind was turning to putty. The silky sound of Cassandra's voice was doing magical things in his ear.

"I enjoyed our own private event last night. Did you?"

"Yes, I did." Greg's voice went husky at the memory. "I enjoyed it very much."

"Good. I'm glad. I did too. I particularly enjoyed the forceful way you bent me over the desk." Cassandra's voice had taken on a seductive tone.

Greg almost dropped the phone again. "Well, yes... I mean, that was... yes..." He had no idea what to say to her or what to do with this line of conversation, but he wanted to see where she would take it.

"I enjoyed the feeling of your hand exploring me, your fingers stroking my wet pussy over and over. And then being fucked by your hard cock, feeling it deep inside me..." Cassandra's deep sultry voice combined with her very descriptive words was having a very physical effect on Greg. He could feel his trousers tightening over his stiffening penis, could feel himself getting flushed. He shifted in his chair and desperately wished he had closed the door to his office.

"Are you still there?" Cassandra asked.

"Yes," was Greg's hoarse reply.

"Do you want me to continue? Are you enjoying this conversation? Are you getting hard?"

"Oh, God, yes. But I need to close my office door." Greg practically crawled over his desk to slam his door, flicking the lock with his thumb. He dove back for the receiver. "I'm back."

"Pesky office doors. I'll continue then: you're fucking me from behind, and your cock feels so good, so hard. You're thrusting it into me, your body slamming against my ass. I can feel you filling me up, pounding into me." Cassandra's voice had taken on a breathy quality, little gasps escaping between the words. "Are you getting harder? Are you touching yourself?"

"Yes." Greg had reached down and was rubbing himself through his clothes, his cock growing harder with each word Cassandra said. He could almost feel her hot breath through the phone. "I am."

"Good. Unzip your pants, reach in and take it out and stroke that hard cock. Feel it like I felt you. Imagine that's my hand on your cock, rubbing you, stroking you. Do you feel me? Does that feel good?"

Greg had never had anyone talk to him like this over the phone. He did as he was told, unzipping his pants as she instructed. His cock was hard in his hand. He looked down and watched as he began stroking himself. Cassandra's silky voice continued in his ear.

"Do you know what I'm doing?" she said. Greg had a pretty good idea. "I'm touching myself. I'm sitting at my desk, with my skirt up and I'm rubbing myself, just like you did last night. I'm feeling your fingers in my pussy, feeling you rub my clit, feeling it growing harder under your touch, feeling myself getting wetter." Greg heard a little cry on the other end of the line, so much like the sounds Cassandra had made last night as he thrust into her.

Greg began rocking his hips up and down in his office chair, his cock thrusting itself into his hand. One small part of his brain wanted her to stop before this got out of control, but the rest of his brain and all of his body wanted nothing more than to continue. He tightened his grip on his cock, stroking it faster, seeing beads of pre-cum forming on the tip.

"I'm so ready, I'm so close. Can you bring me off? Are you close to coming? Do you remember what it felt like, fucking me, feeling me cum as you fucked me hard? I remember and it felt good. I remember what your orgasm felt like, feeling you pump harder and harder into me, feeling your cum explode on me, feeling your hot juices in my pussy... ah... I can feel.... oh, God, I can feel myself.... I'm coming now!" Greg listened as Cassandra's words deteriorated into the sounds of her having an orgasm at the other end of the line, sounds he remembered from last night.

Greg was powerless to stop his own orgasm then, the sounds of Cassandra in his ear driving him over the edge. He felt the shaft of his penis filling with his hot cum and he stroked himself harder and faster, his hips jerking and his cock thrusting into his tightening grip. His stomach muscles contracted, he felt his balls tense and then he exploded. Greg grunted into the phone.

"You're coming in me now. Can you feel yourself in me, pumping your cum into my wet pussy? Does that feel good?"

He looked down and watched as his cock

pumped his hot cum into his hand and onto to the front of his pants. "Yes... oh, God, yes... you feel so good."

"Did you like that?" Cassandra's voice almost purred into the phone. "Was that good?"

Greg was still recovering, his cock twitching in his hand, seeking to pump out the last drops of cum. He watched it dribbling down the side of his semi-erect penis. "Yes... yeah, that was good... very good." Was he supposed to say thank you?

"I'm glad you enjoyed that. I did too. I'm sorry I am not there to lick you clean as I did last night, but sometimes we must make sacrifices. Now, I believe you wanted to meet for drinks? Did you have a time and place in mind?"

Greg's mind was mush; her reminder of how she had licked his cock after their encounter brought back a flood of memories and sensations. He also realized she had asked him a question, to which he had no answer.

"If you do not, may I suggest the Lotus Room at the Peking Hotel? It's off of Green on Lancaster. Say eight o'clock? Will that be acceptable?"

"Um... okay. I mean, yes. The Lotus Room at eight. Yes, that sounds great. See you then." Greg hung up the phone and sat back in his chair. He realized he was still holding himself, his penis no longer erect but sensitive to his touch. He reached for some tissue and cleaned himself as best as he could. The front of his pants had a small stain, but most of his seed had mercifully landed on his boxers. He tucked himself back in his boxers and zipped up his pants. If he wore his suit jacket the stain wasn't that noticeable. Maybe he'd just stay in his office for the rest of the day. He wondered if this was something Cassandra did frequently at work, had phone sex while sitting at her desk. His mind wandered away again, imagining her at her desk, skirt hiked up, her legs spread and her feet, in black stiletto heels he decided, up on her desk. He wondered if she was wearing any panties.

Greg was at the Lotus Room fifteen minutes early, sitting in a dark corner booth, waiting for Cassandra. He saw her through the front windows, walking up the steps of the hotel in heels and a demure business suit. The contrast from last night's costume was sharp; her thick tumble of red curls was now caught back in a sleek tail low on her neck, her suit jacket covering the arms and shoulders that were bare last night. The spiked dog collar had been replaced by a simple silver chain and a loosely tied flowered scarf. She looked like an extremely professional attorney.

Cassandra saw Greg and walked over, her long legs moving beneath the tight skirt of her suit. Greg felt a stirring inside at seeing her. It was more than just animal passion though; he felt truly happy to see her.

"Hello, Greg." Cassandra slid into the seat

next to him. "How are you? Did you have a good day at the office?" Her tone was light and teasing, a playful glint in her eye, even though her words were perfectly ordinary.

"Yes, very productive." Greg wasn't used to women who teased him sexually and he again didn't have any idea how to approach Cassandra. She seemed to enjoy taking the lead. The waitress came and took their order, returning with their drinks. Cassandra took a sip; Greg took a large swallow of his.

"Do I make you nervous, Greg?" Cassandra's perfume was playing havoc with Greg's senses.

"Well, to be honest, I'm not sure how you make me feel. I've never had an experience like last night and then after I thought you'd be on the dance floor; I thought we'd spend more time together. But you'd left."

"Ah, yes, Cinderella leaves the ball, only she left her gloves behind, not a glass slipper." Cassandra laughed. "I don't believe I need a Prince Charming though. For me, the allure of having a clandestine encounter such as we had is to keep the mystery going. The thrill of the hunt, as it were, is just as exciting as capturing the prey, don't you think? Didn't you have a much more enjoyable day today in anticipation of tonight? The unknown is always far more titillating than the familiar. The familiar bores me." Cassandra had been speaking in a low voice, moving closer to him on the seat.

"I'm glad I tracked you down though." Greg took another gulp of his drink. Cassandra was watching him under lowered lids, her head tilted to the side.

"Oh, yes, I am very glad you found me." She placed one hand on his leg, her warm fingers caressing his thigh. "Very glad indeed."

Greg decided to admit he was feeling out of his league. "No woman I've ever known has done to me the things you've done or had sex over the phone with me, or excited me as much as you do." He looked into her green eyes.

"Maybe you've been meeting the wrong women," Cassandra increased the pressure on his leg, gently caressing him, running her hand down the inside of his thigh. "Men should not have all the fun of being the aggressor; women should be allowed to have some fun too. Don't you agree?" She leaned forward, catching his lower lip in her teeth, gently biting him, her tongue flicking over his lips. She released him and he caught her lips with his own, gently sucking them and deepening their kiss, tasting the alcohol from her drink on his tongue. Her hand continued to rub his leg, her forearm occasionally brushing his crotch. He felt the first stirrings of desire stiffen his penis, but he sensed she was holding back from a full-on encounter here in the bar, content with teasing him slowly.

She broke their kiss. "You said you wanted to get to know me better?" she asked, returning to her drink and gazing up at him. "Do you have any questions you'd like to ask? Or... were you interested in getting to know me through actions rather than words? As much as I enjoyed our phone conversation today, I prefer more personal encounters."

"I'd like both. I mean, I'd like to know more about you as a person, talk about personal things, I mean... get to know you better before we... if we..." Greg's mind refused again to come up with coherent sentences. The effect of her body pressed against his, the scent of her perfume and the touch of her hand on him was too much for him to take.

Cassandra removed her hand from Greg's thigh and took another sip of her drink. "All right. We'll have a bit of a conversation. I'll start. I'm an intellectual property attorney at Erskine, Baker and Galang, but you already know that. I've been there three years. It's something I very much enjoy."

"What's intellectual property?" Greg was trying to keep the conversation going, to get his mind working again. "I'm not familiar with that."

"It's patent law. I work primarily in nanotechnology." The look on Greg's face must have given away just how lost he was with that piece of information. Cassandra laughed lightly. "In its simplest terms, it's obtaining patents for very tiny things. Beyond that, there's not much that would interest you or that you would understand, no insult to your intelligence. What do you do during your day, Mr. Finch?"

"I'm an account manager at Peabody-Finch, the Finch is no relation to me, just a coincidence. I basically push numbers around." Greg felt totally inadequate compared to Cassandra. "It's not as glamorous as what you do."

Cassandra smiled. "What I do can be very tedious and exacting. But I do like the discipline it takes to work with clients to help them protect what they've worked hard to achieve. There is a great satisfaction in that. Do you live in the city?"

"Yes, I have an apartment not far from here, on Pierce. What about you?" Greg signaled the waitress for a refill. Cassandra declined a second drink.

"I'm actually just around the corner, which is why I chose the Peking. If necessary, I can make a quick getaway." She tilted her head at Greg, her green eyes sparkling. Again, he realized she was teasing. "Or, conversely, we can make a quick getaway, if we desire." She arched one eyebrow in an unspoken question. "Would you be interested in a quick getaway to my apartment, Greg?" Cassandra reached down, again placing her hand on Greg's inner thigh, running her hand up over Greg's groin. He responded immediately to her touch, his penis stiffening beneath her hand, his body jerking in an uncontrolled spasm. She cupped his cock for a moment. "I take that as a yes."

Greg gulped down the rest of his drink, dropped a handful of bills on the table and scrambled after Cassandra, who had slid gracefully from the booth. He held the door for her and they walked into the cool spring air.

"Will you drive? You can park at my building; leaving your car here for any length of time may get you a ticket." Greg nodded, leading her to his car. He opened her door and watched as she got in, her skirt sliding up, revealing more of those beautiful long legs.

The drive to Cassandra's apartment was short. Greg parked his car and they took the elevator up to the top floor of the building. As they entered the apartment, Greg was momentarily distracted from Cassandra's conversation by the sight from the living room window.

"This view is amazing." He walked to the floor to ceiling window, looking down on the lights of the city.

"Yes, I quite enjoy it." Cassandra dropped her keys and purse on the couch. She walked up beside Greg. "I enjoy being above it all, as it were." They stood for a moment. Greg turned to speak to Cassandra, who put a finger to his lips. "Shhhhh. There's time for talk later." She reached up and kissed him, wrapping her arms around his neck. Greg responded instantly, deepening the kiss, his tongue flicking across her lips, her tongue meeting his.

They continued kissing as they stumbled down the hall, occasionally knocking into the walls, hands groping each other's body. Cassandra worked her way out of her suit jacket, dropping it on the floor. Greg's hands found her breasts. He realized she wasn't wearing a bra; her breasts were barely covered by a sheer silk camisole, her nipples firm beneath his fingers. He pushed her against the wall and kneaded her breasts in his hands, feeling her body shiver beneath his touch. He could feel himself growing harder, felt desire running through him.

Greg reached behind her and worked down the zipper on her skirt. They had made it as far as the bedroom, where she stepped out of her skirt gracefully, and was left standing in her camisole, lace panties and heels, softly lit by the twilight outside the windows. Cassandra reached behind her and pulled her hair free from its ponytail, shaking it out so it covered her shoulders in a flaming wave. Greg had never seen anything as beautiful.

Cassandra began undoing the buttons on Greg's shirt, nimble fingers making quick work of them. She pushed the shirt off Greg's shoulders, hands caressing his chest. She ran her fingernails lightly across his nipples, and then leaned down and licked each one, her tongue flicking across them. Greg looked down, his hands buried in her hair, his cock growing harder as he watched her tongue working him over. Cassandra looked up at him with those beautiful eyes. He grabbed her by the shoulders, pulling her up to him and kissing her deeply, her body pressed against his.

His hands slid down her back, cupping her ass in his hands, rubbing his cock back and forth against her stomach. She reached between them and fondled his growing erection through his clothes, cupping his cock and balls with her hand. She found the zipper on his pants, tugging it down, and Greg let go of her ass long enough to pull off his pants and boxers in one move, stepping out of them and kicking them to the side. He couldn't remember how he'd come to be missing his shoes. And he really didn't care.

Locked in an embrace, they stumbled toward the bed, bumping against the edge.

Greg maneuvered them down on the bed, laying Cassandra down next to him. He pulled back from their kiss, looking down at her body in the fading light.

"You're so beautiful," he said, his voice full of passion. "So very beautiful."

He bent his head to her breasts, licking one nipple through her camisole, feeling it grow hard at his touch, feeling the gossamer silk almost melt beneath his tongue. He watched the material become transparent, saw her hard nipple poking against the fabric. He moved to the other breast, licking the nipple, repeating the process, feeling it grow hard. Soft moans were coming from Cassandra, sounds that were like music to Greg. He looked down at her, the wet camisole clinging to her, revealing more than it covered.

Cassandra shifted her position, reaching down to fondle Greg's cock, stroking the length of it with her soft warm hand. Greg moaned, reaching out to Cassandra, touching her breasts through the wet material, rolling a nipple between his fingers.

"We should take that off, you're going to get cold." Greg tugged on the edge of Cassandra's camisole. She sat up, letting Greg pull the garment over her head. Cassandra pushed Greg back down on the bed, kissing his chest and licking his nipples. She kissed her way down his flat stomach, tracing a circle around his navel with her tongue as she continued to stroke him, watching his cock in her hand as it responded to her touch.

As Cassandra took Greg's hard cock in to her warm mouth, Greg let out a gasp. She slowly licked the slit of his penis, sending shivers through his body. She worked her tongue around the head of his cock, running kisses along the shaft, nibbling it gently with her teeth. Greg watched as she took him into her mouth, the sensations of her tongue, mouth and teeth against his erection almost too much to handle.

Greg felt himself quickly losing control under Cassandra's expert oral ministrations to his cock. He reached down, gently touching her face. "Stop, please." She lifted her head, looking at him. "Please, come here."

He pulled her to him, feeling her weight on his chest, her breasts crushed between them. He plundered her mouth with his tongue, feeling her respond to his kiss. Greg slid his hands down her back, slipping his hands beneath the edge of her lace panties, cupping the smooth skin of her sweet ass. Cassandra straddled his erection, holding his cock with one hand and slowing rubbing the tip of his penis against the fabric of her panties. He could feel through the material just how wet she was, could feel her heat on the head of his cock.

"Take these off." He tugged on the waistband of her panties.

"Tear them." Greg looked up at her, seeing a feral look in her eyes. "Rip them off of me."

Greg grabbed the delicate fabric in both hands and pulled, feeling the material give way, splitting in his hands. He heard Cassandra gasp. He gave another sharp tug and the panties came away in two pieces. He tossed them aside.

Cassandra lowered herself down toward Greg's cock, holding the rigid shaft in her hand, rubbing the tip back and forth against her wet pussy, covering the crown in her rich juices. She shifted her position slightly, touching the tip of his cock to her clit. Greg felt a shiver run through her body as she began rubbing his stiff cock over that sensitive button of flesh. Greg watched Cassandra, her head tipped back, eyes closed, mouth open. He caressed her hips, running his hands up and down her silky inner thighs and up to her full breasts, rolling the nipples between his fingers.

Greg began rocking his hips back and forth in time to Cassandra's motions. He wanted to bury his cock in her, like he did at the ball, to pull her down, feel himself surrounded by her wet warmth. But he also wanted to let Cassandra continue this delicious game she was playing, to keep experiencing this incredible pleasure and torture she was giving him.

Cassandra began rocking back and forth faster, rubbing herself against Greg's cock with more force. Greg could see the tip of his cock glistening with her wetness, stroking back and forth across her swollen clit. She was making little gasping noises, and Greg sensed she was close to orgasm, her hips tilting forward. He wanted to watch her keep using his cock to bring herself off.

"Are you close, Cassandra? Do you feel yourself coming?" Greg had never spoken during sex before. But it seemed to work. Cassandra opened her eyes and looked down at him.

"Yes," she breathed. "I'm so close. Talk to me, fuck me with your words, Greg."

"You're so wet, Cassandra. I can feel you with my cock, feel how hot and wet you are, feel how close you are to coming. I want you to use me to get off, use my cock in your hand. Rub my cock against yourself, bring yourself off, Cassandra. I want to watch you come."

Greg's words had an immediate effect on Cassandra. She began rocking faster, her hips thrusting forward, her gasps turning to cries of pleasure. Greg kept his hands on her waist, feeling her body begin to tremble beneath his touch. Her face took on a look of pure bliss, eyes closed again, head back.

She suddenly gave a sharp cry, lifting her body off Greg's, hips straining forward. He could see the muscles of her thighs tense as her hips thrust forward. She released Greg's cock as her orgasm tore through her. Greg watched in amazement as waves of pleasure washed over her, watched her quiver and tremble, her orgasm taking complete control of her body.

As her orgasm subsided, Cassandra slowly relaxed, lowering her body on to Greg's. He wrapped his arms around her, feeling the final remnants of her orgasm fade from her body.

"That was intense. I enjoyed every minute of it." Greg gently stroked Cassandra's hair, now a wild tangle in his hands.

"As did I," she said. "As did I."

Cassandra lifted her head from Greg's chest, reaching up to kiss him. He returned her kiss, rolling them over so he was on top of her. Cassandra spread her legs, opening herself to Greg.

Greg slid the tip of his cock into Cassandra's pussy, feeling the slickness of her opening. He looked down at Cassandra, saw the look in her eyes that said she was ready for him and he thrust into her, feeling himself finally surrounded by that luscious heat. He ground himself against Cassandra, feeling her contract around his shaft.

Greg placed his hands on either side of Cassandra's shoulders, holding himself above her, watching her face as he began to thrust into that delicious warmth, pulling back slowly and pushing forward, the full length of his cock buried in Cassandra. Her orgasm had left her very wet and he felt the slickness and heat of her as he rocked his hips back and forth.

Cassandra matched him, pushing up against him, rolling her hips from side to side when he held himself deep inside her, making his cock move in a different way. He continued thrusting into her, speeding up his thrusts, the passion building in him.

They continued this pace, each meeting the other's thrusts, fucking each other in a steady rhythm. Cassandra moved under Greg with a fluid grace that excited him. He'd never felt so completely in tune with a woman before. There seemed to be no line between where he ended and she began; they were like a well-oiled machine that worked perfectly.

Cassandra drew her knees back, pulling her legs up further. Greg shifted position, and Cassandra draped her long legs over Greg's shoulders, rolling her hips up, giving Greg a totally different angle of penetration. He pushed even deeper into her, thrusting harder, feeling Cassandra push against him. He looked down at her and again thought there was nothing so beautiful as this woman in the throes of passion, a passion he was part of. That thought fueled his desire, a wave of emotion washing over him.

Greg's cock and hips took on a life of their own as his orgasm started building. He could feel a heat in his solar plexus, the muscles of his stomach starting to tense. His cock felt incredible, the delicious pressure inside building to an almost unbearable level. He heard himself grunting in time to his increasing thrusts into Cassandra. He was so very close to coming but he wanted to continue this experience as long as possible.

It was the sound of Cassandra's voice, rough with passion that sent him over the edge. "I'm ready, Greg, I'm ready for you to come in me. Come in me, Greg, take me over the edge with you."

He could hold back no longer. His balls contracted, the shaft of his cock filling with liquid heat. He thrust quickly into Cassandra then, his orgasm bursting from his cock, his hot cum pumping into her. He heard her cry out beneath him, her hips rising to meet his thrusts, her body starting to shake and tremble with another orgasm. His own body began to tremble with the force of his orgasm, his thighs quivering as his muscles tensed.

His cock continued pumping into her, seemingly without end. He looked down at

Cassandra, watching the waves of her orgasm course through her body, her head back. She continued to cry out, her expression a mix of pain and pleasure.

He felt his body begin to relax, the orgasm beginning to subside. His arms were quivering and he lowered himself down slowly, easing his weight off Cassandra but keeping his cock seated in her, feeling her orgasm begin to fade from her body.

Cassandra opened her eyes, looking at Greg. He reached out and stroked her cheek, then pulled her close to him, tucking her against his chest, wrapping his arms around her. She relaxed against his chest, resting her head on his shoulder.

"That was amazing," Greg said. "You're amazing." He kissed her forehead. "I've never felt anything like that."

Cassandra was quiet for a moment. "Yes, it was."

Greg was dozing off. He felt Cassandra shifting beside him as he fell into a deep, well-earned sleep.

"You need to leave now." He heard her talking from what seemed like a great distance away. Cassandra was getting out the bed, slipping into a silk robe and tying the sash around her narrow waist. "I have an early day tomorrow."

Greg woke up slowly. He didn't want this feeling to end, not the just overwhelming sexual attraction he felt for Cassandra, but the feeling of just being with Cassandra. The fleeting thought that he was falling in love with her briefly crossed his mind.

"When can I see you again? Are you free tonight?"

"Give me your cell number and I'll call you when I'm available." Greg got out bed, finding his pants and fumbled in his wallet for a business card. Cassandra handed him a pen and he wrote his cell phone number on the back.

"Here, this has all my contact information at the office as well."

"I have your office number. Or have you forgotten our phone call so soon?" She stood before him, the fullness of her breasts outlined through the sheer silk of her robe. Greg wanted nothing more than to reach out and run his thumbs across those breasts, feel the nipples grow hard beneath his touch.

"Greg?" He realized he was standing naked staring at Cassandra's breasts and she had asked him a question.

"Oh, sorry." Greg actually felt himself blush. "I mean... well... what?"

Cassandra laughed lightly. She reached up, wrapping her arms around his neck. "I said, I enjoyed our time together tonight and asked if you did as well, but I sense it was a rhetorical question." Greg wrapped her in his arms, feeling the silky fabric against his skin, warmed by her body. He smelled the perfume of their sex on her. He pulled her closer, pressing himself against her, bending to kiss her full lips. He slid one hand up to cup one perfect breast, skating his thumb across the nipple, which reacted just as he had imagined, growing hard beneath his touch. He felt a shudder run through Cassandra's body, felt her gasp, sensing her arousal.

"Cassie," he ran a line of kisses down her neck. "Have I told you how much you mean to me? I think I'm falling in love with you, Cassie."

He was surprised when she abruptly broke their embrace, an unreadable look crossing her face. He thought for a moment she was going to slap him.

"You should go, Greg." Her voice was shaking. There was something close to fear in her eyes.

"I'm sorry..." Greg reached for Cassandra, but she turned away. "I said too much too soon. You do mean a great deal to me. It just slipped out. I didn't mean to scare you. I don't expect you to feel the same, but that is how I feel."

Cassandra turned back to Greg, regaining control of her expression and voice, her tone cool and her look closed and remote. "I think we both need a good night's sleep. I'll call you, Greg, when I'm available. I'll leave you to get dressed." She retreated to the bathroom, closing the door.

Greg let himself out of Cassandra's apartment, bewildered by this turn of events. He'd had no conscious plan of telling her he thought he loved her and realized it was too much too soon, but her reaction confused him. She had looked both angry and terrified by his words, and close to tears. He drove home and spent the few short hours until his alarm went off tossing and turning, wondering how to fix this, how to undo the damage those few words had caused.

Greg was miserable at work, tired from lack of sleep and bereft at the thought that his burgeoning relationship with Cassandra was now over. He tried calling her at her office but got only her voicemail; the cool and efficient sound of her recorded voice was no comfort. He eventually dialed the firm's main number and was told by someone who said they were Ms. Holland's assistant that she was unavailable for calls but would he like to leave a message? He hung up.

Taking a detour on the way home, Greg drove to Cassandra's apartment building. He wasn't sure this was a good idea but he was starting to feel desperate. If he'd ruined things completely, he rather just get this painful part over with and move on.

As he stepped out of the elevator on Cassandra's floor, he saw her door open and a man walk out into the hall. Cassandra, dressed in the same robe he'd last seen her in, stepped into the doorway, reached up and kissed the man. The kiss was filled with passion and Greg felt rooted to the floor, almost numb and unable to turn away.

As the couple broke apart, Cassandra saw Greg. A momentary look of shock crossed her face. The strange man from her apartment ignored Greg, walked passed him and punched the button for the elevator, got on, the doors closing behind him.

"Greg." Cassandra said Greg's name softly.

Greg's trance was broken and he walked the short distance to Cassandra's apartment. She was still standing in the doorway, watching Greg.

"Who was that?" Greg's voice was shaky.

"Come in, Greg. I'm not dressed to be standing in the hallway." Greg stepped into the apartment as Cassandra closed the door behind him.

"Who was that?" Greg asked again.

"Greg, sit down. You look like someone punched you in the stomach. Would you like a drink?" She moved toward the kitchen, returning with two glasses of amber liquid. Greg tossed his back without registering what it was. Cassandra took a sip of hers.

"Do you want to tell me what's going on here?" Greg could feel the warmth of the alcohol competing with the anger that was replacing the shock, which was now wearing off.

"If you mean Peter, which I assume you do, there is nothing going on. Or more precisely, the same thing is going on that is going on with you and me."

Greg frowned at her. "How can you say it's the same thing? It's not the same thing at all. We have... had... it's different. I thought we had something special."

"Greg, I thought I had made myself clear. I'm not interested in anything other than the pursuit, the thrill of the hunt, as it were. And when I am successful in my pursuit, both parties benefit from some extremely enjoyable physical encounters. But there are no strings attached; nothing beyond what has already happened. We've enjoyed a few very wonderful days here and I would have wanted it to continue, but you seem to have misunderstood my intentions. I cannot give you anything other than what I already have. I'm not interested in anything more complicated."

As she spoke, the pit of Greg's stomach dropped and any warmth, either from anger or alcohol, disappeared. He looked at Cassandra in disbelief.

"You're kidding. You do this all the time? This is how you are with all the men you meet?"

"No, I'm actually very particular about the men I spend my time with. I have very high standards and excellent taste. I do not "do this" with just any man I come across. Each man I pursue is unique in some way. You are very appealing to me, on many levels. Obviously there is a very strong sexual attraction, but there's more than that." Cassandra's voice trailed off and she abruptly rose from the couch, turning away from Greg.

"I am very sorry, Greg, that you were hurt by this, that I did not intend. But again, I thought I had been clear. I thought you understood." Greg realized she was again very close to tears, which baffled him even more than her explanation.

He rose and stood behind her. He placed a hand on her shoulder, but she moved away from him. "I think it's best if you leave, Greg. I really have enjoyed our time together." She walked to the apartment door, placing one hand on the door knob. She turned to face him. "Goodbye."

Greg walked woodenly toward the door. "I'd like you to think about this, Cassandra, to think about us. I can't imagine you're happy living like this, moving from one empty encounter to the next, without any love. I can give you the one thing no one else can—my heart." Before she could resist, Greg leaned down and kissed her, trying to convey in that one kiss all the passion and love he felt for her, even though she claimed it was not what she wanted.

He felt her respond to his kiss, felt her body move toward him. He also felt her tears against his face. She broke the kiss, moving back from Greg. He looked deep into her eyes. "I can't believe you're telling me the truth, Cassandra. Your emotions are written all over your face. And they're saying something completely different to me than your words."

"I am telling you the truth." Cassandra opened the door. "Please leave." Tears were streaming down her face.

Greg walked to the elevator, hearing the door close behind him. He had no idea what just happened. He felt like someone had punched him in the stomach.

The next few days passed in a haze for Greg. He was distracted at work, lost his appetite and wasn't sleeping. His co-workers were starting to ask about his health. He knew he should snap out of this funk, but he still thought of Cassandra.

He sat morosely at his desk, the production numbers for the month still unfinished, somehow mocking him as a failure. The thought that he might need professional help crossed his mind, not for the first time.

"Snap out of it," he said out loud. He took a deep breath and started clicking the mouse, moving numbers about on the screen. His phone rang.

"Finch." There was silence on the other end of the line. "Greg Finch." Greg was ready to hang up but he thought he heard sounds on the line. "Greg Finch here. Who is this?"

"Cassandra Holland here. And now we know where everyone is. Hello, Greg."

Greg almost dropped the phone. "Are you there?" Cassandra asked. "Greg?"

"Yes... I'm here. Why are you calling me?" Greg felt a stirring in his chest; either his heart was going to stop completely or start beating wildly. He really wasn't sure which it might be.

"I... well... I'm calling..." The normally poised and articulate Cassandra seemed at a loss for words. "I called because I wanted to talk to you. About the other day. I... we... can we meet? I really would rather do this in person, not over the phone."

"You expect me to come back for more humiliation? Do you really think I'm in the mood for that? Or are you going to use me again just for sex? I'm not someone, or something, you can just use for your own games. You've hurt me, Cassandra, you've hurt me a great deal." Greg's voice had risen; a co-worker turned to stare as he walked past Greg's door.

"You're right. I have. But I did take your advice, I have thought about us. And I'd like the chance—one more chance, if that's all I get—to see you. Please, Greg, give me one more chance." Cassandra was almost pleading.

"All right," he relented. "Where do you want to meet?"

"Can you stop by my apartment after work?"

"Yeah, okay. I guess I can do that." Greg hung up the phone, unsure of exactly what just happened. He found himself torn by conflicting emotions; he'd resigned himself to never seeing Cassandra again, but now she was asking to see him. It was all too much. He poked around with his spreadsheets for a few minutes and then decided he wouldn't get anything accomplished until he saw Cassandra. He turned off his computer, grabbed his jacket and left the office.

Cassandra opened her apartment door before Greg had even finished knocking. He had the impression she'd been watching through the peephole for him. He was shocked by her appearance. Even after passionate sex she had managed to look composed and in control. But this Cassandra was drawn, with dark circles beneath her eyes, her hair carelessly pulled back from her face. She was wearing a robe, not the silk one he'd seen before, but a rumpled cotton one. To be honest, she looked like hell.

"Cassie, are you okay?" Greg had no idea what to do or say.

"Please, Greg, come sit down. We need to talk." She led him to the couch.

"Cassie..." he started.

Cassandra held up one hand. "Please, Greg, let me say what I need to say. It's been a rough few days and I want to say this to you before I lose my nerve." Cassandra took a deep breath. Greg had a fleeting vision of someone contemplating either a life changing decision or a dive from a very high ledge.

"I told you once that I didn't want a complicated relationship, that the familiar bores me. In truth, I find the familiar scares me; getting to know someone, but also having them get to know me. I prefer to build walls, to keep men at a distance. Not too far away, but no closer than I let them get. But you, Greg, you got through my walls, you got to close to me... you got too close to my heart. And that scared me."

Greg could see a vein beneath the pale skin on Cassandra's neck, he could see her heart beating rapidly. His impulse was to hold her, but both his wounded feelings and her apparently fragile hold on her self-control kept him from doing that.

Cassandra took a deep breath; her voice had grown quiet and shaky. "I did love someone once, loved him very much. Someone who called me Cassie. No one calls me that anymore. I don't like it. Or I didn't like anyone, any man, calling me Cassie. I thought he loved me, I thought he felt about me the way I felt about him. But it turned out he had no feelings for me, other than purely physical. Maybe I was naïve, maybe I wanted to believe something that wasn't true, or maybe he led me on. In any case, my heart was shattered when he told me how he really felt about me, or to be more accurate, how he didn't feel about me." Tears had been forming in Cassandra's eyes and they spilled over, running down her cheeks.

Greg's heart melted at the sight of her crying. He moved over and placed an arm around her, pulling her into his embrace. She resisted; he felt her body stiffen. But her strength to resist was gone and she relaxed, letting Greg hold her, curling up on the couch next to him.

"I decided that no man would ever control my emotions again, that I would control every situation, satisfy my needs and desires and find men who felt the same way. I wasn't going to open myself up to that kind of hurt again, but I wasn't going to lock myself away either. And it seemed to be working, at least until I met you. My plans fell apart." Cassandra looked up at Greg, shifting on the couch, kneeling beside him.

"I know I've hurt you terribly; I know exactly what you're feeling. And it's breaking my heart all over again, that I could have done to you what someone did to me. I can't make very many promises to you right now, Greg, but I can tell you that—if you can in anyway forgive me for how I have treated you—I'd like to try to start over. To have a relationship... some kind of a real relationship... together... I mean... with you..." Cassandra's voice faltered. She was leaning forward, watching Greg's face intently, apparently waiting for some kind of sign he would agree.

"I need time to think about this, Cassandra. You're right, you've broken my heart. I've been trying to get over you as best I could, trying to erase from my memory all the encounters we've had."

Cassandra sat back, looking down at her hands clasped on her thighs. "I understand. I don't blame you. It was a long shot that you'd agree. But it was a long shot I needed to take."

"I didn't say I didn't agree. I haven't been doing a very good job of getting you out of my mind." Greg reached out and wiped away a stray tear from Cassandra's face. "I can't make any promises right now either, but as strange as it seems, this is the best I've felt in days. I'm still hurt; you've hurt me a great deal, Cassandra. But underneath all that I think I still am in love with you. As foolish as that might seem."

Cassandra looked up at Greg, a faint light of hope in her eyes. She seemed at a loss for words. Greg gently drew her to him, tenderly kissing her lips. She responded to his kiss, cupping his face in her hands. Greg's body responded to her touch, although his mind told him this was a foolish thing to do. But his body won and he pulled her gently against him.

Their lips met, tentatively at first then with growing intensity. Greg felt something different in Cassandra: she was less distant, more relaxed in his arms. For the first time he actually felt an emotional connection coming from her, not just his own feelings. It went far beyond just the physical connection they had experienced.

That subtle change affected Greg in a dramatic way. He pulled Cassandra to him passionately, his kiss deepening, his lips almost rough against her mouth. She opened her lips to him and their tongues met, sliding against each other, moving from one warm wet mouth to the other.

Greg lowered Cassandra down on the couch, settling himself between her legs. She lay back, watching as he tore open the front of her robe, looking down at her beautiful full breasts. He had grown hard during their kiss and his cock was straining against his pants, rubbing against Cassandra's stomach, begging to be released. With one hand, she reached down and undid the zipper on his pants, pushing them down his hips; he gasped as she took his cock in her warm hand, stroking it. Greg bent his head to one perfect breast, taking the nipple in his mouth, flicking it with his tongue as he sucked on her, feeling the nipple grow hard in his mouth. He crushed the other breast in his hand, rolling that nipple between his fingers. Cassandra cried out in pleasure beneath his touch.

Greg slid one hand down her stomach, slipping his fingers into her wet slit. She was already wet and swollen with desire. He stroked her, drawing her wetness over her clit, rubbing it, pinching it between his fingers.

He felt Cassandra shudder beneath him, felt the pressure on his cock increase as she stroked him harder. She ran her thumb over the sensitive tip of his cock, where beads of pre-cum had started to form. He could feel himself growing harder still and he thrust against her hand. He wanted nothing more than to fuck her right then, to pump himself into her wet pussy, to take her forcefully and release all the built up emotion from the past few days.

He released Cassandra's breast, shifting on the couch, kneeling between her legs and pushed her knees apart with his body. She responded by pulling her robe further away and sliding one leg up over the low back of the couch, the other leg falling open, revealing her wet and ready slit to Greg.

He grabbed her by the hips, sliding her roughly up the front of his thighs, pulling her to his rigid cock. She was totally pliant in his grip, apparently sensing his need to dominate this encounter.

Greg grabbed his cock with one hand and looked down at her, wet pussy spread before him. He looked at her face, saw in her eyes she was ready to let him take her and so he did.

He pushed into her in one stroke, thrusting his cock to the hilt into her warmth and wetness. He felt her buck up, arching her back, pushing herself against him, grinding her hips back and forth. He pulled back, grunting as he thrust into her again and again. And each time she met him fully, emotions now burning brightly in her eyes.

Greg could feel himself building to an orgasm very quickly. He wanted to pump his cum into her, to start their relationship over with this orgasm, to claim her as his now, under his control. He was surprised by the force of his emotions, emotions he had never felt before, that were now driving his orgasm.

With one final thrust he pounded into Cassandra, releasing his hot load, feeling her body momentarily tense, then felt her pussy contract violently around his cock. Her body shook beneath his with the force of her orgasm. Greg continued thrusting into her, his cock pumping out more of his hot juices, mixing and melting with hers.

As their orgasms gradually faded, Cassandra slid herself back on the couch, pulling Greg down on top of her. He was still breathing heavily as he pillowed his head on her breast.

"Cassandra..." Greg gently brushed a strand of flaming red hair from Cassandra's forehead.

"Shhhh..." She laid a finger on his lips. "Call me Cassie. Cassie Holland here, and Greg Finch here. And now we know where everyone is. And where they should be... right here together."

5 THE ART OF LOVE

Nick Scott stepped back from his latest canvas, paint spattered across his bare chest and arms. He absently wiped one hand on the back of his jeans, adding to the smears of color already there. The studio smelled of oil paints, turpentine and carried the spicy scent of clove oil, something Nick added to the paints on his palette to help keep them from drying too quickly while he worked.

This canvas was the latest in a series of works featuring one particular woman. At least Nick tried to think of the works as a series; anyone seeing his studio would have called her his obsession, and that bothered him more than a little.

Each canvas depicted her in various settings and poses. That alone wasn't remarkable, but what made these canvases different was that Nick had never actually met this woman. She'd never sat for him as a model.

He'd noticed one day that the empty apartment in the building across the alley was occupied. He'd never paid much attention to his neighbors until he caught a glimpse of this new tenant. And he was instantly mesmerized, especially after she'd installed a ballet barre in front of her living room window. She was diligent about doing some kind of routine daily. Nick assumed she was a professional ballet dancer.

He didn't know her name but that didn't matter. He sketched and painted while watching her across the alley between their buildings. He'd walked around the block one evening and tried to find her name above the buzzer to her apartment, but as with many single women in New York, there was only an initial and last name: S. Reynolds. Or maybe it was J. Petersen. He'd tried counting windows and matching up the numbers and he'd narrowed it down to those two. He had lingered, his finger above the buzzers, half wanting to press either one, wanting to meet her. But he didn't press them. He had returned to his studio and painted her instead.

Nick knew he was on the verge of becoming a stalker, but the woman held him captive. The first time he saw her, she'd apparently just come back from a date. He'd been working on a painting of a landscape when he saw her light come on in the living room. Her apartment glowed in the darkness and he moved to his window to watch her.

She was dressed in a simple halter dress,

her arms and shoulders bare. He was immediately struck by how pale her skin was, even in the middle of June. She was like porcelain. Nick noticed in a not entirely painterly way that she was very well proportioned. Her legs were long, her waist narrow above slender hips and her breasts were round and firm without overpowering her frame. She had a dancer's body but it was also lush, at least from his vantage point.

As he continued to watch her, he had the overwhelming urge to capture what he was seeing. He dragged the easel with the half-finished canvas over to the window. He grabbed a stick of charcoal and began drawing over the work he'd already started. He worked in broad strokes, capturing her grace, her lines, her innate beauty.

She poured a glass of wine and unpinned her hair, releasing a cascade of ebony curls down her back. Nick felt a jolt of heat deep within him at the sight of all that dark glossy hair against her pale skin. He shook his head, momentarily confused by this. He'd painted from dozens of models over the years and they never excited him in any other way but artistically. He had remained professional with all of them, no thought other than capturing their form in paint ever crossing his mind.

Sophie discovered soon after moving in that the guy across the alley watched her. One night, she had come home from a watching a late movie. She sensed she was being watched and looked across the alley, saw the guy and freaked out. She had immediately gone into the bedroom and pulled the drapes.

After her initial panic, she was irritated and considered calling the cops, but quickly realized he was an artist. He pulled his easel over next to the large window in his apartment, and she realized he was painting her. Her irritation quickly disappeared. In fact, Sophie had been very pleased; she was a dancer and thoroughly enjoyed being in the spotlight, even if it was just the peeper guy across the way.

Sophie's dancing career had recently ended with an injury and she missed having every eye in a theater focused on her and every move she made. Even though it was just one pair of eyes watching her now, she was strangely happy. Any anxiety at being watched faded and she quickly grew to looking forward to their daily sessions together.

Sophie found she was occasionally aroused by him watching her, something that was surprising but not unwelcome. She had no illusions he found her sexually attractive, but knew there was no reason for him to continually paint her if he didn't find interesting. She knew he had done several canvases with her; there had been various sizes of canvas in rotation over the past few weeks.

Coming in from work one day, Sophie was restless, full of pent up energy, and she threw herself into her workout. The artist had been painting her the entire time. She could see smears of paint on his chest and arms. Apparently he was as caught up in her emotions as much as she was. His painting style had been particularly wild, broad gestures and strokes capturing whatever it was he was seeing from his window.

Sophie finally collapsed on the floor, spent from her workout. She was glistening with sweat and heat, not only from the exertion but with a building sexual tension. She decided today was the day to see just how far her neighbor would go to watch her. She knew she risked scaring him off completely, but she somehow sensed he'd not shy away from a different view of her.

Sophie walked into her bedroom, pulling open the drapes she always kept closed; she had felt she needed some privacy. But today she was brazen, ready to have him watch her, no matter what she did. She glanced up at the window, saw he was still there, paintbrush still for the moment.

Nick watched the woman during her workout, apparently possessed by some type of restless energy. He'd never seen her move with such intensity. She finally dropped to the mat in a heap. He'd watched her, thinking his time with her for the day was over. Then she stood up and walked into the bedroom where, much to Nick's amazement, she opened the drapes. He watched, afraid to move, afraid to break whatever spell had been cast.

With careful movements she began stripping off her leotard, peeling the garment from her lithe body, sliding it down her legs and gracefully stepping out of it. She turned, facing the window, and stretched her arms over her head, her breasts fully exposed to the artist. She brought her arms down, running her hands over her breasts, feeling their weight in her hands, gently rubbing the nipples with her palms, feeling them grow hard at her touch. She could see the artist had moved closer to the window; he was still watching her. She felt a thrill deep within her at the realization. She crushed her breasts together, kneading them with her hands, a gasp of pleasure parting her lips.

She sat down on the bed, facing the window. She slid her hands from her breasts down her flat stomach and over her hips and legs. She brought her hands back up the insides of her thighs, pushing her legs apart, spreading herself open for the artist to see. She glanced up and saw he was still standing there. She saw he had put down the paintbrush and was rubbing his hand over the front of his jeans, obviously aroused by what she was doing. She felt an incredible rush of power, knowing she had this control over him.

Nick could barely breathe as he watched the woman. He knew he should turn away but he sensed she was doing this for him, somehow acknowledging that she knew he watched her. His rational mind told him to walk away. But his body was reacting in very pleasurable ways, even as it was keeping his feet rooted to the floor. His jeans were pulling across his growing erection; he found he was rubbing himself, slowly stroking and kneading his cock through his pants.

Sophie lay back on the bed; from this position she was looking almost directly up at him. With a flush of pleasure, she realized he was looking right down at her. She wanted to watch him, to see how far he would go. Would he pleasure himself as she was doing? She wondered if he knew she was watching. How could he not know?

She began slowly rubbing her hand over her already swollen pussy, feeling the soft skin beneath her fingers. She gently spread herself open, exposing herself, bending her knees and drawing her feet up on the bed. She started slowing sliding one finger into her wetness, drawing that finger up and over her clit, feeling it grow harder beneath her touch. She continued slowly teasing her clit for a few moments, circling it with one finger, amazed at how wet she was.

She began responding then to her own fingering, her hips rising and falling in time with her fondling. With her other hand she slipped two fingers into her slit, slowly sliding them in and out in time to her rocking hips. As she became more aroused, she moved faster, pumping her fingers in and out of her wet slit. She continued rubbing her clit, now swollen and hard and exquisitely sensitive, the wetness from her pussy coating her fingers.

Nick couldn't resist. His cock sprang free of his jeans as soon as he undid the zipper and button. He grabbed himself then, a sound between a sigh and a moan escaping him. He watched her, stroking himself as she fingered her clit and pussy, sliding his cock in his clenched hand to her rhythm.

As she worked her fingers in and out of herself, she looked up at the artist. With a jolt of pure pleasure, she saw he had his cock in his hand, stroking it in time to her own thrusting fingers. Her eyes traveled to his face and a current of electricity ran through her as she met his eyes. They were hot with passion and something she couldn't quite identify: embarrassment or guilt at being caught? She wasn't sure. But it was clear he knew she was watching him. And he wasn't turning away.

She felt an incredible orgasm start to build in her. The entire process of being watched while she played with herself was more erotic and exciting than she could have imagined. A stray thought told her she should be afraid, but the look in his eyes as he watched her somehow made her feel safe. Odd to feel safe as a total stranger watched you masturbate from his apartment window.

Sophie's hips were rising and falling, lifting off the bed. She took her fingers from her pussy and grabbed one breast, kneading it, pulling on the hard nipple. She was rubbing her clit faster now, gasping as her orgasm started. She lifted her head, looking up at the artist as he watched her, seeing in his posture and in his eyes that he was close as well.

Then Sophie's orgasm tore through her and she lost all awareness of anything other than the incredible feelings flowing through her body. She cried out, pushing her hips off the bed with her feet, thigh muscles straining, her whole body shaking with the force of her orgasm.

Nick watched in amazement and awe as the

woman brought herself to orgasm, her hand almost a blur as she rubbed her clit, the other hand now clutching the bed cover. He felt his own orgasm start, felt an incredible heat building at the base of his cock, his balls tensing and filling his shaft with liquid heat. He watched her shake and tremble on the bed, hips straining upward as if searching for something. He imagined being there with her, feeling the heat of her passion, her pussy working his hard cock as she held him in her warmth.

As Sophie's orgasm began to fade, she propped herself up on her elbows, looking up at the artist. She gasped at what she saw. He was standing, legs apart, eyes closed, hips thrusting forward as he pumped his cock in his hand, a look of pure pleasure on his face. She had the overwhelming desire to touch him right now, to run her hands over his balls, gently raking her nails over them as he trembled on the verge of his orgasm, sending him over the edge.

With a hoarse cry, Nick threw his head back as his orgasm burst from him, shooting a stream of hot cum on the window. His hips rocked forward, stomach muscles contracting as he continued to pump his cock with his hand, shooting another stream of his load on the glass. He watched as his cock kept pumping out more hot liquid, more than he thought possible. He finally rested his forearm on the window, dropping his head against his arm, as his orgasm slowly subsided, pearly drops of cum dribbling from his semi-erect cock. He was breathing hard, his chest heaving.

When his cum hit the window, Sophie gasped and involuntarily jerked as if her thoughts had triggered him, as if the hot liquid could reach her from across the alley. She walked to the window, watching as he shot load after load of cum against the glass, his orgasm finally slowing, the artist leaning against the window, his chest heaving.

As his breathing returned to normal, Nick straightened. He looked down at the woman. She was standing at her window, watching him intently. Before he could even think to turn away, she put the tips of her fingers to her lips and blew him a kiss. Then she pulled the blinds and was gone.

The next day, Sophie was wiping down tables at the café when she saw the artist walk past the front windows, head down, apparently lost in thought. She stopped wiping, the cloth hanging limp in her hand. He pushed open the door, looking up and looking directly into Sophie's eyes. There was a moment of silence. Sophie had the distinct impression he was wishing right then that the ground would open up and swallow him.

"Hi. Have a seat. What can I get you?" Sophie broke the silence, gesturing to a cleaner table than the one she had abandoned.

"Um... well, ah... I'll just have a coffee...

black." Nick wanted to bolt but sat down where she'd pointed. "Thanks."

Sophie bustled behind the counter preparing his coffee and brought it to his table. "My name is Sophie Reynolds," she said as she placed the cup in front of him. "It's nice to meet you... in person." She smiled, holding out her hand. Nick hesitated, then shook her hand. "I'm Nick Scott. It's nice to meet you too."

"Can I sit for a minute?" she asked.

"Oh, well... yeah, sure." Nick had no idea what to do, other than point to the chair across from him. "Please."

"I'm glad you stopped in. I've wanted to meet you for a couple weeks now." Nick was totally flustered. As much as he'd wanted this to happen, he was totally unprepared for this encounter or being this close to her... to Sophie. Sophie. He knew her name now.

"This is embarrassing." Nick decided to just brazen this out. There was no use in pretending they hadn't been watching each other. "I've wanted to meet you too."

Sophie smiled. "I think we're having a conventional meeting after already having a rather unconventional couple of weeks."

Nick laughed. "Yeah, I guess that pretty much sums it up. Now what?" Nick took a drink of coffee.

"Well, I'd like to see what you've been painting."

Nick almost spit his coffee on the table. "You want to what?"

"I want to see your work. I want to see the

paintings you've done of me. Don't your other models get to see your work?" Sophie's voice had taken on a teasing tone. "At least I'm not asking for payment for sitting for you. At least, not yet."

"You seem to know something about art, or at least modeling."

"The college I went to had a fine arts department. There were always artists hanging out at dance rehearsals. I dated one for a short time."

"You're welcome to come by and see what I've done. If you're free tonight, stop by." Nick was actually feeling somewhat more confident now that he'd met Sophie. He was pleased that she'd turned out to be friendly and open, so far, about their unconventional relationship. He was still a little embarrassed about watching her the night before, but he was hoping she wouldn't bring up that subject in public.

"Actually I am," Sophie said. "I could stop by around eight o'clock. Would that work for you?"

"Yeah, that works. I'll have time to get things cleaned up. My apartment is my studio, and it usually looks more like a studio than an apartment. I'll try to make it resemble an apartment by tonight." Nick finished his coffee. "I'll see you later then. My name's on the buzzer. I'm guessing you know which building it is." Sophie smiled again. Nick wished he had paper and charcoal; her smile lit up the room.

Sophie watched him walk out of the café, heading off toward their block. She was relieved Nick seemed like a normal guy, that he appeared to be surprised to see her at the café. At least she took it to mean he really wasn't a stalker. And he turned out to be taller than she thought, which for some reason she found very appealing.

Nick walked home in the afternoon sunlight, his mind a tangle of thoughts. He was glad to have finally met Sophie, after the initial shock of seeing her at the café. She must have just started working there; he usually stopped in during the day when he was tired of his own coffee and apartment. But he was also still mortified at coming face to face with her after watching her last night. He blushed a little, remembering the scene, which still aroused him, making him hard. He'd played the whole thing back in his mind several times; he remembered every move she'd made. It had been surreal without being able to hear her. In his memory, his mind added the sounds, the small gasps and moans. He imagined he knew what her final cry of pleasure sounded like as her orgasm tore through her.

Nick let himself into his apartment, surveying the disarray. He had a couple hours to try to make it less of a mess and more like a place to entertain Sophie. He gave the matter a moment's thought. It was totally wishful thinking, but he decided he'd start with the place he hoped they'd end up and headed off to clean the bedroom.

Nick heard the buzzer and pressed the intercom to let Sophie in. She arrived at his door, her ebony hair out of the sleek ponytail she'd worn at the café, cascading in waves down her back. She'd changed from the jeans and T-shirt she'd been wearing to a soft blue dress that set off the color of her eyes.

Nick had tried very hard not to watch her getting ready. He'd set one of the larger canvases on the easel and pulled it in front of the window, effectively blocking the view. He wanted to be surprised; he did not want to become any more of a voyeur in her life, now that he'd met her.

When Sophie was getting ready, she was momentarily puzzled by the fact that she could no longer see into Nick's apartment. That meant he was no longer watching her. She thought that was an interesting development. Had meeting her in person been a letdown, somehow seeing her in the flesh a disappointment of his imaginary vision of her?

"Hey there," Nick greeted, waving her in. "Welcome. You didn't have any trouble finding the place, did you?" Nick seemed in a very good mood as he ushered Sophie into the apartment.

"Well, yes, I did need to do a MapQuest search and program my GPS," Sophie answered back, smiling up at him. She caught a glimpse of something in his eye that was missing earlier, a higher level of confidence maybe. She thought he really had been caught off guard at the café, taken totally by surprise.

"Can I get you something to drink? I have water, lemonade, wine—there's always coffee— or something a little stronger? You can set your purse here." Nick motioned to a chair near the door and then moved to the tiny galley kitchen.

"If you have a bottle of wine open, I'd love a glass." Sophie perched on one of the bar stools on the other side of the counter separating the kitchen from the rest of the apartment. "This is a nice apartment. It's very organized for being so tiny." She looked around. "Although it's bigger than it looks from my place."

Nick winced a bit in embarrassment at her acknowledging they watched each other. "Your line of sight only lets you see the corner by the window, really only a little bit of that part of the room. There's the whole other side of the room that you'd never be able to see, where the table is and the door to the bedroom and bath. However, I'm sure the kitchen is exactly as tiny as it would appear from your place." He set her wine on the counter. "You can fit two people in here if one sits on the counter while the other stands perfectly still and does nothing more than wield a can opener. It's definitely not designed for making a seven course dinner. But it's perfect for me, since the coffee maker is the most used appliance and three coffee cups don't take up that much room."

Sophie laughed, taking an experimental sip of wine. "This is good. You must know something about wine and not just coffee if you're serving this."

"Something I picked up during grad school was a taste for good wine, even though I had no money at the time. Good wine and good coffee beans and I'm set." Nick moved into the living room. "Would you like to see the paintings? It's kind of hard not to, since they take up most of the usable space here."

Sophie nodded, sliding off the stool. Nick had a series of shallow shelves covering one wall where he kept works that were not framed or still drying. Sophie came to stand next to Nick, looking at almost a dozen paintings, all of her. She was momentarily at a loss for words. Each painting was exquisite, even those that were unfinished.

She moved closer, examining each one. Some showed her at the barre, caught in a mid-pose, arms extended or legs taut. Others showed her in more relaxed poses, standing or sitting, still dressed in her dance clothes, graceful but more contained. All of them were set in what appeared to be her apartment, but made to look like a stark dance studio, the backgrounds dark and lacking detail, but her figure always painted in exquisite detail, bright against the somber background.

Sophie was mesmerized by each painting. It was eerie in a way, the amount of detail he'd captured from his vantage point, but her overwhelming sense was one of awe at the amount of work he'd put into each canvas, the apparent loving detail. She could almost sense that he'd been caressing the canvas with his brush, using it as an extension of himself, capturing not only her form on the canvas but the emotions he felt while painting them.

One canvas in particular caught her attention. In it she was standing at the barre with one hand resting lightly on the pale wooden apparatus, almost caressing it, looking out the window, a mixture of naked emotions on her face; there was hope in her eyes, but exquisite sadness as well. She moved closer, trying to remember if she had ever stood like that, looking out the window, feeling that same mixture of sadness and hope, longing and regret.

"When did you paint this?" she asked Nick.

"It was the first week after you installed the barre. You were hesitant that day, really tentative in your moves, like you weren't sure if the barre was going to let you use it. Like you were meeting an old friend who you thought was mad at you. It was one of the first pieces I did."

Sophie was silent, her back to Nick. Her lack of response made him think he'd finally gone too far, that she'd finally realized he was a crazy stalker and she'd either slap him or toss wine in his face and storm out. But he realized she was crying quietly. He moved toward her, gently placing a hand on her shoulder.

"Are you okay?" Nick's voice was soft, unsure of her answer. Sophie's voice was far away as she answered.

"I had an injury to my knee that had ended my dancing career. I felt like a failure, and like the one thing in my life I loved the most had let me down. But I really missed dancing. So I finally had the barre installed. I walked around it for days, afraid of it. Eventually it all came back. But I also realized I could never have what I had before; that was gone. And you caught all those feelings on this canvas. It's amazing."

Sophie turned to Nick with tears on her face. "This is exactly how I felt that day: meeting an old friend and hoping they still liked me. And I discovered they did. But also realizing the relationship could never be what it was, that it had to be something different."

Without thinking, Nick bent down and kissed Sophie, then quickly pulled away. "I'm sorry." He stepped back, embarrassed.

Before he knew what was happening, Sophie stepped forward, arms around his neck, kissing him back. He found his arms wrapped around her, kissing her with more passion than he realized he felt. Even feeling all that passion, he broke their kiss.

"Wait. I want to apologize for watching you yesterday. I've never done that before. I think I got a little obsessed with watching and painting, forgetting that you weren't a consenting part of this arrangement. I sort of stopped viewing you as real, or started seeing you as more than real, if that makes sense. You were here in my apartment, in the paintings; you were always on my mind. I think I got carried away. And I crossed the line. I feel terrible about watching you yesterday."

Sophie looked up at Nick, her arms still around his neck. "Nick, what you saw yesterday, you were meant to see. I've known for a while that you've been painting me. I was

irritated at first but only for a very short time.
I realized what you were doing and in a way,
I've been posing for you. I like the attention. It
made me feel like I was in front of an
audience. And yesterday... yesterday was as
much for me as it was for you. I wanted you to
see me, to watch and participate. I wanted us
to have more than just the living room
together." Sophie looked up at Nick, seeing the
amazement in his eyes. "I wanted you to
watch me, Nick. I wanted that." She reached
up and kissed him, hard. "And now I want to
do together what we did separately last night.
Take me to bed. Make love to me, Nick."

They renewed their kiss, their tongues
exploring each other's mouths as their hands
touched each other's bodies. Nick's hands rose
to her breasts, feeling the weight of them
through the soft material of her dress. He felt
his erection starting to grow, felt it pressing
against Sophie's stomach. They worked at
taking off each other's clothes, laughing as
they fumbled with buttons and hooks. Nick
yanked off his T-shirt as Sophie pulled the
zipper down on Nick's jeans and stripped
them down his legs. He kicked them away.

Nick was trying to find some fastening on
the back of Sophie's dress. She pulled away
from him, smiling. "It unties." She undid the
tie at the side and the dress fell open. Nick
slid his hands inside the dress, pushing it off
her shoulders. The garment fell in a puddle on
the floor. Sophie was left in just her bra and
panties, some kind of shimmering material
that barely concealed anything.

Nick looked down in something close to awe

at having Sophie in his arms. She was incredibly beautiful. He could see her tight nipples pressing against the sheer fabric of her bra. He reached out and ran his thumb across one nipple, feeling a tremor run through her. Sophie arched her back, gasping with pleasure. Nick rocked his hips forward, pressing his cock against her stomach. Sophie reached between them, grabbing Nick's penis and stroking it firmly. He moaned softly, looking down to watch his cock moving in her hand.

"Sophie..." Nick had so much he wanted to say to her, but words seemed inadequate. He pulled her to him, kissing her deeply, trying to convey all the passion and emotion he felt for Sophie at that moment. He felt her respond to his kiss. "Sophie, I want to make love to you." He picked her up, carrying her into the bedroom, thanking whatever deity was listening that he'd taken the time to change the linens.

Nick placed her gently on the bed and lay down beside her, covering her mouth with a kiss, his hand finding one perfect breast and fondling it. He trailed a line of kisses down her neck, across her shoulder and down to that breast. He flicked the nipple with his tongue, sending shivers down Sophie's body, feeling the nipple grow hard. She ran her fingers through his hair, arching against his mouth.

He took her nipple into his mouth then, sucking it gently, hearing Sophie moan. He increased the intensity, sucking harder, feeling something primal unfurl deep in his stomach. He loved Sophie's breasts, the nipple and areola puckering in his mouth as he sucked them, feeling her breasts grow full and heavy with her arousal. He moved to the other breast, repeating the process, sucking on that nipple until it was hard. He moved back and forth between the two, licking between them, kissing them, leaving them both sensitive and thoroughly wet.

Sophie's eyes had grown dark with passion, her pupils dilated. She was almost dizzy with the arousal Nick's tongue had created as he sucked and kissed her breasts. She tried to reach down to Nick's cock, but he slipped down her body, kissing a line to her navel, flicking his tongue in and out of it, something that sent waves of pleasure through her.

But Nick didn't stop there. He changed position on the bed, settling between Sophie's legs, spreading them and using his fingers to gently spread the lips of her pussy, loving every second of watching her. He stroked one finger gently against the soft folds of her pussy, feeling how wet she was. Sophie had gone completely still beneath his touch. He looked up at her and found she was watching intently, one hand fondling a breast, gently pulling at the nipple he had so recently sucked with such pleasure.

He returned to his task, sliding one finger into her, feeling the heat and wetness. He drew that finger out, sliding it up and over her clit, drawing her juices over that little hill, feeling it grow hard as he continued to rub it gently. He felt Sophie's breathing increase slightly, felt her hips start moving gently in time to his touch.

Nick continued rubbing her now swollen clit for a moment longer. He bent down then, spreading the lips of her pussy further with his hands, gently licking her, following the same path his finger had taken. She was incredibly smooth and he could taste her on his tongue; she was sweet and salty at the same time. He worked his tongue up to her clit, flicking it with the tip of his tongue. Sophie let out a gasp and he felt her shudder under his touch. He swirled his tongue over her, feeling her wetness mix with his saliva. He realized he'd grabbed his cock with one hand, slowly stroking himself as he stroked Sophie with his tongue.

As she became more aroused, Nick began to suck on her clit as he had sucked on her breasts. The reaction from Sophie was instant. She arched her back, pushing her hips off the bed and crying out. It was so much like what he'd seen the day before, when he'd wanted to be there with her. And now he was. He felt an instant reaction in his own cock, feeling it jerk in his hand, and he tightened his grip on himself.

He worked her clit with his tongue and lips, licking, sucking and kissing that little mound of flesh, taking Sophie for a wild ride. The sensation of Nick's tongue on her clit were incredible; she felt herself building to an orgasm, but she wanted to come with him inside her. She twisted away from him, gently pulling his hair, lifting his head from her pussy.

"I want you inside of me when I come, Nick. Make me come with your cock." Sophie's words and eyes were almost begging him. Nick left that warm and beautiful place he'd been kissing and slid up Sophie's body. He was still holding his cock, feeling the beads of pre-cum that had formed on the tip; going down on Sophie had been just as arousing for him as it had been for her. He was ready to feel his cock in all that wetness.

He rubbed the tip of his cock over her clit and pussy lips, coating him with her luscious fluids. She twisted her hips, raising them off the bed, seeking more of him in her. He pushed the tip of his cock into her, watching her face. "Now, Nick, please. Fuck me hard."

Nick drove himself into her then, feeling her take all of his cock. She was tighter than he'd imagined; he wondered if dancing made a difference. And then he didn't care; he had no other thought than to make love to Sophie.

He thrust into her, filling her up each time with the length of his cock. Sophie met every thrust he made, raising her hips to meet him fully, grinding her hard and swollen clit against him as their bodies met. Nick sensed she was close to the edge; he felt his own orgasm building inside him, his balls and cock filling with a familiar liquid heat.

He thrust into her harder, faster, her breath coming in short gasps. She was pulling the nipples of her breasts, rubbing them between her thumb and index finger. He pushed himself up from Sophie's body with extended arms, looking down at her beneath him. He watched as she looked down as well, saw her eyes widen as she watched his cock pumping in and out of her body. Sophie hadn't realized just how much she got off on watching herself having sex, of watching a big cock being thrust into her over and over. It was what finally sent her over the edge.

With a short cry, she bucked against Nick, her orgasm tearing through her, catching her by surprise. Nick watched as Sophie's body shook beneath him. He wanted to watch the whole experience but his own orgasm wouldn't wait. He thrust into her with several short fast strokes, his cock releasing the first of his cum into Sophie. His own cry was hoarse as his cock and balls pumped into her. He felt liquid warmth surround him, their combined orgasms flooding through them. They were both breathing hard, both spent and satisfied as the final waves of pleasure washed over them. Nick pulled out of Sophie, collapsing at her side. Sophie stretched, feeling more relaxed than she could ever remember.

Later they lay in each other's arms, Sophie's head pillowed on Nick's shoulder, absently tracing patterns on his chest with her finger.

"That works far better than each of us alone in our own apartment."

Sophie looked up as Nick spoke. "Yes, I agree. Much better." She sat up. "Speaking of working together, when do you want me to start sitting for you in person, rather than you window peeking at me?"

"You can sit for me whenever you want," Nick said. "You know I'm always here. Is tomorrow too soon?"

"I think tomorrow is perfect," Sophie said.

 ❧

Sophie was looking for something to wear for her first official modeling session with Nick. She tore through her stash of leotards and dance wear. Most of her daily outfits Nick had already seen. She laughed at herself; she was going to sit for an artist and she was acting as if she were going on a date.

She decided on just a simple lyrical dance dress with an asymmetrical hem. It seemed like something Nick might like to paint her in, something simple but interesting. She was running late, so she threw a coat over her outfit and dashed around the corner to Nick's building. She arrived breathless and rang the buzzer.

Nick opened the door, laughing at her flushed appearance. "Are you okay? You look like someone's been chasing you."

"No, I'm fine. I was late so I ran, literally, around the corner." She tossed her coat on the chair by the door. She walked over to look at the prepped canvas. "What did you have in mind for a pose?"

"I wasn't really sure. I just gave myself a pretty generic backdrop to start with. I thought maybe I'd do some quick sketches of different poses, something I haven't obviously been able to do with you before." Nick grinned. "It's going to be interesting to actually have control of the session, and the model, now."

Sophie laughed. "I'm not sure how 'controllable' I am, but I'll give you different poses. Where do you want me?" Nick took her to the corner of the room where a wooden chair stood.

"Let's have you start by just sitting on the chair or standing with your hand on the back. Something simple." Nick grabbed his sketch pad and sorted through his charcoal. Sophie walked and turned the chair so her right side was facing Nick, the chair in front of her. She placed her hands on the back, gracefully extended one leg behind her in an arabesque.

"How long can you hold that?" Nick asked, sketching in broad strokes.

"As long as you need me to," was the reply.

"Okay, show off. Let me know when you get tired, or if you just want to change position. I don't want to spend a lot of time on these; I want some quick studies of you from different perspectives than what I've got." Nick worked quickly, capturing Sophie's elegant lines, the black charcoal moving across the cream colored paper.

Sophie was aware of Nick's intense scrutiny, his eyes roaming over her body, and as had happened before, she found she thoroughly enjoyed being the center of his attention. Over the course of the next hour or so he had her change positions, standing with the chair or alone and finally sitting on the chair. She felt relaxed and limber, even though this wasn't truly a workout.

Nick was thoroughly in his element working with Sophie. She took direction extremely well and was able to adjust her poses to exactly what he was looking for and then hold them for what seemed an eternity without moving. He felt time stand still as he worked. An hour had flown by without him even realizing.

"Let's take a break, a real one. Do you want

something to drink? Wine or something?" Nick stood and stretched. He'd been sitting on the floor, Sophie sitting across from him. She stretched her arms and leaned over to look at the sketch.

"Wine would be great. This is really good, Nick. It's amazing." She was kneeling in front of the creamy papers, sorting them out on the floor until they formed a rough circle around her. She studied each one carefully as if she'd never seen either a ballet dancer or herself before.

Nick brought her the wine, pulling the chair over and sitting down. "I'm glad you like them. They're really rough but it's such a joy to have someone who is so beautiful to draw. And who holds still so well." Sophie looked up and laughed.

"You get used to holding still in ballet. Or at least you learn how to control your muscles. I'm thinking more ballet dancers should be artist's models. Some of the same skills are required." She took a sip of wine. "Oh, this is good." She took a larger swallow.

"Don't get all tipsy on me here. I still want you to sit for the rough-in for the painting. I can't have you wobbling all over, after the great performance you just gave." He held out a hand and helped Sophie to her feet. They stood for a moment, fingers interlaced, both feeling the electric current generated by their touch. Sophie's lips parted with an involuntary gasp. Nick held her a moment and then leaned down and kissed her quickly on the lips. "Come on, we've got work to do. I'd like you barefoot for this, sort of like a 'ballerina at rest' kind of pose."

Nick watched as she removed her slippers. He had Sophie sit on the chair, moving her limbs until he found an arrangement he liked. Touching her skin, seeing her breasts and nipples through the sheer fabric of her dress was starting to have an effect on him. He walked to the canvas and started roughly sketching an outline with charcoal. After a few minutes, he started to laugh.

"What's so funny?" Sophie asked.

"Out of habit, I keep looking for you in your apartment, forgetting you're sitting right here. I glance out the window, and wonder where you've gone to."

"Maybe you're the one who's had too much wine, or you've inhaled too many paint fumes." Sophie started to laugh.

"Hey, hold still. No laughing allowed. This is serious." Nick was mock stern with her. She immediately resumed her pose, a smile playing round her lips. "Yes, sir."

Nick worked quickly, blocking out her form on the canvas. He was conscious of Sophie's eyes watching him. She was positioned in such a way that she would be looking directly at the viewer of the painting, meaning she was looking directly at Nick. He was amazed by the intensity he saw and hoped he would be able to capture that when he started painting. He was struck again by her beauty and grace; even sitting still she conveyed energy and life.

Sophie watched Nick working to capture her image. He'd taken off his shirt and she was stuck by just how muscular his chest and arms were, how flat his stomach was. While she'd been aroused before just knowing he'd been watching her, seeing him right here doubled the effect. He was a very handsome man and physically incredibly exciting. She felt a stirring low in her stomach, making her shiver involuntarily.

As he worked, Nick noticed a not-so-subtle change in Sophie's appearance. He'd pulled off his shirt, as was his habit, and she'd immediately grown flushed, her pupils dilating. Her breathing quickened and she trembled ever so slightly. Seeing her arousal made his cock stiffen, pulling his jeans tight. He stepped back behind the easel, hoping to conceal what was soon going to be a large and very visible erection, if he didn't gain some kind of control.

While he worked, Sophie was intrigued to notice Nick was getting an erection. He tried to hide it but she could see the bulge in his pants. This brought another wave of sensation washing over her, causing her to catch her breath. She saw Nick look over at her suddenly and she tried to gain control. But she knew this was going to be a losing battle. She could feel all sorts of changes happening in her body, changes she could not conceal from Nick much longer.

The sound of Sophie's gasp was too much for Nick. He dropped the paintbrush on the floor. He bent for the brush but before he could pick it up, he heard Sophie speak.

"Leave it." Her voice was husky. She stood and crossed the short distance to stand before Nick. Without any conscious thought, he reached out and grabbed her by the shoulders, pulling her to him. She came to him eagerly, twining her arms around his neck, pressing her lithe body against him. Nick groaned as she rubbed against his erection. He could feel her breasts and hard nipples pressing against his bare chest.

They met for a kiss that seared both of them with heat. Nick groaned again, opening his mouth, seeking the heat and warmth of Sophie's mouth. She responded by parting her lips to him, their tongues meeting, playing back and forth. Nick slid his hands down Sophie's body, grabbing her hips, feeling the taut muscles beneath the firm skin. He moved his hands back to her round ass, cupping it, spreading her with his hands, rocking his hips forward, his cock pushing against her warm body. He realized she was wearing only a thin pair of panties beneath her dress.

She was making noises deep in her throat and he felt her reach between them, struggling to find the zipper on his jeans. He moved back, giving her access. She undid the zipper and pulled his jeans down, releasing his hard cock, now almost fully erect. He pulled her back to him, reveling in the feeling of rubbing himself against the soft fabric of her dress, the warmth of her body and the delicious friction creating an intense heat on his rigid shaft.

Sophie felt Nick pressing his quite large erection against her and wanted to feel that cock against her bare skin. "Undress me, Nick. Make me naked. I want to feel my skin against yours."

Nick grabbed the bottom of her dress and pulled it up over Sophie's extended arms, dropping the garment to the floor. She was left standing in only her panties. Nick stripped them down her slender legs and she stepped gracefully out of them. Before pulling her into his arms, he stood looking at her.

"God, you're beautiful." Nick's voice was soft but intense with emotion. Sophie felt a wave of heat start from her center, moving rapidly through her limbs. She felt like she was full of liquid energy.

"So are you Nick." She walked into Nick's embrace, their naked bodies coming together, each feeling the intensity of the other's passion and arousal. Nick gently thrust his hips back and forth, rubbing his shaft against her soft skin, his hands again on her ass, her soft thighs pressed against his. Sophie responded by lifting one leg, sliding that silky smooth leg up Nick's leg and hip, opening herself up to Nick. He slid one hand from her ass to her pussy, feeling her wetness, making her moan with pleasure as he stroked the outside lips of her slit. He slowly slid one finger inside her, amazed at how hot and wet she was. His cock twitched in anticipation, Sophie feeling it moving against her, hearing Nick moan deep in his throat.

"Fuck me, Nick, fuck me now... right here." Sophie practically growled the words in Nick's ear. The effect of her naked body in his arms coupled with her rough language brought a fresh wave of sensation washing over Nick. He reached down and grabbed his fully erect cock, sliding it into the soft wet folds of Sophie's body. He thrust upward, entering her fully, feeling her take the entire length of him, heard her gasp. He held them like this for a moment, enjoying the feeling of being inside Sophie again, feeling he'd found home.

He was quite aware of Sophie's strength as she held herself against him on one leg. He looked in her eyes and saw her arousal and excitement and began moving himself inside her, rocking his hips back, thrusting forward again slowly, savoring the feeling of pushing the entire length of his cock into that hot wetness. He kept this same pace, never breaking their eye contact, watching the arousal and heat intensify in her eyes. The effect on him was incredible, magnifying his physical pleasure, connecting him with her in a way he'd never had with any woman before.

Sophie's body reacted to Nick with wave after wave of pleasure, like a small series individual orgasms. She watched his face and saw in his look just how much he was enjoying this experience, more than words could convey.

Nick began thrusting harder, unable to hold back much longer. He felt Sophie's pussy begin to tighten around him, felt the urgency in her movements. She was rocking her hips back and forth in time to his thrusts, the foot of her raised leg sliding against his own ass, the soft skin of her inner thigh rubbing against his hip. He found this incredibly stimulating. He caught a glimpse of their reflection in the window which was acting like a mirror.

"Sophie, look. You can watch." He nodded at the glass. She turned her head and he heard her gasp.

"Oh, God, Nick. Look at us. Oh, Nick, make me come, I want to watch you make me come." Again her words in his ear triggered an instant reaction in his cock.

Nick spread his legs for leverage and hesitated a moment. He could feel his orgasm building, feel the warmth start to coalesce in his stomach, moving down, growing hotter as his balls began to tense. He thrust hard into Sophie then, his cock filling with liquid heat. There was no holding back now. He thrust into her hard several more times, watching her face as she watched their reflection in the window. She could see his cock sliding in and out of her and she lifted her leg higher, giving Nick even more access and allowing her to see the full length of his cock disappearing into her pussy.

Nick could see her eyes grow wide as she watched him thrusting hard into her, her lips parted and her breath coming in short gasps. Her breasts, caught between them, were full and heavy, the erect nipples pushing against his chest. He felt his cock explode then, the first shot of his hot load pumping into her.

Then Sophie screamed, eyes never leaving the window, watching as Nick's hard cock pounded her, feeling her own orgasm rip through her, spasms starting in her pussy and radiating out to the rest of her body. Nick felt her heat contract around his pumping cock, as he continued to thrust into her, watching her watch them. Her body shook violently and he tightened his hold on her as she was lost to her orgasm.

Nick felt Sophie sag against him, the

aftermath of her orgasm leaving her limp. He held her to him, her leg slowing sliding back to the floor. She was breathing hard, her forehead on his shoulder, her arms still around his neck. His semi-erect cock had slipped from her, releasing a flood of his their combined juices. Nick could smell the intoxicating scent of their sex.

"Come on." He scooped her up and carried her into the bedroom. He laid her gently on the bed. She looked beautiful in the soft glow from the open doorway, her hair a tangled dark mass on the pillow, her face flushed and relaxed, looking up at him with a satisfied look. The term afterglow came to mind and he thought her picture, as she looked right now, should be placed in every dictionary alongside the definition.

Sophie reached up and pulled him down next to her on the bed. "Nick, that was incredible; you're incredible. I've never felt anything like that." She leaned over and kissed him, one hand on his chest. "I want this feeling to never end. It's like the best rush I ever had dancing but without any of the pain. I don't want this to ever end." Nick kissed her back, pulling her to him, wrapping his arms around her.

"I don't want it to end either. I think though we'd eventually need to get some food. Or, I'd need coffee," he said. She smiled up at him. "But for the near future, I don't see why we need to leave this bed."

"But I do have to leave. I have the early shift tomorrow." Sophie pulled a mock pout. "You, however, get to be lazy and stay in bed."

She leaned down and kissed Nick again.

"I wish you could stay. But it's late. I'll walk you home." They managed to find clothes and shoes and Nick escorted Sophie to her apartment door, leaving her with one final kiss.

Sophie woke to the annoying sound of a buzzer. She rolled over, smacking the alarm clock, trying to make the noise stop. But it continued. Sophie finally realized it was the door; she frowned at the clock, finally focusing on the time. It was just past six in the morning. Who could want to see her at this time? The fleeting thought that it might be Nick passed through her mind, giving her a rush of emotions. But she'd practically just left there; she assumed Nick was sleeping.

She padded to the door, pulling her robe around her. She hit the intercom button and said hello. The voice that came back to her shocked her. It was her ex-boyfriend Kurt. She took an involuntary step back from the intercom.

"Hello? Hey, Sophie, let me in. It's raining." Sophie hit the buzzer and then walked to the door, watching through the peephole until she saw him standing at the door. She waited until he knocked, then opened the door.

Even though he'd dumped her, broken her heart and kicked her out of their apartment, her stomach still did flip flops seeing him. His physical presence had always affected her; even when they were in the throes of an argument she was still attracted to him. She had mistaken that physical attraction for love, but learned the hard way it was not.

"What are you doing here, Kurt?" Sophie tried to keep her voice steady, tried not to give away her emotions with a shaky voice.

"I've come to see you, Soph. Are you going to invite me in?" Sophie realized she was blocking the door. "I'm not going to bite you."

Sophie moved into the apartment, letting him in. She closed the door behind her. "What do you want, Kurt?"

"I came to apologize, Sophie. I came to tell you I was wrong and want you to come back." It was just like Kurt to make a pronouncement and expect her to just accept it, especially when he decided it was the time and place to do so. It had been the constant underlying friction and struggle in their relationship. She had finally stopped going along with everything Kurt said and it resulted in their last, and she had thought, final argument. She had left shortly afterward, or more accurately, Kurt had asked her to leave. That demand she had obeyed.

"Kurt, it's barely morning. You can't just waltz in here and tell me you apologize and expect me to pack up and move back in with you. That was why you asked me to leave, because I wasn't jumping when you said, wasn't following your commands. No more, Kurt. I'm not doing that anymore." She crossed her arms over her chest, her face in a scowl. She glanced out the window and noticed Nick's light was on but she couldn't see him. She didn't want Nick to see Kurt. She pulled him toward into the bedroom, a perplexed look on Kurt's face.

Nick had been unable to fall asleep after Sophie left. He was full of energy and restlessness. He'd paced for a time, thought about a walk but realized it was raining. He finally pulled out the brushes and paints and began working on the canvas he'd started with Sophie. Out of habit he'd glanced down at her apartment, expecting to see it dark, imagining her to be asleep after their night together.

Instead he saw her light was on. He moved closer to the window and realized she was talking to a man, obviously having a heated discussion. Nick couldn't tell if Sophie was angry or just excited. She was too far from the window to see her face and the man had his back to the window. Nick watched for a moment and then felt his heart sink as Sophie took the man by the arm and pulled him into her bedroom. The blinds were drawn, the rest of the apartment dark.

Nick stood for a long moment, his emotions swirling, his body numb. He realized he'd dropped his brush; he looked at the paint splatter on the floor. He turned away from the window, went to his bedroom and closed the door.

"Sophie, why are you rushing me off to the bedroom?" Kurt sat on the edge of the bed. "You're too angry with me to have sex, even I can see that." He leaned back on the bed. "Unless this is how you plan on making up with me."

"No, Kurt, I'm not having make-up sex, or any other kind of sex, with you. You're not staying. I just... didn't want... there's neighbors who can see in and the blinds were open. Anyway, you're not staying. I'm not coming back, you're not changing my mind and I don't want to see you anymore." Sophie's words came out in a rush, her emotions churning.

"Sophie, I want you to think about this, about us. I want to make changes. This has been really hard for me, since you've been gone. I miss you. I want you to come back. I can admit I was wrong. Can't you even accept that?" Kurt stood before her, placed his hands on her shoulders and looked down at her. "If I can change, can't you at least meet me halfway?" He bent his head, catching her lips with his.

Sophie's resistance melted under Kurt's familiar and passionate kiss. He sensed her relax and pulled her to him, deepening their kiss. She could feel the heat of his body, his familiar scent and her body began to go through the familiar excitement she felt in Kurt's embrace. She wrapped her arms around his neck, pressing herself against him. She felt his desire, felt his erection growing, pressing against her body. As he rubbed himself against her, the friction and heat against her was incredible.

Kurt pulled her robe off her shoulder, exposing one breast. His hand slid down, cupping her breast, rubbing his thumb across the nipple. Sophie arched her back against his hand, her body coming alive on its own, reacting under Kurt's hands. Her head tipped back as Kurt trailed a line of kisses down her neck, along her collarbone and shoulder, all the while gently fondling her hard nipple.

Sophie signed, running her hands through Kurt's hair. She opened her eyes and looked at him, seeing him kiss the top of her exposed breast. But instead of Kurt, she saw Nick. Nick, who had not long ago been making kissing that breast.

With a gasp, she pulled away from Kurt. She pulled her robe up to cover herself and stumbled back a few steps, away from his grasp.

"What the hell, Sophie. What are you doing?" Kurt stood there, a black frown on his face, his erection making a bulge in his pants. "What's the matter?"

"I'm not doing this again, Kurt." Her voice was shaking, both from anger and from the residual heat of passion. But the passion was fading as the anger increased. "You need to leave. Now."

Kurt followed her to the front door, lit only by the growing daylight outside the living room window. "You're making a mistake, Sophie." His voice had taken on a rather menacing tone she had never heard before and really did not like.

"No, Kurt. I'm making a decision. And I'm making the right one this time." She held the door. Kurt hesitated, then stormed into the hallway. As she was closing the door, he turned back.

"You're making a mistake," he repeated. "This is your last chance. I walk away and we're really done. Is that what you want?" In response, Sophie closed the door in Kurt's face.

Sophie sat shaking on the bed. She'd almost given in to her desires, gone ahead and had sex with Kurt. As much as her body had wanted that, she knew it was the wrong thing to do. Nick crossed her mind again, not as the sole reason for not giving in, but one of many.

She realized with dismay she was going to be late for work. She showered and left the apartment, relieved Kurt wasn't lurking outside her building.

Nick was waiting for the coffee to finish brewing when he heard the buzzer. He glanced up at the clock and realized it was probably Sophie. He contemplated not answering the buzzer but decided if he was going to get his heart broken, he might as well do it now and get it over with.

He pushed the buzzer and moments later heard her knock. He opened the door and walked away, letting her find her own way in. She followed him to the kitchen, taking up her place at the counter.

"Nick? Are you okay?" Sophie asked.

"Fine," Nick almost spat the word at her, surprised by his sudden anger. He turned back to the coffee, grabbing a mug and pouring himself some. He held the pot, tipping his head at Sophie. "You?"

"Um... no, I'm fine. Nick, what's wrong?" Sophie was confused and bewildered by Nick. She obviously didn't know him very well, but this didn't seem like the person she'd spent time with in the past few days.

"What's wrong?" Nick slammed his coffee mug down on the counter, spilling coffee. "Why would anything be wrong?"

"Nick, you're scaring me." Sophie had grown pale. Nick's outburst seemed totally out of character for him.

"Sorry." He wiped up the coffee with a paper towel. "Look, I don't think this is a good idea anymore."

"What's not a good idea? Me being here? What happened?" Sophie was beginning to think Nick had seen enough of the scene with Kurt to be upset. "Are you upset over Kurt?"

"Kurt? Is that his name?" Nick finally met her eyes. She could see he was not angry as much as hurt. The pain in his eyes was obvious. Sophie reached across the counter and touched the back of Nick's hand. He pulled away as if he'd been burned by her touch.

"Nick, you don't know the whole story. You're jumping to conclusions."

"So tell me the story, Sophie. Tell me why I see you taking another man into your bed, after leaving here, after we... you and I... what we had together. Are you telling me everything you've said and done these past days has been a lie? Or some way to get back at me for watching you? You know I've told you how I feel about what I did, that it wasn't right. But you told me that didn't matter, that it was something you enjoyed. Was that all a lie too?" Nick had grown pale, his hands shaking. Sophie got up and walked around the end of the counter. She reached for Nick, tried to hold him but he backed away.

"No... don't..." She walked right through his protests, wrapping her arms around him, hugging him to her. She could feel him trembling through his shirt.

"Nick, what you saw wasn't what happened. Come on, come sit with me." She pulled him to the couch, Nick following behind.

"Kurt is my ex-boyfriend. He came to tell me he wanted me to come back to him, that he decided he was wrong. When you saw me take him into the bedroom, it was so you wouldn't see him and wouldn't jump to this conclusion. But I guess my idea backfired."

Nick looked confused. "So he came back to get you, but you made him leave? Nothing happened?"

"Well, not exactly nothing. It's complicated—I hate that phrase—but it is." Sophie saw the pain in Nick's eyes and tried to explain. "There's always been a huge physical attraction between Kurt and me. I know that's not what you want to hear, but let me finish. He did try to start something, and my body started going along, which is what always happened before; I just went on autopilot. And that's what always got me in trouble. I'd go along with him, feel so good and loved and cared for afterward that I thought all our problems would go away. But that never happened. They were still there after the glow faded away; it was all just an artificial kind of thing. Anyway, yesterday he did kiss me. And I responded. And we started down that same path we always took." Sophie stopped for a breath, realizing she was almost babbling in an effort to get the words out fast enough to erase the look of pain in Nick's eyes.

"But I stopped. I stopped myself and then I stopped him. It wasn't what I wanted or what would have been good for me. I did it for myself. But I also did it for you... or us... or what could be between us." She reached out and touched Nick's cheek. "Nick, I thought about you and remembered why I didn't want to have anything to do with Kurt. I was still feeling the glow from our lovemaking from last night and it made me feel strong enough to say no to him. It wasn't the artificial feeling I was used to with Kurt. It was strong and good and had your caring behind it. And it made me able to stand up for myself and speak my mind. And to make Kurt leave my apartment. Which he did. Unhappily, but he left."

Nick wasn't sure how to take in everything that Sophie had told him of if he even could. His thoughts and emotions were tangled.

"Sophie, I don't know what to think." Nick looked down at his hands, clenched in his lap.

"I know, and I'm sorry. I wish with all my heart you hadn't seen him there. You did, but now you also know the whole story. Nick, if I could erase all that from your mind, I would. All I can ask is that you try to believe what I'm saying, that Kurt isn't a part of my life." She took Nick's hands in hers. "Nicky, look at me."

Nick raised his head, looking at Sophie. He wanted to believe her and had no reason not to. "Nick, I'm not interested in renewing anything with Kurt. What I am interested in is right here, right in front of me. I'm interested in you, Nick, and seeing where this relationship can go."

Sophie leaned forward and kissed Nick softly on the lips. She felt how tense he was, felt his lips taut beneath hers. She tried to convey in that one kiss all the passion she felt for him, how much he meant to her. She felt Nick gradually relax as she deepened her kiss. She also felt something wet on her cheek. She pulled back and realized tears were running down his face.

"Oh, Nicky. I'm so sorry." She reached out and held him, felt him shaking as he cried silently against her shoulder, all the emotions he'd held inside finally finding release.

"Sophie," he said. "I didn't realize how much you mean to me until I saw you with Kurt in your apartment." He raised his head. "Men aren't supposed to cry, are they?"

She smiled at him, brushing the hair back from his face. "Nick, it's okay. It's been a roller coaster day, for both of us. I think you're allowed to cry if you want."

"Sophie, have I told you how much I love you?" Nick took Sophie's face in his hands. He leaned down and kissed her lips. Sophie responded to his kiss, opening her lips, meeting his exploring tongue with hers. She felt a swelling of emotion in her chest at Nick's words, not just the burgeoning sexual attraction Nick aroused in her but a deeper feeling of contentment she never felt with Kurt. She momentarily broke away from Nick.

"You know, all the time Kurt was explaining why I should come back, he never said he loved me. You've said it more since I've known you than he ever did." She looked into Nick's eyes. "And I love you, Nick."

6 LAW OF ATTRACTION

Ben walked into the Crooked Bean Coffee House and took his place in line. The shop wasn't as hectic as usual; maybe they hired another barista. The Bean was sometimes lacking in customer service, but the coffee was worth the wait, plus it was right around the corner from his office.

When it was his turn, Ben had his head buried in a legal brief. He didn't look up as he ordered his regular coffee. He heard a woman's voice asking a question, glanced up, and completely forgot where he was or what he was doing. All he could register were a pair of blue eyes, the bluest eyes he'd seen, set off by a thick fringe of black bangs. And a pair of lips, lush and deep pink that he thought looked like rose petals. He had never thought any woman's lips could look like rose petals. He also thought he'd like to kiss them, right then.

"Are you interested?" came the question again. Ben resumed breathing and looked down at the flier she was holding out to him, relieved she hadn't read his mind. "We're playing tonight at the Barrymore. I know it's a Monday, but you're welcome to come. If you're interested, that is."

"Um, yeah." Ben took the flier and turned away from the counter, looking down at the colored paper, realizing the girl behind the counter was the lead singer.

"Sir? Hey, you forgot your coffee." He heard the girl's voice again.

The next guy in line punched him in the arm as Ben walked away. "Dude, your coffee."

Ben turned back to the counter. "Oh, sorry." The girl smiled up at him. "No problem. It's Monday, you're allowed to be forgetful." She took his money, gave him his change and he grabbed his coffee. She smiled again, and Ben's mind turned to mush. He took a step backward, stumbled into the guy behind him and almost spilled his coffee. He mumbled an apology and managed to reach the sidewalk without any more incidents. Already late for work, he jammed the flyer in his coat pocket.

It was Jane's first weekday at the Crooked Bean and so far things were going well. The manager was cool; he said she could pass out fliers for her band, as long as she didn't fall behind serving customers. The place was pretty busy for a Monday morning. She realized it must be the businessmen heading to work. All she saw as she pulled shots was a sea of suits and ties, all dressing bored-looking guys. But the band either rehearsed or played most nights so for now this worked with her schedule.

Jane and the other barista were working their way through another rush when she saw the guy two customers back in line. There was something different about him, something that stuck out from the crowd. For one thing, he was about her age, not older like the rest. He looked serious and had his nose buried in a stack of papers. But there was something about his posture, about the way he held himself that caught Jane's attention. She timed it right so she was the one to wait on him. She took his order and then offered him a flier. His reaction was not what she expected. She wasn't sure if it was his reaction to the flier or to her, but he seemed totally taken by surprise and at a complete loss for words. As she waited on the next customer, she wondered if he'd be at the show. In the back of her mind, she hoped he would be.

Ben made it to his office without being too late. He took a seat at his desk, fished the flyer out of his pocket and turned on his computer. He did a quick internet search for the band and came up with several reviews of their gigs. They seemed to be quite popular and had good reviews. He was impressed.

Music had been a passion of Ben's since college. Even in law school he'd managed to see various bands ranging from some really bad ones to some that had gone on to make a name for themselves. It had been a long time since he'd gone to a show. Beth, the woman he occasionally went out with, liked the symphony and the opera, which he didn't mind. But she didn't like local bands or anything she called weird, which included pretty much everything but the symphony or the opera. He thought she only went to those events because they were socially appropriate and doubted she even liked them. But Beth was out of town at the moment, so he was free to indulge in something fun. He found he was really looking forward to seeing this band and the lead singer. He glanced down at her picture again and noticed what looked like a tattoo on her leg, high up one slender thigh, partially covered by her skirt. He squinted at the grainy photo. He wondered what that tattoo was, and his mind wandered away, wondering exactly how short of a skirt she'd need to wear to see the whole thing.

The Barrymore was an old theater revamped as a music venue. It had a nice ambience; some old touches of the grand theater had been left behind, such as the stars on the ceiling. As the house lights dimmed, hundreds of tiny lights set in the ceiling came on, creating the illusion of a starry night sky. It had always been one of the things Ben loved about the place. They'd also left in some of the old velvet theater seats along the back, removing enough to make an open area in front of the stage. Ben took a seat in one of them, waiting for the band to start.

The crowd was a pretty good size. He was happy he'd decided to come out for the show. As he was watching the crowd, he noticed the girl from the coffee shop, the singer in the band, talking to a group of people. As she moved away, she caught his eye. He gave a small wave and was pleased when she smiled and walked over.

"Hey, thanks for coming out. I'm glad you decided to catch the show." She perched on the edge of the seat next to Ben. "I'm Jane." She extended her hand.

Ben took her her hand. "I know. I mean, I read it on the flyer. I'm Ben." He was surprised when she didn't immediately release his hand. She held it a moment and smiled. Ben felt the gentle pressure of her fingers, the soft skin against his. He realized they were staring at each other, a subtle tension running between them.

"Well, Ben, it's nice to meet you," she said softly. Someone called Jane's name and she turned to wave. "I need to go. We're getting ready to start. Listen, though, will you stick around after the show? We could grab a drink or something, or just talk?" She looked hopeful and Ben found himself agreeing.

The show turned out to be great. Jane had a real stage presence and a clear voice that was capable of a wide range of emotions. He found himself sitting forward in his seat, focusing intently on her face as she sang. In a word, he found her mesmerizing.

When the show ended, Ben watched the milling crowd, waiting for Jane. She walked through a side door, flushed and excited. She spotted Ben and walked over. He was struck by her delicate bone structure and petite but curvy frame. On stage she carried herself with such strength she appeared taller, somehow more substantial. Here, next to him, she was truly a pocket Venus.

"Did you like the show? What did you think?" She was standing next to him, her hand on his arm, looking up into his eyes. Her lips were parted, those lips that looked like rose petals, lips that looked like they should be kissed.

"You were great. I really enjoyed it." Before he thought about it, he bent down and kissed her. As they broke apart, she looked startled for a moment. Then Ben saw a spark of passion in her eyes. She reached up, wrapping her arms around Ben's neck, kissing him fully. Ben kissed her back, pulling her up against him. He could feel the delicious curves of her body against his. He involuntarily tightened his embrace, feeling something stirring deep in the pit of his stomach.

Jane broke away first. "Oh, wow. Sorry. I get a little carried away sometimes. I've been told I lack impulse control." She laughed up at Ben. "You don't seem to mind though. Let's go. There's a place I like just around the corner. We can have a drink if you like, and talk a bit."

"I think I'd like that." Ben followed her out of the Barrymore, marveling at the way Jane affected him. They walked the short distance to a little bar. Ben knew the place; it was a popular hangout for local bands and their fans, and two members of Jane's band were at another table. They took a small table in the corner, ordered a beer and started talking. Ben had never been one for making small talk, but with Jane, he found words flowed easily.

They left the bar when it closed. Ben had totally lost track of time. They had been engrossed in each other, sharing their respective life stories. They discovered they both hated cilantro and loved music. Ben found himself laughing more than he had in a long time, relaxing with Jane. She was refreshing, held unconventional views, and wasn't afraid to share them. He marveled that he could be so comfortable with someone he'd just met. Jane was equally as comfortable with Ben. Conservative guys in suits were not usually her type but she decided in Ben's case she shouldn't judge a book by its cover.

They walked back to Ben's car. "Do you need a ride?" he asked.

"Well, yes, actually. That would be great. I got a ride here with the drummer. If it's no trouble, that is."

"It would be an honor to escort you home." Ben unlocked the door and held it for Jane. She got in, her skirt sliding up a bit, revealing more of her curvy thigh and creamy skin. Ben was momentarily distracted by the glimpse of the tattoo visible on Jane's leg: the edge of a leaf and what appeared to be a flower. He found his glimpse of her tattoo quite arousing, and wanted very much to find out what the tattoo looked like, to slide her skirt higher, run his hands up that creamy leg, revealing more of the tattoo, and Jane...

He realized she'd said his name. He

mentally shook himself. "Sorry. What did you say?"

"I said, thanks for the ride. I'm not far from here. I hope it's not out of your way." Jane was smiling up at him with a mischievous grin. She'd noticed the reaction to seeing her leg as her skirt slid up. She playfully tugged the hem of her skirt just a little higher, teasing Ben. She heard him draw in a breath, his lips parting, as if he'd seen something he really wasn't supposed to see but wanted to see more of. Jane was intrigued by this reaction and also excited by it. There was something both innocent and worldly about Ben that was quite arousing.

"Oh, sorry. I mean, no, it's not out of my way. Even if it was, I'd still give you a ride," Ben stumbled out an answer. Jane laughed. "I think I'd like that ride," she said, making a double entendre out of his innocent comment.

Ben followed her directions to her flat. They made small talk in the car, sensing they were passing time in a comfortable way before something was going to happen. There was an awareness running between them, a heightening sense of sexual tension. Ben opened her door when they arrived, Jane sliding out of the car.

"Do you want to come in? We could have something to drink, some coffee or something?" Jane looked up at Ben. Rather than answering, he tilted her chin up and kissed her, slowly and lingeringly, gently running his tongue over her lips. She responded to his kiss, lifting up on her toes, wrapping her arms around his neck. Ben held her gently; the only real contact between them their lips. Jane took Ben's lower lip gently in her teeth, sucking on it, tugging it briefly before running her tongue over it. Ben felt a surge of pleasure run through his body and he responded to her kiss by pulling her closer, almost lifting her off her feet. He broke their kiss reluctantly.

"I think I'd like to come in," Ben said, his voice husky. Jane smiled up at him and his second unintentional turn of phrase.

The moment they were behind the closed door of Jane's apartment, they were in each other's arms. Ben folded Jane against him, crushing her mouth with his, feeling her breasts against his chest, feeling his own response to her body in every fiber. His cock began to stiffen, pressing against Jane through their clothes.

Jane was amazed at the swiftness of her arousal. She found Ben extremely attractive and began to make little whimpering sounds as soon as he started kissing her. It was obvious Ben was aroused as well; she could feel his growing erection against her stomach as he held her tightly, his hips pushed forward, thrusting himself gently against her. She responded by reaching down and rubbing her palm up the length of what appeared to be a nice sized cock. She felt him shudder against her, a moan escaping his lips. He said her name then, and leaned down, kissing her with such passion and force it almost took her breath away.

As Jane continued to massage his stiffening cock, sending waves of desire coursing through him, Ben ran his hands underneath Jane's skirt, up her bare legs to her hips, sliding them down over the sweet curve of her ass. She was wearing a thong, her ass bare in his hands. He moaned again, squeezing her ass, spreading her, massaging the smooth warm skin in his hands.

Jane felt a shudder run through her at the touch of Ben's hands on her bare skin. She began working the zipper on his pants, wanting to feel him, to see his cock in her hand. She undid the button of his pants, tugging them down, his erection catching on the waistband of his boxers. She pulled at the elastic, freeing his penis from the confines of his clothing, breaking their kiss to look down at her hand holding his hard cock.

Ben looked down as well, the sight of her holding him in her delicate hand making him harder. His penis gave an involuntary jerk, his hips moving forward as if seeking more contact. Jane met his eyes, saw his passion and desire and began moving her hand up and down the shaft, running her thumb up over the sensitive tip of his penis, feeling him shudder beneath her touch. He closed his eyes, lips parted; the sensation of her warm hand stroking him was incredibly exciting. She continued stroking him, watching, enjoying the sight of that big cock in her tiny hand while Ben's hands were on her body.

Ben moved one hand from her luscious ass, sliding it between her legs, feeling the satin material of her thong. He ran his middle finger over the material, feeling her heat and how wet she already was. He slid his fingers inside the edge of the thong, pulling it aside and slipping a finger in her luscious warmth and wetness. He felt Jane whimpering against him, swiveling her hips as if seeking more contact.

He obliged, sliding two fingers deep into her opening; Jane gasped with pleasure. She increased the pressure on his cock as he worked his fingers into her pussy, feeling the hot slickness of her, fingering her as she continued stroking him.

Ben worked his middle finger deeper into Jane, stroking her with the pad of his finger, seeking one certain spot inside her. Jane suddenly let out a cry, her hips thrusting forward and her stomach muscles contracting. He increased the pressure on that spot, stroking it, rubbing it with his middle finger.

Jane was straining against him now, her knees bending slightly, hips pushing upward, seeking release. She was gasping against his chest, still holding his cock tightly but lost in her own pleasure, no longer stroking him. He held her tightly against him as he worked his fingers more aggressively into her pussy. She was shuddering against him now, on the verge of coming. He wanted to make her come, to bring her off and watch. He didn't have long to wait.

As Ben's fingers worked their magic inside her, Jane was almost overwhelmed with sensations. She could feel herself building to an orgasm, feel herself peaking. She suddenly cried out, her head back, her body wracked by spasms of pleasure. She'd never experienced anything like this, the intensity was amazing. She felt liquid squirt from her pussy, felt it running down the inside of her leg as waves of intense sexual pleasure ran through her body. Ben watched her as her orgasm flooded over his hand, watched as his fingers, still buried in her pussy, thrust into her. There was a look of pure bliss on her face, a smile on her lips. She was limp in his arms. He slowed his thrusting fingers, gently stroking her as her orgasm faded, then sliding them from her, rubbing his palm over her soft mound.

He felt her contractions and spasms subside, sensed she was coming back to reality. She opened her eyes, a look of amazement on her face. She smiled up at him, regaining her balance and reached up to kiss him. He responded to her kiss, seeking her tongue with his. He began to massage one perfect breast through her shirt, feeling the hard nipple beneath his finger.

They made swift work of the rest of their clothes, Ben stripping Jane's shirt over her head revealing full round breasts barely restrained by a lacy bra. She pushed her skirt down, wiggling her hips as she worked the garment over them, pulling her soaking wet thong off in the process.

Watching her take off her skirt, that little wiggle of her hips, tipped Ben over the edge. He pulled Jane to him roughly, grabbing her ass in his hands and grinding his cock against her stomach, his mouth crushing hers in a kiss. His cock felt like it was going to explode at the touch of her skin against him. He wanted her right then, right there. Jane seemed to read his mind.

"Fuck me now, Ben, I want you to come

inside me, come like you made me come." As she spoke, she turned, her back to Ben, putting her hands on the arm of the couch. "Take me here, like this. Fuck me hard, Ben." She bent forward, looking over her shoulder, spreading her legs, showing Ben her beautiful ass and the wet pussy he'd just been fingering.

Without any hesitation, Ben grabbed her hips and thrust himself into Jane's slit, a deep primal sound somewhere between a moan and a growl escaping him. She took the entire length of his rigid shaft, crying out with pleasure. Ben pulled back, held himself with just the crown of his cock in Jane, wanting to experience again the sensation of thrusting himself fully into her. He looked down at his cock, covered in her juice, glistening wet, the veins visible beneath the skin. He saw her perfect ass in his hands, the smooth skin, saw the swollen lips of her pussy holding him tight. Jane had reached down and was fingering her clit. Ben saw her fingers rubbing that hard button of flesh, knew she was getting into this as much as he was. Seeing his cock in her and watching her finger herself sent him over the edge.

With a hoarse cry, Ben pumped hard into Jane, thrusting repeatedly, his hips driving his rigid cock deep into her each time. He slammed into her with increasing speed, Jane's pussy welcoming him. She was gasping beneath him in time to his pounding, cries of pleasure fueling his thrusts. He could feel her fingers brushing against him as she continued rubbing her clit, bringing herself closer to her second orgasm.

Ben felt himself close to the edge, the feeling of pressure and heat building low in his stomach, moving to his balls. He could feel his cock filling with heat, feel that heat working toward the tip of him. With a final thrust his orgasm burst from him, shooting his cum deep in Jane's pussy. He felt her contract around him, sensed she was coming too and heard her cry out.

She started rocking her hips in time to his thrusts, working her clit with her fingers, bringing herself off while Ben continued pumping his load, his cock still working to shoot into her. He held himself in her then, grinding against her ass, his orgasm almost over as Jane still bucked back against him, the waves of her orgasm continuing to consume her.

They were both breathing hard when their orgasms finally began to subside. Ben slid his cock reluctantly from Jane, wanting to stay buried in her warmth. She turned around and he held her, feeling her breasts pressed against him as her breathing slowed. She looked up at Ben, smiling.

"That was incredible. I've never had anything like that happen before. You're amazing."

Ben actually blushed. "Well, truth be told, I've never had anything like that happen either. I'm not a stud by any means. You're just very easy to ... um, well..." He was at a loss for words. He had never discussed sex with a woman afterward.

"To stimulate?" Jane laughed. She kissed

him lightly. "I was going to say 'easy to please'," Ben replied.

"Do you want to spend the night? You're more than welcome to."

"I can't." Ben looked at his watch. "I need to be to work in exactly four hours. I think I need to get some sleep, and I know if I stayed, we probably wouldn't sleep at all." He smiled down at her, kissing her forehead. "I really need to go." He reluctantly let go of Jane, gathered his clothes, and made an attempt to get dressed. Jane left the room briefly, returning in a robe, tying the sash around her waist.

"When can I see you again?" Ben asked, buttoning his shirt, thinking that sounded a little desperate.

"Anytime you want." Jane reached out and finished the last couple buttons. "We're rehearsing tonight, but if you want you can stop by here about nine or so, or I can stop by your place. I think we'll be done by then. Give me your cell number and I'll call you if we run late."

Ben handed her a business card. "This has all my contact information. I have a brief to work on, so if you don't mind, you can swing by my place when you're done. It will be a great reason to stop working." Jane tucked the card beside the phone.

"Okay," Jane said. "We're set for tonight. Do you want me to bring a late dinner? I can stop by Jimmy Chow's on the way home from rehearsal. Do you like Chinese? They make a really great lemon chicken and yang chow rice."

"I love Jimmy's. I think that sounds like a plan," Ben said, tucking in his shirt and stuffing his socks in his pocket.

Jane wrapped her arms around Ben's waist. "This was a fantastic night. I'm so very glad you decided to come to the show."

Ben kissed her, eventually tearing himself away from her embrace. "Me too. I really need to go." She let him out, closing the door softly behind him. She leaned back against it, smiling to herself.

Ben was only an hour late for work the next day. He didn't think that was too bad, all things considered. He'd gotten home, crashed into bed and, it seemed, was immediately woken by the alarm. He'd hit the snooze a couple times, then decided to hell with it and just set it for an hour later. He'd showered and gotten dressed in record time, thankful he had no clients till that afternoon. He knew he'd be exhausted but he didn't care. He was exhausted for a good reason; he'd had fun and he'd had great sex with Jane. Not from studying or working all night.

Feeling pretty pleased with himself, he set to work on the brief in front of him. He was deep in thought when there was a knock on the door. He looked up. His father was standing in the doorway.

"Doris tells me you were over an hour late today. Care to tell me why?" As owner of the firm, his dad tended to ride him hard about work. It was expected Ben would follow in the old man's footsteps, inherit the firm one day. Doris was his secretary and knew everything that happened in the firm, particularly as it concerned Ben.

"I would think you'd have enough work to keep Doris busy without having to spy on me," Ben looked up at his dad, a teasing glint in his eye. But he was met with a stony glare from the older man.

"I don't believe this is the time for jokes, Ben. I'm serious. Beth called last night looking for you. She said you weren't answering. This is highly unlike you." Ben's father gave him the same look Ben had seen when he was in school and hadn't received a high enough grade to satisfy his dad.

"Dad, I'm not a child. I was out, I didn't hear the phone, I didn't think to check messages and I was late this morning. Taken as a whole, I'm not sure that's enough to convict me of anything, much less charge me. Can we talk about something else?" Ben watched his father struggle for a moment. He knew the old man really wanted to let him have it but he also knew Ben was right.

"Fine. Just don't make a habit of this. And speaking of Beth, she was looking for you to discuss tonight." Ben's father was referring to the Black and White Ball, an event his father sponsored each year. Ben disliked the event, which he'd attended a few times. It was a networking device and while he understood the need for networking, he disliked the artificiality of sponsoring an event just to meet other lawyers.

"That's tonight? I thought it was on Tuesday." Ben's mind raced. He'd promised to take Beth, even though he really didn't want to go. She felt it was important for them to be seen. She practiced at a different firm and was very much into the "see and be seen" ethic. So as a favor he'd said he'd take her.

"This is Tuesday, Ben. The Ball is tonight. Beth will be back today on the one-fifteen flight from Chicago. You had better pull yourself together here. I still don't know what's gotten into you."

Ben knew it was Jane that had gotten into him, but he couldn't really tell his father that. He thought about Jane and remembered he had a date with her. This day was starting to go downhill fast. Maybe he could get ahold of Beth and tell her he wasn't going. Ben realized his father was still talking.

"At any rate, your mother and I expect to see you at the Ball no later than eight o'clock. Understood?" Ben nodded. His father strode out of his office. Great, Ben thought. Between his father, his mother, and Beth there was no way to get out of this thing. He'd have to call Jane and reschedule.

With a start he realized he had no way to get ahold of Jane. He had forgotten to get her number. He called the Crooked Bean but she wasn't at work and the guy who answered wouldn't give out her home number. He did an online search for her name but she wasn't listed. He tried a reverse address search but no luck. He thought about driving over there, but he'd have to walk home, get the car, drive to her apartment. He couldn't leave work for that long and not have his father, with an earful from Doris, on his case any more than he already was. Ben felt trapped and miserable. He buried himself in his work until it was time to go home.

He ran home from work and then drove to Jane's. He rang the buzzer but there was no answer. She'd said the band was rehearsing, but he had no idea where that would be. His heart sank. The only thing he could do was leave a note on his door explaining the confusion and hope she'd be okay with that.

He went back home and got ready for the Ball. He put on his one and only tuxedo, managed to get the tie tied correctly and was just heading out to get Beth when there was a knock on the door. He had a fleeting thought it might be Jane and opened the door in anticipation. But it was Beth, resplendent in a floor-length white satin gown, which looked like something his mother would wear. In fact, this may have been one of his mother's old dresses. He shook his head in disappointment.

"Nice to see you too, Ben," she said, as she walked into his apartment. "Where have you been? I've been trying for days to get in touch with you." She perched on the edge of the couch. Beth never sat; she always perched or stood. It was something he'd always been slightly annoyed with, and tonight it seemed to bother him more. The woman seemed incapable of relaxing.

"Have a seat, Beth. I'm not quite ready." Beth remained where she was, looking at him with narrowed eyes. Ben left the living room to get his wallet and cell phone. He checked it for messages and saw there were quite a few from Beth, but none from Jane. He also realized the ringer was off and remembered turning it off at the show. He returned to find Beth still perched on the arm of the couch.

"What's going on with you? You're acting rather odd. And where were you last night? I tried calling you but you never answered."

"Yeah, Dad told me. I was out."

"'I was out' does not explain where you were." Beth was not giving up on this. Ben cut her off.

"Look, we need to go or we'll be late. Why are you here anyway? I thought I was picking you up." Ben had written a brief note to Jane explaining he'd be out but back later and would she please call. He couldn't put her name on it now, since Beth was here. He taped it shut and stuck another piece on it to attach it to the door. He looked at Beth.

"If you'd bothered to check your messages, you would have known why. And now the reason is irrelevant. We do need to leave though." She walked past him to the door. "Coming?"

"Yeah, go ahead. I need to find my keys." He grabbed them and the note as she walked into the hall. He locked the door and then stuck the note to it. It was the best he could do for now.

Ben and Beth arrived at the Ball and tracked down his mother and father, thereby avoiding another lecture. His mother and Beth began an instant critique of every other woman in attendance and his dad started pointing out certain individuals he felt Ben should meet during the evening. Ben was already starting to get a headache at the thought of spending the evening networking among his father's business associates. He was regretting not having the balls to just say no.

Beth appeared and asked him to dance. He began moving her mechanically about the floor, feeling an overwhelming desire to bolt. Beth kept after him, asking him what was wrong, why he was so distant. He finally couldn't stand it any longer. He steered her to the edge of the floor, let her go and took a deep breath.

"Look, you know I hate these things. I'm not here because I want to be. And I'm tired of having to explain what's wrong with me to everyone. There's nothing wrong with me. In fact, I've never been better. So I'd appreciate it if you'd just leave me alone." Ben turned and stormed out of the Ball, leaving a stunned Beth looking after him. He'd just reached the car when his phone started ringing. He fished it out of his pocket, hoping it might be Jane but knowing it would be Beth. The caller ID showed Beth's number so he ignored the call. It rang twice more before he got out of the parking lot. He ignored those as well.

He drove to his apartment and was relieved to find the note still on the door; he hadn't missed her. He took it off and let himself in. It was still early, although he didn't know how long bands rehearsed. He took off the tux and put on sweats and a T-shirt. He was exhausted from lack of sleep and the argument with Beth. He lay down on the couch, relying on Jane's arrival to wake him up. He fell asleep.

Jane's band had gotten done rehearsing much earlier than she'd anticipated. She made a quick stop at Jimmy Chow's, getting dinner for her and Ben. She was looking forward to a late dinner and seeing Ben again, and anything that followed. She had enjoyed the entire evening with him, from performing while knowing he was in the audience, to spending hours talking with him after the show. She went over the details of their time at her apartment, her body tingling at the memory. Ben had been passionate and aggressive, something she liked in guys, but she'd also had a real connection with him on other levels besides just mind-blowing sex.

She'd parked down the block from the address he'd given her. As she collected the Chinese carryout bags she'd heard voices and recognized Ben's. She straightened and watched as he walked down the stairs of his building, dressed in a tuxedo, and escorting a statuesque blonde woman. They got in Ben's car and drove away. Jane felt her stomach drop. She turned woodenly back to her car, got in and drove home.

When she got to her block though, she found she didn't want to be alone. She was hurt and confused. She pulled out her cell phone and dialed up Ethan, the drummer from the band. He was up for dinner and company. He said he'd be there in 20 minutes.

Jane warmed up the now cold food, set out plates and opened a bottle of wine. She poured herself a glass, drank it and poured a second. Ethan arrived and they ate dinner, talking about the gig they had on the weekend, going over the set list and other details of the show. They finished the first bottle of wine, or rather Jane did. She opened a second and they moved to the living room.

Ethan and Jane had slept together a few times since they'd formed the band. Jane thought he was okay in bed and they'd always had a good time. And she knew he wasn't interested in anything long-term. Neither wanted to ruin working together in the band; they knew sex was as far as it would go and both were okay with that.

Ethan started kissing Jane while they were sitting on the couch. He moved his hands over her breasts, cupping one, gently squeezing it. Jane responded, arching her back into his hand. She returned his kiss a bit sloppily, a little drunk. Ethan deepened their kiss, laying her down on the couch. He continued fondling her breast, his other hand working its way up her leg beneath her skirt. She moved her legs, bending one knee and throwing her leg over the low back of the couch, dropping the other foot to the floor. She could feel Ethan's erection rubbing against her stomach. He reached down and unzipped his pants, pulling his cock from the confines of the fabric. He continued fingering her beneath her skirt, rubbing her with his hand. She was slowly getting aroused at his touch. She wasn't sure if she was fuzzy-headed from the wine, but something was off, something didn't feel quite right.

Ben woke with a start, imagining he heard someone knock. He looked at his watch; it was well past midnight. He didn't think bands rehearsed this late. He wondered why she hadn't called. He paced restlessly for a time, then thought the hell with it, grabbed his keys and drove the few blocks to Jane's apartment.

Jane shifted her hips, pulling her skirt up further. Ethan looked down at her, stroking his cock. "You're so beautiful, babe. Are you ready?" Jane nodded her head; although physically she was aroused, mentally and emotionally she was miles away.

Ethan entered her slowly, pumping in and out in a steady rhythm. She knew his style, steady and consistent. He wasn't adventurous but she wasn't looking for that now, she was looking to fill an emptiness inside. She started thrusting up to meet him, twisting her hips to bring her clit more in contact with him. He propped himself on one elbow and buried his head on her shoulder. With his free hand he rhythmically massaged one breast, occasionally tweaking the nipple. Jane knew from experience he could go on like this for a long time unless she took the initiative.

Ben had gotten as far as her apartment door before thinking this may not be the best idea. He'd feel bad if he woke her up. He'd feel worse if she told him she hadn't wanted to see him. But he was here so he decided he might as well knock.

Jane reached down and started to massage her clit, rubbing herself in time to Ethan's thrusts. She started gasping as her arousal increased, little cries escaping her. With her other hand she reached down beneath her leg and began to rub Ethan's balls.

Ben's hand was poised at the door when he heard noises from inside. He hesitated, thinking it was the television. But he recognized Jane's voice, or more precisely the noises he heard her make last night. He leaned closer, hating that he was eavesdropping but powerless to stop. He also heard deeper noises, male sounds that definitely weren't coming from Jane.

Ethan felt her fingers stroking his balls and moaned. He raised his head, changed his position and started pumping harder into Jane. She tipped her hips up, giving him a different angle of penetration. Ethan began moaning deep in his throat, thrusting into her with force, making Jane cry out.

Ethan came quickly then, pumping in short thrusts, his cock shooting his load into Jane. She tried hard to bring herself off, but Ethan was finished before she even started.

Ben was horrified at the unmistakable sounds of Jane having sex in the living room. He realized he was still standing with his arm raised, ready to knock on the door. With a pain in his heart he turned and almost ran from her building. He wasn't a prude and realized he didn't have any particularly solid relationship with Jane—he really didn't have any relationship with her—but he thought he'd read her a little better than that. She didn't seem like the kind to stand him up for sex with another guy.

Jane struggled to sit up beneath Ethan, tugging her skirt down in the process. He sat back, pulling his jeans up and tucking himself inside. He zipped up his pants, leaned over and kissed Jane.

"Thanks for dinner, Janie. I liked the Chinese. I gotta go. See you at rehearsal tomorrow." Ethan let himself out and Jane was left alone. She felt worse than she did before. Sex with Ethan had only made her feel emptier. Plus she was getting a headache from the wine.

She threw the rest of the Chinese food away and went to bed. Maybe she'd sort all this out in the morning. With a sinking feeling, she realized she was scheduled to work the early shift at the Bean. This was turning out to be one hell of a day.

Ben spent another miserable night not sleeping. He walked to the Bean for his coffee, wondering how things could change so rapidly in just 24 hours. He contemplated skipping the coffee this morning but realized he couldn't alter his entire life because of one unfortunate evening. Besides, he'd been getting his coffee from the Bean long before Jane started working there. It was his coffee shop, not hers.

Carrying that belligerent and, he recognized, entirely childish attitude with him, he got in line. He didn't see Jane behind the counter. Maybe he'd be spared from having to see her today. Just as he reached the counter though, Jane came out to the front from the back, carrying a tray of cups. She saw Ben and almost dropped the whole thing. The look she gave him could have scalded water, it was so full of anger. Ben frowned. What did she have to be angry about? It wasn't him having sex with someone else.

"Can I help you?" The petite blonde barista was speaking to Ben. Jane glared at him and walked to the counter.

"I'll take this one, Leslie. He's got special needs." Jane practically spat the words at Ben. She motioned him to the end of the counter, taking him out of the line of other customers.

"What are you doing?" he asked, totally perplexed.

"What am I doing? What are you doing? Or I should say, who did you do? Who's the tall blonde in the evening gown?" Jane was almost hissing her words at him. "I bought you dinner, I drove to your apartment and I see you leaving with... with that Amazon."

"You saw me leaving... you saw me leaving for the Black and White Ball with Beth." It suddenly dawned on Ben what she was talking about. "But you were having sex with someone. I heard you."

"Heard me? Where were you?" It was Jane's turn to look perplexed.

"I was outside your door. I came over to find out why you'd stood me up. I was just about to knock when I heard him... you... heard you having sex with him... with someone."

"Oh..." Jane lost some of her anger, looking down at the floor. "Well, yeah, there is that... but you'd stood me up to go to some fancy dress ball with... Beth. Who is she? How could you do that?"

"Jane, I didn't run out and have sex with someone after having sex with someone else the night before. Or rather, the same day, since I'd just left your apartment that morning." Ben was still hurt and angry with her, a tiny part of him wanting to understand but most of him really pissed off at Jane.

"Ben, there's a whole lot of stuff here you don't know about." She looked at her watch. "Look, you're late and I have to get back to work. Can we meet later? I think we both have a lot to explain, and to understand."

"Fine." Ben walked toward the door, Jane following behind.

"We don't have rehearsal tonight. I'm done here at two o'clock. I can meet you when you're done with work." Jane felt the first glimmer of hope that there really was a logical explanation for all of this.

"How about your apartment at six o'clock? Give me your cell phone number just in case." She scribbled her number on an order slip on Ben stuck it in his coat pocket. "Okay. We're set then. Your place at six o'clock and we both know how to reach the other." Jane nodded.

Ben was late for work again. He knew at some point Doris would report that fact to his father, who would be at his door asking him what was wrong. Plus he'd have to explain last night, leaving the Ball and leaving Beth. Ben put his head in his hands. This was not how he wanted to spend his day.

True to form, his father was knocking on Ben's door after lunch. "You've got some explaining to do, Ben." Rather than stand in the hall, his father came in and sat down across from Ben. He reached across the desk, turning the flyer for Jane's band around, frowning as he read. "Well, this explains a lot." He stabbed a forefinger at the date. "This is where you were Monday night. Seeing some band. Seeing this girl from the band?" Ben's father frowned at Jane's image, visible tattoos, long black hair framing her pale face, her stage make up dark and dramatic. To Ben she looked beautiful, but to Ben's father she was the epitome of everything he didn't want his son associating with.

"My God, Ben. She's a tattooed girl in a band. I suppose she has piercings in inappropriate places. What could she offer you? Why would you choose to associate with someone like this, when you're dating Beth?" Ben's father looked at him, expecting an answer.

"Well, Dad, I'm not 'dating' Beth. I occasionally squire her to events to 'see and be seen' but I'm not in a serious relationship with her. She may think we're a couple, and you and mom think we're a couple, but I don't. And second, Jane..." His father snorted at the sound of her name "Jane is not some tattooed and pierced stereotype, she's a very talented singer, and she's a great person, open and genuine." Ben didn't know if he was trying to convince his dad how great Jane was or himself.

"Anyway, who I see on my free time is really none of your concern, Dad." Ben was working hard on mastering his father's dismissive tone, but he knew he had a long way to go. It didn't work with his dad.

"Ben, you're not thinking clearly here. This girl has some kind of negative influence over you and it's not good. You need to cut her from your life and get your head on straight."

"Okay. That's it." Ben found he was suddenly very angry. "Dad, I am thinking straight, I'm thinking straighter than I have for a long time. I'm not interested in a relationship with Beth. She's incapable of relaxing; she never sits down, she perches." Ben's father started to speak but Ben cut him off. "I'm not done. You may be able to push me around here at the firm; it is your firm, after all. But you are not allowed to dictate who I decide to see. Jane is someone I care about, someone who is real and honest and actually sits on furniture." Ben had a brief mental image of Jane; the last time she'd been near any furniture, he'd had her bent over the arm of a couch, pounding her from behind. He shook his head.

"Jane is someone I want a relationship with. Not Beth." Ben's father seemed shocked by Ben's words. Ben was surprised himself. He thought that what he'd heard through the door of Jane's apartment had ended any feelings he had for her, but apparently he was wrong.

"And now, before it's too late, I'm going to find Jane and figure out how to salvage what we have, or had, or could have." Ben stood up. "If you'll excuse me, I've got to go."

Ben took the stairs to the street two at a time. He glanced at his watch; Jane said she worked until two o'clock. If he ran, he could catch her. He didn't want to wait until six o'clock to get this straightened out; he wanted to get it straightened out now and get on with whatever was next. And he hoped 'next' was a relationship with Jane.

He rounded the corner down the street from the Crooked Bean, catching sight of Jane just walking out the door. He sprinted the last half block, calling her name. She turned, caught off guard, surprise on her face. She waited for him.

"Ben. What is it?" She looked alarmed as he caught his breath. "Are you all right? Is something wrong?"

"Yeah. I mean, no. I'm fine," he said. "I need to talk to you. I don't want to wait until tonight. Come on, walk home with me." He tugged her arm, turning her in the direction of his apartment. Jane followed along.

"Look, I'll start. The woman you saw me with is Beth. I've known her since law school. She practices at a different firm than I do. Our parents are friends. Anyway, our relationship is sort of like an arranged marriage."

Jane looked startled. "You're getting married to her?"

Ben rushed on. "No, we're not getting married, it's nothing like that. But the whole relationship is based on appearances, not on any real feelings for each other. Our parents think we're the perfect couple, that we complement each other. We went out a few times in law school, when neither of us had time for any serious relationships. When it came time to go to these things my father arranges, it was just easier to take Beth than look for someone else. She loves those things, those artificial gatherings, the networking, all that. She's good at that stuff. I hate them."

They'd reached Ben's apartment. He let them in. "You want something to drink? Have a seat." He motioned to the couch.

Jane sat. "I'll have whatever you're having. Or a beer, if you have one."

Ben watched her sit back on the couch and suddenly laughed.

"What's so funny?" Jane looked up. "Do I have something in my hair? Did a pigeon poop on me?" She reached up, gingerly touching her head.

"No, just something I said to my father. I'll explain in a second." He came back from the kitchen, handed her a beer and sat down next to her. She took a healthy swallow of hers, and Ben did the same.

"So, anyway, Beth and my parents all assume because we've been going to these events over the years, or I take her to some prominent social event, we're dating. They all believe we're eventually getting married. Which we're not." Ben took another swallow of beer.

"The night you saw me—saw me and Beth—Tuesday night. God, it seems like ages ago, but that was what, yesterday?" Jane nodded. "I'd completely forgotten about this event my dad sponsors. I'd promised to go, to take Beth. My dad reminded me that morning. I didn't have any way of getting ahold of you. I didn't get your cell phone number, the Bean wouldn't tell me your number and I couldn't leave work to come to your place to explain. Then Beth showed up unexpectedly at my place and all I could do was leave a note on the door, hoping that you'd understand and we'd get together later. But you saw us leave, I guess, and then, well, you were hurt and confused."

Ben's rush of words finally trailed off. "And then... I left Beth at the dance. We had a fight and I left her there. I guess I've left her permanently, if you can leave someone you're not actually seeing. I came home, waited for you, fell asleep for a bit, and then went looking for you. And heard you in your apartment."

Jane had taken all this in, her face a kaleidoscope of emotions. She understood a whole lot more about what she'd seen, but now she was really embarrassed to explain her activities that night.

She took a deep breath and dove into her explanation. "After I left—after seeing you and Beth together—I felt horrible. I went home, but I didn't want to be alone. I called Ethan—he's the drummer in the band—and asked him to come over for dinner. And to have sex. We've hooked up a couple times over the years. Neither of us are interested in anything long-term; it's always been a friends-with-benefits kind of thing. We're far better as band mates than soul mates. But he was here, and that's who you heard. And I feel terrible about that."

Jane looked up at Ben. "It didn't fix anything, being with Ethan. I felt worse afterward, like I'd done something really wrong, and I still had this big emptiness inside, like I was missing a piece of my heart. I would have undone it all in an instant, rather than hurt you." She reached up and touched his face.

Ben leaned down and kissed her. "I think we've both been through a whole lot in a really short time," he said. "But I do know this: you are the person I'm interested in trying a relationship with. I'm making a conscious choice to see you, if you want to see me, rather than just go along with the status quo. Does that sound like something you'd like, Jane? I'm willing to start this all over again, to forget what happened—well, to forget the bad stuff that happened—and keep repeating the good stuff."

Jane turned to him, wrapping her arms around his neck. "Yes, Ben. I think I'd like that. I'd like that very much." She kissed him back then, probing his lips gently with her tongue. "Can we start repeating the good stuff right now? Like what happened the other night?" Ben looked down at her, at the teasing glint in her eye.

"You bet. But not here, not on the couch." Ben stood up, pulling Jane with him.

She frowned lightly. "And why not?"

Ben laughed. "Okay, here's the story; it might not make sense to you, but it's important to me. When I was telling my dad the reasons Beth drove me nuts, one of them is her inability to relax. She perches on the arms of things, like the couch. I said one of the reasons I loved you was because you actually sit on furniture. But the image that flashed in my mind when I said that wasn't of you sitting on a couch; it was of the other night, of you bent over the arm of your couch and, well—you remember what we were doing." Ben looked down at her, smiling. "It may not have been the best image to have while arguing with my dad, but it was a pretty hot image of you."

The look on Jane's face made Ben stop. "What's wrong? Did I say something wrong?" He realized she was crying. "Hey, what's the matter?"

"Nothing's wrong. You said you loved me. Did you mean that? No one's ever said that before." The vulnerable look on Jane's face touched Ben.

"I guess I did say that, didn't I? It must be true then. I never lie." He bent down to kiss her lips. "I love you, Jane, amazing as that sounds. 'Love at first sight' is such a cliché, it's one of those things you find in those sappy romance novels, where the hero saves the heroine from danger, they fall madly in love and they live happily ever after. I think though, if this were our romance story, you're the one who's saved me."

"How so?" Jane was smiling up at him through her tears. "How have I saved you?"

Ben pulled her close, kissing her forehead. "You made me realize what's important to me, that I need to choose what I want rather than going along with what everyone else expects. You've opened up my eyes, and my heart. I don't think I'm going to go quit my job just yet, but I may start questioning if I really want to take over the firm someday. It's always been expected of me, but no one's actually asked me if that's what I want. You've basically derailed my life, Jane, and sent me down a totally different track."

Jane laughed. "So I've made your life a train wreck?" She punched him lightly in the arm. "You're funny."

Ben leaned down and kissed her again, more firmly on the lips this time. "Maybe so. But weren't we heading off to start making new stuff happen? I believe we have a date with a different piece of furniture... the bed." Ben's teasing tone had changed to a more serious one. "I want to make love to you, Jane, in a proper bed." He took her by the hand, leading her to the bedroom.

They stopped next to the bed. "Jane, I really did mean it when I said I love you. This is all new for us, but that is how I feel. I don't need you to feel the same, at least not yet." He bent down and kissed Jane. She ran her hands up the side of his face, twining her fingers in his hair. He pulled her to him, pulling her hard against his body, wanting to feel all of her against him.

Jane could feel Ben's erection growing, pushing against her. She wanted, as before, to see and feel it. She pulled the zipper down on his pants, reaching in to rub his cock, feeling it stiffen at her touch. Ben had worked his hands underneath her T-shirt, pulling it up as he reached for her breasts. He tugged at it and Jane reluctantly let go of his cock as he slipped the shirt over her head. He looked down at her perfect breasts, full and round, contained in a black satin bra that made her skin seem even more porcelain-like. Ben had never seen such a beautiful contrast between skin and material.

He ran his hands up over her breasts, feeling the cool satin over her heated body, the soft skin of the tops of her breasts. He had the sudden desire to feel his cock between those breasts. He had no idea how to ask Jane for that though.

Jane had taken his cock back in her hand and was slowly stroking it, watching Ben fondle her breasts. "Um, Jane... could I... would you? I'm not sure how to ask you for this."

Jane looked up at him. "Then show me what you want, Ben. If I can, I'll do whatever you want." He looked into her blue eyes, amazed at her trust in him.

"Okay." His voice was husky with anticipation. "Just sit on the edge of the bed. I think that will work."

Jane sat down, curious to know what Ben wanted. He reached down and undid the clasp at the front of her bra. She started to slip the straps off her shoulders, but he stopped her. "No, leave it. Leave it on, but unhooked." Ben moved forward a step, still hesitant. Jane took a guess at what he wanted.

"Here, is this what you want?" She took his cock in her hand and guided it between her breasts. Ben could only manage to nod his head. He pushed his hips forward slightly and Jane released her hold on him, using both hands to push her breasts together, still partly covered by the black bra, gently squeezing his cock between them. She looked up at Ben, whose eyes had grown dark with passion.

"Go ahead, Ben. Fuck my breasts. Slide your cock up and down. It feels good for you and it feels good for me. That's all that matters." She began kneading her own breasts, massaging Ben's cock as she massaged her own breasts. Ben began slowly thrusting his hips back and forth, his cock sliding up and down against the soft skin.

Jane heard him gasp and she looked up at him, smiling. "Does that feel good? Is that what you wanted?" Ben nodded again. "Then this should feel better."

As Ben thrust forward, Jane bent her head and licked the tip of Ben's penis. At the touch of her tongue, she heard him gasp and felt his cock jerk. He pulled back, holding still for a moment and then slowly thrust upward again. Jane again licked his cock. This time Ben didn't pull back and Jane ran her tongue around the head of Ben's penis.

Ben watched as Jane continued to use her tongue on his cock every time he thrust forward. He could see his cock glistening, could see her breasts growing wet as well as he moved against her, as she continued to push her round firm tits against his cock. He was starting to groan with each stroke, starting to increase his thrusts. He knew if he kept this up, he could easily come all over Jane's breasts and face.

As arousing as the image of his creamy cum coating her breasts and dripping onto the black satin was, he really wanted to make love to Jane, to have her feel as much pleasure as he was.

"Stop." He finally managed to get the word out. "I want to make love to you now, please." Jane looked up. She stood, sliding her body along Ben's, keeping contact with his cock.

He kissed her then, a hard passionate kiss. He gently lowered her to the bed, reaching down to slide her panties from her legs. Somewhere along the line she'd lost her pants and he'd taken off his shirt, but he really couldn't remember when.

Jane lay beneath him and he looked down at her beautiful body. He ran a hand down her stomach, watching as he slid it between her legs, over her pussy, feeling her heat and warmth. He looked up at Jane, leaning down to kiss her full lips.

"I'm ready for you, Ben. Please. I don't want to wait." Jane's voice was low, her words sending a wave of passion through him. He positioned himself between her legs, gently easing them apart, and guided his hard cock into her wet slit. He felt her opening up to him, felt her pussy taking his cock. He pushed into her slowly, enjoying the feeling of her soft warmth surrounding him.

Jane pushed against Ben, taking all of him into her, feeling him fill her up. She swiveled her hips back and forth, rubbing against him. He pulled back, pushing himself up with his arms so he could watch his cock entering her, watch her pussy accepting him. Jane watched Ben, saw the look of passion and love on his face. Seeing him so open caused a flush of emotions to run through her. She made a soft noise, almost a sob, in her throat.

Ben looked up at the sound, startled that she was crying. The look on her face was one of deep emotion, happy emotions. He pushed himself back into her, watching her face. "Are you okay?"

Jane nodded her head. "Yes, Ben. I'm way beyond okay." She smiled up at him. "I'm perfect."

Ben lowered himself to kiss her. Jane wrapped her arms around his neck, holding him to her as he began thrusting into her, moving faster, feeling their mutual passions build. He felt more than heard Jane gasp against him and sensed she was getting close. He broke their kiss and looked down at her.

"I'm so close, Ben." She was surprised by how quickly she was ready to come. "Make me come, Ben. I want to come now, with you inside me." She began thrusting up against him and Ben answered her thrusts, pushing himself into her more deeply, moving in rhythm with her.

Suddenly she arched against him with a sharp cry. Ben kept stroking into her, feeling her orgasm wash through her, marveling at the look of pure bliss on her face. He wished he could know what it felt like to be Jane when she had an orgasm. He slowed his thrusts as her orgasm faded, watching her face until she opened her eyes and smiled at him.

"Was that a good one?" Ben asked. Jane laughed. "With you, apparently they're all going to be good. It was rather sudden though." She pulled him to her, kissing him hard. "And now, it's your turn." She pushed him over, rolling on top of him, keeping him inside her. She straddled his hips, moving herself where she wanted to be and began sliding his cock in and out of her, setting a steady rhythm, taking him fully into her with each stroke.

He reached up to fondle her breasts, running his thumbs across the hard nipples. He could still see the damp trail left from his earlier adventures there; the image of his cock sliding between them and of watching Jane licking the head of his penis came flooding back, triggering the beginnings of his orgasm. He grabbed Jane's hips, pushing her down on his erection, thrusting up into her, seeking the pace that would get him off. Jane responded to his urgency, moving faster over him, letting him thrust as he needed into her.

When his orgasm hit, it shook Ben to his very core. He cried out, throwing his head back, his cock pushing upward into Jane, pulsing as it shot his hot cum into her. He thrust upward again and again, pumping more of his load into her pussy. Jane watched Ben in the throes of passion, unable to take her eyes from his face.

Ben's orgasm finally subsided, leaving him spent and satisfied. Jane slid off of him, lying beside him, gently putting one silky thigh over his cock. She snuggled into his shoulder, Ben wrapping his arms around her. After a few minutes, she spoke.

"So now we've initiated two pieces of furniture, my couch and your bed. What do you want to try next?" She looked up at Ben, a teasing glint in her eye.

Ben laughed. "Well, we could start on the kitchen next. I have a complete dining room set you know." He leaned down and kissed her. "And when we run out of what we own, we'll just go buy more."

7 THE STRENGTH OF LOVE

Mark Fanning had swept Emily Monroe off her feet, literally. The first time they met had been at a political fundraiser for Mark's brother, Paul. Emily was working with the catering staff, setting up the buffet line. She had run smack into Mark coming around the corner of the catering tent. The collision between his 6 foot 4 inch athletic body and her 5 foot 4 inch petite frame had sent her sprawling on the ground, Mark barely flinched at the impact.

Being a well-trained perfect gentleman, Mark had helped Emily up off the ground and set her on her feet. Emily was angry at this oaf for being where he shouldn't be at this event. Mark had been annoyed at someone getting in his way while he was looking for Paul. But both forgot their anger and annoyance, 2losing themselves in the current of electricity that ran between them. Neither had ever believed in love at first sight; both changed their minds after that day.

They were married two months later, much to Mark's mother's dismay. Estelle Fanning could not understand how her son could marry someone so common; the woman was a cook, for heaven's sake. She could barely manage to say Emily's name without making it sound like she had tasted curdled milk. Estelle had tried all avenues to find something to discredit Emily in Mark's eyes. She had worked hard for those two brief months before the wedding, employing private detectives to uncover some dirty secret about Emily or her family, but to no avail. All Estelle discovered was Emily's small town upbringing where her parents owned their own café for 25 years. Emily had gone to Le Cordon Bleu in Paris for her culinary training. Estelle was momentarily impressed by that. But she hired Paris-trained Le Cordon Bleu chefs, she did not sit down to dinner with them. And that was certainly not the caliber of woman to whom she wanted her son to be married. Fanning women may work, but they never served.

Emily and Mark were blissfully happy for their first year of married life. They had moved into the family compound outside of Houston, to one of the outlying guest cottages, again, to Estelle's annoyance. But they craved their privacy. They had discovered on their first night together, after the fundraiser that the chemistry between them sexually was beyond what either of them had expected. Mark was very surprised, but also very intrigued, by a sexually adventurous side of Emily. She was curious, willing to try new positions and techniques, and not afraid of employing a few toys either.

She had brought long red silk ties to their bed one night, tying Mark's hands and feet to the bed posts and requested firmly that he remain still. For Mark, who was usually the one in charge, being restrained and totally out of control of the situation, especially during sex, was a mind-blowing experience. Emily had done things to various parts of his body with her hands and tongue that he could never have imagined. Being powerless to touch her and to surrender completely to her ministrations had given him one of the most intense sexual experiences of his life. She had brought him to the edge repeatedly, leaving him in a heightened state of arousal for hours. His final orgasm had left him almost faint.

Emily loved being married to Mark, except for Estelle. She knew the woman did not approve of their marriage, but she had hoped Estelle would eventually accept the relationship and that her attitude would change, or at least mellow. But Estelle's remarks had become more cutting, her barbs sharper, and she had started turning the rest of the family against Emily. More alarming was that she had begun insinuating that Emily was having an affair. She was driving a wedge between Emily and Mark, and even though Mark knew in his heart Emily was devoted to him, the poison Estelle poured over the relationship began to erode away at his trust of Emily.

Emily was heartbroken when Mark, in one

angry outburst, accused her of having an affair. Emily sobbed as Mark left the guest cottage and went into the main house, apparently moving out and leaving her. She missed her husband, her lover, and her best friend. Now shunned by the rest of the family and isolated in the guest cottage, she accepted her parents' invitation to join them in Canada, where they were staying for the summer. She had quickly packed a bag and flown to a tiny town on the New Brunswick shore. Her parents had provided comfort and advice, and Emily came to the conclusion that there was really no future with Mark if he continued to believe Estelle's lies. She had left a note at the cottage with her new location, in the hope Mark would follow her, but he had not. She was convinced Estelle had finally won.

She had her remaining belongings packed and shipped, and settled into life in Canada. The Maiden Inn at the Shore was looking for a chef and was delighted to have Emily work with them. She began to feel she was getting her life back on track. As part of this new life, she found an attorney and initiated divorce proceedings. She had the papers sent to Mark and nervously waited for his reply, if he were to make any.

When Mark had gone to the family house, he thought it was short term, till he cooled off. But his mother had shown him convincing evidence that night that Emily was having an affair; there were pictures and a signed report from one of his mother's private detectives. The proof seemed valid. She advised him to remain at the main house. He could not imagine why Emily would have an affair; as much as she enjoyed sexual adventures, he didn't think she was planning on turning him into a cuckolded husband. He was deeply hurt and confused and blindly took his mother's advice.

When Mark received the divorce papers from Emily, he was stunned. He had no idea where Emily had gone, and it had driven him wild. He had returned to the guest cottage a few days after their fight, but had found her gone, with no indication where she was. His mother's private detectives said they had been unable to locate her. He was heartbroken. Shortly after that, a mover came and packed the rest of Emily's belongings, removing every last trace of her from the cottage. Estelle had told Mark the mover had only the address of a storage facility in Emily's home town as the destination for the belongings.

Mark found the name of the attorney on the envelope, located in a small town on the Atlantic Ocean in New Brunswick. He chartered a plane to the nearest airport, arriving the following morning. He had an idea to start looking for Emily at the most logical place she would be, a kitchen. The town boasted three inns. He picked the closest, The Maiden Inn, within walking distance of his hotel.

The Inn was a prominent building in the center of town. He walked through the lobby, turned into the dining room, and ran smack into Emily. She staggered backward, the tray in her hands clattering to the floor.

"Mark! What are you doing here?" Emily

was stunned to see Mark standing before her.

"I've come to find you. I've been looking for you and then I get divorce papers. You leave without a trace... what do you think... how could....." His voice had grown louder and several guests turned to watch. Mark was used to holding sway in a courtroom; he was a bit out of place in the dining room of a luxury inn.

"Mark, not here. Come on, we can use one of the unoccupied guest rooms to talk. There's no other place that's private." They left the dining room, Emily grabbing a room key from the front desk. She spoke briefly to someone behind the counter and motioned him up the stairs.

She opened the door to a luxurious room, dominated by a huge four-poster bed. Mark started talking before the door was even closed. "Emily, what is going on? Why did you leave without telling me? Why a divorce?" Emily closed the door and took a deep breath.

"Mark, you left me. You moved out of our home, into your mother's house. You never came back, never checked on me, and never called. What was I supposed to think? I left you a letter explaining where I was going, the address here in Canada with my parents. I left messages at the house, left messages at your office. But you never called, never came to find me." Emily was close to tears, but held them back.

"Emily, there were no letters or phone calls. I came back to the cottage after I cooled off, but you were gone. Mother said you'd left in the middle of the night. She'd gone to check...

she said she'd gone to check on one of the guest cottages, that there was a problem with a broken window... she said vandals... and when she checked ours, you were gone. She never said there was a letter for me. There were no phone messages; Janice at the office never gave me any messages."

"Mark, you do know Estelle is behind this, don't you?" Emily believed she knew the truth, knew the depths of Estelle's treachery. She didn't know if Mark understood how much Estelle really hated Emily or their marriage.

"Emily, I know my mother doesn't like you or approve of our marriage, but I don't know if I'm willing to believe she went so far as to make up you having an affair. I'll ask you once more: did you have an affair? Who is the guy in the pictures my mother showed me? Who else would you have been hugging and kissing outside of the Saint Jacques Hotel, and then gone inside with?"

"No, Mark, I did not have an affair. Do you really think I would have done that to you, to us? As far as hugging and kissing someone..." Realization dawned on Emily. "Did you say the Saint Jacques? Those photos were of me with Monsieur Jarre, from Paris, from the Cordon Bleu. He works at the Saint Jacques now and we had lunch. That was over six months ago. I thought I told you about him."

Emily could see a slowly dawning realization in Mark's eyes, along with a deep sadness. "Emily, maybe we've been... I've been foolish. Maybe my mother has worked to poison our marriage. I really don't know what to think anymore." Mark moved toward Emily, who had been standing stiffly with her back against the door. "But I do know that I love you and want you back home with me." Emily looked into Mark's eyes and realized he was starting to understand the lengths Estelle would go to in order to keep them apart. "Emily, I'm so sorry."

She moved into his arms, placing her head on his chest. She could feel his heart beating through his shirt. He tilted her chin up and looked in her eyes. "I'm so sorry," he repeated. He bent to kiss her, his lips soft on hers. She returned his kiss and felt the passion ignite. At least that hadn't diminished. Mark sensed this as well and deepened the kiss, probing her lips with his tongue. Emily reached her arms around his neck, stretching to kiss him more deeply.

Mark held Emily in his arms, felt her breasts caught between them and pulled her closer. His body remembered this feeling and he felt himself stiffen in response. He pulled her closer still, hands now on her back, moving down to cradle her ass in his hands. His body responded, his erection growing larger, pressing more urgently against Emily's firm stomach.

Emily felt Mark's erection and the passion in his kisses, and as excited as it made her, she had reservations about going any further. Her emotions were in a tangle and she hadn't had enough time to process this new development. But Mark's hands on her, pulling her closer to his body, fueled her need for more contact with him. Abandoning her better judgment, she gave in to the physical sensations washing over her and, to Mark's surprise, reached down and placed a warm palm on his burgeoning hard-on. She rubbed her hand over his hardness, feeling his cock move beneath her hand, hearing Mark's sharp intake of breath as he broke their kiss. "Emily..." he gasped. "Oh, God, I've wanted you for so long."

They ravished each other like wild animals, Emily shedding her chef's jacket, Mark pulling his shirt over his head. Emily made quick work of the zipper on Mark's pants, giving her access to his now fully erect penis. Before Mark could react, she knelt before him, taking the shaft of his cock in her hand and licking the slit in the tip of his penis with her tongue. Mark closed his eyes, his head back, a groan of pleasure coming from deep within him. Emily began working her tongue further down the crown, licking and nibbling as she moved his cock further into her mouth.

Emily looked up at Mark. "Watch me, Mark, watch what I'm doing." Mark opened his eyes as requested, looking down at Emily, seeing the head of his penis sliding past those luscious pink lips, into the soft cavern of her mouth, feeling her tongue surrounding him with warm wetness, her eyes never leaving his face. He wanted to thrust himself into her, to fuck her mouth, but he didn't want to take control just yet. He felt their reunion was too new, their truce too fragile. He held still, holding back, letting her have her way with him. Besides, letting Emily have her way usually resulted in some pretty fantastic experiences.

Emily worked Mark's rock hard cock further into her mouth, alternately sucking on it and thrusting it in and out of her mouth. She had learned early in their relationship that Mark really enjoyed oral sex; she also found great pleasure in sucking his cock. It made her hot and wet; the temptation, as always, was to touch herself while she pleasured Mark. But she knew from experience that holding back was also exciting. Besides, she was still wearing her pants.

Emily watched Mark closely; she knew when he was close to the edge, close to coming in her mouth. That wasn't her plan, so she gently removed him from her mouth, keeping her hand around the shaft of his wet hard rod. She stood then, Mark working the buttons and zipper on her pants, pulling them off of her, leaving her in her bra and panties.

Mark picked up Emily, his hands grabbing her backside, spreading her ass, slipping his fingers into the cleft of those perfect cheeks, feeling the heat of her with his hands. She wrapped her silky thighs around his hips, her arms around his neck. The silky feel of her panties, stretched across her wet pussy, sliding against his now extremely sensitive erection was almost more than he could stand, after having his cock so expertly sucked on by Emily. Her breasts were pressed against his chest, pushed up from her bra, the nipples hard and erect, pressing against the lacy fabric.

Mark carried her to the bed, putting her down on her back, laying himself down between those silky thighs. They kissed deeply, tongues playing in each other's mouths. Mark reached for one perfectly round breast, rubbing the nipple through the lace; Emily arched her back against Mark's hand, the rough sensation of the fabric against her rigid nipple was intense.

Mark was rubbing himself against her now, the friction of her panties making delicious heat spread across his cock. He sat back and knelt between her legs, reached down and ripped the panties, tearing them off of Emily's hips. He watched her eyes darken with passion; he knew as much as she liked being in control, she liked him to be forceful as well.

He looked down at her, at her wet pussy now visible as she lay beneath him. He thought there was no sight more beautiful than his wife, naked and ready for him. His hand had found his cock; he realized he was gently stroking himself, and Emily was watching him. He saw her reach down between her own legs, her fingers finding her clit, rubbing slow circles around it, sliding her index finger into her wet honey hole. They watched each other masturbate, each anticipating their coming together. Emily withdrew her finger and slowly slid it into her mouth, licking it with her tongue. This was Mark's undoing, spreading his knees and grabbing Emily by the hips, forcefully pulling her across the bed toward him and his waiting cock, a cock that was almost twitching in anticipation. He used his hand to guide his rod to the pink lips of her slit, her hand closing over his in eager anticipation. "Are you ready?" he asked.

"God, yes, Mark... I want you in me... I want you to make me come."

Mark hesitated a moment longer, looking into Emily's eyes, eyes that were almost begging him to thrust into her. He couldn't resist; he pushed into her, pounding into that hot, wet abyss. He heard Emily scream, matching her noises with his own sounds. He pulled back and thrust into her again and again; each time she took the full length of his cock into her, she felt as if he were reaching into her chest. Mark had a long, full cock; to Emily it seemed it had gotten even bigger since the last time they'd made love.

Mark continued his thrusts, pounding her hard, his balls slapping against her ass. They were making the bed creak. It occurred to him that their noises might draw some attention from the Inn's staff; he had completely forgotten where they were. Either Emily had the same thoughts, or she was very eager for an orgasm. He could feel the walls of her pussy tightening around him and she was thrusting her hips up to meet every stroke of his cock.

Mark shifted his position, changing the angle of his penetration and the effect on Emily was immediate. Her face grew flushed; she closed her eyes and arched her back, her body starting to shudder uncontrollably, her hips rising up, twisting and grinding her pussy against him. He watched in amazement as his wife had one of the most intense orgasms he'd ever witnessed. He momentarily forgot about his own imminent orgasm, thrusting once more into that hot hole, but not pulling back.

Seeing Emily totally lose herself to her own orgasm was intense: watching her breasts quiver, still contained in the lacy bra, the nipples thrust against the sheer lace. He felt her buck sharply against him, her hot juices flowing out of her, her hands clenching the bed covers, her whole body shaking with the force of her release.

Emily's orgasm took her totally away from her surroundings; she could feel her body wracked by intense and uncontrollable spasms, the center radiating out from some place deep inside her. She arched against Mark's cock buried inside her, the one point of contact with reality. She twisted against him, grinding herself on his shaft. She felt her insides turn to liquid, felt the hot rush of her orgasm spurt out of her. She heard herself scream, but could not stop.

Mark felt her intensity subsiding as his own peaked. He could not remain still any longer; he ground his hips against her wet pussy, feeling her juices running over his testicles. His balls were tensing, the pressure building; his cock felt like it was filling with molten liquid. He pulled back, and with a loud grunt, thrust quickly and violently into Emily once, twice, three times, feeling his cock explode then in his own orgasm, spurting hot cum into her, mixing with her own juices. He continued to push into her, each thrust accompanied by a guttural sound, each thrust releasing more hot juices into that now-pliant pussy.

Emily watched as Mark's own orgasm

overtook him. She loved watching him when he came. His athletic body grew tense, his hips tilting forward, thrusting his massive cock into her. If the angle was right, she could watch that cock as it pumped into her, could see the veins become engorged, the thrusts becoming faster and more intense. She almost came again watching him, seeing the muscles in his solar plexus contract as he shot his hot cum into her, feeling that liquid heat inside her body. She could see the creamy liquid coat his cock as he pulled back, his cock still pumping out his load.

Panting and finally spent, he looked down at Emily. A smile of satisfaction played over her face. He pulled his still-hard penis from her, rolling onto his side next to her on the bed. His cock was slick and wet, still twitching in spasms.

A knock on the door brought both of them to their feet. "Emily? Are you still in there?" a voice asked.

"Who's that?" Mark hissed.

"It's Patty, from the front desk. I told her I'd only be a minute. I thought we'd have only an angry argument, and you'd leave." Emily made a dive for her clothes, grabbing pants and jacket, but coming up empty-handed on underwear.

"Um, yes, Patty... I'm fine. We'll be down in a minute." Mark was trying to get his shirt on; it was still buttoned, but inside out. Emily saw him grab his one of his socks and stuff it in his pants pocket. She started to giggle, momentarily distracted from their plight.

"Stop laughing, this isn't funny," Mark

growled. He was very concerned about his image, but she doubted anyone in this tiny Canadian town knew, or cared, who Mark Fanning was.

"Sorry, it's just... well, your shirt is on inside out. This is like high school." Giggles still shook her slight body. "Look, no one knows you here, no one will care about you. It's me I need to worry about." She was dismayed at having to get dressed without her underwear.

"I'm going up to change, you go down and leave and then I'll return the key." Emily turned to straighten the bed. "Um, well... there's no hiding the evidence we were here." Emily pointed to the rumpled bed covers. Quite a large wet spot was clearly visible. "If you didn't have such large orgasms, this wouldn't have happened."

Mark looked at her sharply, but saw the teasing glint in her eye. "Yeah," he said, "Same goes for you, Emily." He planted a hearty kiss on her lips, and then bent to retrieve something from under the bed. "May I present you with your panties, my dear?" He bowed and held out the ruined silk panties to her. She made a grab for them, but he held them out of her reach.

"Hey, come on. We need to leave." Emily made one more attempt to but Mark held them higher. "No, I think I'll keep these. I may have a use for them." He stuffed them in his pocket, along with the other sock, and opened the door a crack.

"Coast is clear," he murmured. Mark turned to her. "You live here now?" She nodded. "I'll call you later. We can have dinner... somewhere other than the Maiden Inn."

"Okay. Now go." Emily pushed him out the door. She bolted up the stairs to the third floor to her room, grabbed a fresh pair of panties and clean pants and changed. She tore a comb through her hair, checked her face in the mirror and flew back down the stairs. She'd had no time to think about the consequences of what she'd just done. What she did need to do was get back to work and worry about Mark later.

Mark walked back to his hotel, his body relaxed from sex but his mind twisted with conflicting thoughts. He believed Emily now when she had said that she had not had an affair. He still could not completely believe that Estelle had done so much damage. There must be a logical explanation for all this that did not include all these Machiavellian dealings by his mother. He believed she always had his best interests at heart, but did not believe she would go to such lengths to drive Emily from his life.

Mark drove his rental car to pick up Emily at the Inn. They drove several miles down the coast to a small waterfront restaurant Emily was interested in trying. Mark asked questions about her work, what it was like living in a small town. She told him how much she enjoyed the Maiden's Inn; the pace suited her, and she was given free rein in the kitchen. She loved having fresh seafood to work with on a daily basis.

The evening was warm so they decided to take a walk down to the sea front. Both were strangely nervous with each other, tentative in bringing up certain subjects.

"Emily," Mark finally began. "Do you need to give notice at the Inn, give them time to find a replacement chef?"

"I'm not leaving the Inn," Emily replied. "Did you think I was going back to Texas with you?"

"Yes," said Mark. "Why would you stay? I thought now that we have everything cleared up, that there's no more misunderstanding, you'd come home with me."

"Mark, things may be clearer for you, but nothing's changed for me. Your mother still hates me, your family still shuns me, and I would have no different of a life in Texas now than I did before I left." Emily was amazed at Mark's belief that just because he had a clear picture of how his mother's interference had ruined her life, everything was somehow fixed.

"But you can't still want the divorce, can you?" Mark looked at her in disbelief.

"To be honest, Mark, I don't know what I want right now. I think it's too soon for me to make any decisions."

"But what about today, what happened between us. You can't deny that we're still amazing together, that we belong together. That should count for something." Mark was incredulous at Emily's attitude.

"Amazing sex has never been our problem, Mark. It's something else: it's a level of trust that's been broken. It's that you have always put your mother ahead of our marriage. Your mother is obviously an important person in your life, but she's driven a wedge between us and you were oblivious to all that was going on. You refused to see what was happening to us, to me." Emily had grown progressively angrier. They had stopped walking. Emily pulled her sweater closer to her shoulders, even though the night was warm. Her emotions had come to the surface, the force of them making her shiver.

"Mark, you can't expect me to undo the emotional impact of everything that's happened with one afternoon of sex, even fantastic sex. That's an unrealistic expectation."

"Emily, I'm not leaving without you." Mark planted his feet, facing Emily. He put his hands on her shoulders, shaking her. "You mean more to me than anything, but you have to understand that my mother is my mother. She has always been there for me. But, I'm not leaving without you," he repeated.

"Mark, let go of me, you're hurting me." Mark had dug his fingers into her shoulders. He let go, stepping away from her. He rubbed a hand across his face. "I'm sorry. This is all so frustrating."

"You can't just proclaim what you want and expect it to happen. I am not something you can force into place just because you want it to be." Emily turned away from Mark and started back down the sidewalk. "I'd like you to take me back to the Inn now."

They drove back to the Maiden Inn in silence. Mark opened the door for Emily. "I'll see you up to your room," he said.

"No, Mark. I don't think so. I need time to think."

"I'll call you tomorrow then," Mark said.

"No, Mark, don't. Listen, just let me have some space here. I'll call you in the next few days. Will you be staying or going back to Texas?"

"I said I'm not leaving without you. I'm staying here until you're ready to come home with me." By the stubborn set of his jaw, Emily knew Mark had made up his mind.

"Suit yourself. You know where I am and I know where you are. Enjoy yourself while you're here." Emily turned and walked up the stairs to the front door of the Inn. Mark watched her enter the Inn and disappear.

Emily spent the next few days deep in thought. Finally she came to some sort of decision and called Mark at his hotel. He answered on the first ring. She asked him to pick her up at the inn at five-thirty.

Mark was waiting outside the inn at five-fifteen. Emily came down the stairs and he opened the car door for her.

"You're early, although I didn't expect you'd be late." Emily reached up, kissing Mark's cheek.

"I needed to get out of that place. Estelle's been calling all afternoon, but I don't want to talk to her. She's been driving the hotel switchboard operator nuts with her insistence that she be put through to my room. Between her calling the hotel and my cell phone, I've spent most of my day avoiding her."

"Did you tell her where you were going?" Emily settled herself in the passenger seat.

"No, I didn't tell her where I was going. I left in a bit of a hurry. I'm sure though it would have taken her all of 10 minutes with her security team to locate me. I don't really care if she knows where I am. She's not the important issue right now. I don't want to talk about her, I want to talk about us. I want to hear what your decision is." Mark started the car, driving away from the Maiden Inn.

"Mark, I want you to listen to me. This has been one of the hardest decisions I've made. I don't want the divorce, but I am not coming home with you, at least not yet." Mark's expression reflected his disappointment.

"What can I do to change your mind? Tell me what I need to do to get you back home." Mark was almost pleading.

To Emily's dismay, Mark had driven them back to his hotel. "Come on up to my room and we can talk more."

"I'm not so sure that's a good idea, Mark. Let's go walk down by the water. Maybe after dinner." Emily led the way toward the waterfront. "It's a nice night for a walk."

They took the boardwalk down to the ocean. Mark held Emily's hand. "You're telling me you don't love me anymore, is that it Emily?" Mark's voice was soft, full of hurt and pain.

"Mark, I do still love you. I will never stop loving you. But back in Texas, I thought you had stopped loving me." Emily was near tears.

Mark stopped walking, pulling him into his arms. She broke down then, crying against the soft material of his shirt. "Emily, it's okay. It'll be okay. We'll make this work."

She looked up at him, and he brushed the tears from her cheeks. Her eyes reflected the moonlight, tears making them glow softly. Mark took her face in his hands, bending down to kiss her lips. He tasted the salt of her tears. He looked down at her, brushing the tears away. Emily sniffled.

"Mark, leaving Texas was the hardest thing I ever did. I felt abandoned and alone. But living with Estelle now would be impossible. Even if you realize just a tiny portion what she's done, the wedges she's driven into our relationship, you're always going to be influenced by her. She has power, not only as your mother but as a very powerful political figure. She could, and probably would, ruin your career. It may come down to you having to make a choice between her and me."

Mark looked stunned. "Is that what you think, Emily? That she's going to make me choose?"

"As much as it hurts me to tell you that Estelle knows no bounds in her dislike of me, yes. I would bet her phone calls to you today have been ultimatums: it's either her or me." Emily was quiet a moment, looking down at her hand in Mark's. "She's made those same calls to me today. The difference is, I answered the phone."

Emily looked up at Mark. "She's told me she would pay me off to disappear, that she'd give me a million dollars to stay in Canada, pay me to change my name and never make contact with you again."

Mark took a step away from Emily, dropping her hand. "You are kidding. Wait, no, you wouldn't kid about this." Mark ran his hands through his hair. "This is unbelievable. This is my mother we're talking about."

"I know, Mark. And it's a horrible thing to think. You'll have to take one of her calls to find out what she really wants, but I wouldn't be surprised by what she says."

Mark pulled out his cell phone, hitting speed dial and waiting a moment as the call went through. Emily saw his face darken and it was several moments before he even spoke.

"Mother, stop—you haven't let me even say hello. Stop talking for a minute." There was a pause. "Yes, I'm here with Emily." He looked at Emily; she could see the frustration and anger building in his eyes.

"Yes, you've already told me about Emily's affair. I've talked to Emily about that and I know the truth." Another pause. "No, I don't believe you. I believe her. She's my wife and I trust her word... Yes, you're my mother but... no, I don't believe you." Emily could hear a voice coming from Mark's cell phone as Estelle was apparently now yelling on her end.

"Mother. Estelle, you listen to me for a minute. What you're asking me and what you've asked of Emily is unacceptable. You cannot pay off Emily, you cannot blackmail her and you cannot order me to return." Mark took a deep breath, listening for a moment. Emily watched the color suddenly drain from Mark's face. She reached out and touched his arm. Mark looked at her, his mouth open in disbelief.

"You can't be serious, Mother. You're asking me to choose between you and my career, and Emily? You'd make your own son decide something like that?"

Mark was silent for a moment. "I made a decision when I married Emily that she was going to be part of my life. I'm not changing that decision now. If you're forcing me to choose, then it's the woman I'm married to." There were several moments of silence and then Mark's voice grew cold.

"No, Mother, you're making the mistake and you're the one who will regret this. I'm sorry it had to come down to this, but you've given me no choice. Goodbye."

Mark clicked his cell phone shut. He looked at Emily in stunned disbelief. "You were right." His voice was low and shaky. "She asked me to choose. How could she do that? What kind of mother asks her son to choose between his family and his wife?"

"She did and you have." Emily wrapped her arms around Mark. "And now you know the depth she'll go to in order to keep us apart." She reached up, kissing Mark. "And I think now you can take me back to your hotel room. I think both of us could use a stiff drink and a good fuck to clear our minds."

Mark laughed out loud. "Emily, you have a dirty mouth, and a dirty mind. But I think you're right. All I know is that I want you and you're here." He pulled her toward the front door of the hotel. "And I want you in my bed."

∞

"This is nice." Emily looked around Mark's hotel room. "I've never seen the guest rooms at this place before. I think we may need to make some changes at the Maiden."

"Emily, do you ever stop working?" Mark handed her a glass of scotch. Emily smiled.

"Old habit. Always checking out the competition." She took a sip of her drink and coughed. "Nice and smooth. Are you trying to get me drunk?" Emily set the glass on the bedside table, kicked off her shoes and threw herself across the bed.

"Sorry, it's all they had in the minibar. You did say you wanted a stiff drink though." He sat down next to Emily on the bed, swirling the ice in his glass. Emily reached out and touched his leg.

"You look seven ways sad, Mark. I'm so sorry this had to happen." Mark sighed, looking down at her, a sad smile playing around his mouth.

"Yeah, well, I have you and that's all that matters. It just hurts that she'd make me choose." Mark tossed back the rest of his drink, setting the glass on the floor. "But I want that good fuck you mentioned earlier."

Emily smiled up at Mark. "I'm all yours, always have been, always will be." Mark leaned down, covering her with his body, trailing kisses up her neck, flicking his tongue over her skin. He reached her ear, pulling the lobe into his mouth, sucking gently. Emily moaned softly beneath him.

Mark ran one hand over her flat stomach, up to her breast, cupping one in his hand. He ran his thumb over the nipple. "There's far too much material between my hand and your breast, Emily. I think we need to fix that." Emily smiled up at him.

"Same could be said for you. There are just entirely too many clothes on both of us." Emily sat up, fingers working the buttons on Mark's shirt as Mark tried to find the fastenings on Emily's dress.

"Emily, how the heck do you get out of this?" Emily laughed.

"Pull the tie at the back of my neck." She turned on the bed, her back to Mark. He pulled at the tie and the top of Emily's halter dress fell forward. Mark reached around Emily, cupping her breasts in his hands, kissing the back of her neck. Emily tilted her head, giving him access to her neck as he trailed a line of kisses down her bare shoulder.

"If you had no intention of sleeping with me, why did you wear a dress with such easy access and apparently no underwear?" Mark murmured against her neck. "I think you had something like this in mind all along."

"A girl can dream, can't she?" Emily turned to Mark, reaching up to kiss him, running her tongue over his lips, opening her mouth to his probing tongue. Mark's hands were still on her breasts, tweaking her nipples, pulling and rolling them between his fingers, sending waves of sensation coursing through her body. She shivered against him.

Emily ran her hand up the inside of Mark's thigh, not surprised to find his cock already hard, straining against his pants. He groaned softly as she rubbed the length of his erection with her warm hand. She felt him twitch against her hand.

"I've missed this so much, Emily. I've missed you." He looked down at her, watching his hands at her breasts. "You're so beautiful, Emily." He kissed her, searing her lips with his.

Emily worked the button and zipper of Mark's jeans, fumbling to free his cock from the confines of his clothes. She finally pushed him back on the bed, sitting up beside him, tugging down the zipper. His erection sprang free, even bigger than she remembered.

"Well, someone's happy to see me." She took his cock in her hand, gently stroking him, looking down at his massive cock in her small hand. "And I'd say by the lack of any underwear, you were looking to get lucky tonight too."

Mark shrugged, a lopsided grin on his face. "A guy can dream, can't he?" He lifted his hips, sliding his jeans down his legs. Emily pulled them free, dropping them to the floor. She undid the last of the buttons on his shirt, pulling it open, leaning down to kiss his muscular chest.

Emily moved to straddle Mark's hips, leaning forward to flick a tongue over his nipples, moving from one to the other. Mark's hands were in her hair as he groaned softly at her touch. He rocked his hips back and forth, trying to get some contact between Emily and his cock, but she held herself about him, just out of reach.

"Emily, no teasing me tonight. I want you. I

just want to feel myself buried in you, to connect with you. I just want a good fuck, okay?" Emily looked down. Mark's eyes were almost begging her.

Emily smiled down at him. "You want a good fuck, you've got it." Emily pulled her dress over her head, her hair crackling with static. She sat back, letting Mark guide his cock into her pussy with his hand, settling down on him slowly, letting him fill her completely. She looked down. Mark was looking up at her with something like awe in his face; it was almost like they were making love for the first time again.

"Oh, God, Emily." Mark's voice broke. "I've wanted this for so long. I've missed you so much." Emily realized Mark was close to tears. She leaned down, kissing him gently, letting his cock slide slowly out, holding him there, with just the crown of his cock inside of her.

"I've missed you too." She sat back, sliding him back into her wet pussy. As he filled her fully, she circled her hips, rubbing her pussy against his body. He groaned, placing his hands lightly on her hips, letting her set the pace. She pulled back again, repeating the motions, working his cock in different directions, sensually gyrating over him. She reached up to cup her breasts, working the nipples with her fingers. She knew Mark enjoyed a good show and she was determined to give him one.

Mark was rocking his hips forward in time with her movements, starting to circle his hips, matching her rhythm. Each time she came down on his cock, his movement brought her clit in contact with his body, sending waves of pleasure through her. She started moving faster, wanting more contact between her clit and his body, aching for that little button of flesh to be touched. She finally looked down at Mark with dark eyes.

"Mark, rub my clit, touch it please." Mark reached between her legs, finding her swollen clit, pulling the wetness from her pussy up and over it. He began rubbing it in slow circles with his fingers, in time to Emily's twists and thrusts, watching her every movement as she swiveled her hips and rode his cock.

Emily looked down at Mark, watching him watch her; it got her hot both watching and being watched. She ran her tongue over her lips, moaning softly.

"Is that what you wanted, baby? Does that feel good?" Mark's words were making her even hotter. She nodded her head.

"That feels incredible, you're making me so hot." Her voice was low and seductive. "Talk to me, Mark. Tell me what it feels like fucking me."

Mark grinned, a wicked glint in his eyes. "You really are a dirty girl today. I like this side of you. And fucking you is fantastic, feeling my cock..." Mark thrust up sharply into Emily. "... Inside you, filling your pussy..." Another thrust. "... Holding me... feeling how wet you are..." Mark growled out the words, picked up his speed, thrusting upward with every word. He was holding her hard now, moving her in time to his increasing thrust. Emily reached down and placed her hand where his had been, rubbing her clit with her own fingers. She saw Mark watching her rubbing and touching herself and heard him take in a sudden sharp breath.

Emily sensed he was building up to his orgasm and, as aroused as she was, she wanted him to come first, wanted him to take his pleasure. He was starting to grunt with each stroke, lips parted, eyes looking at her, every part of her, from her hand still clutching one breast to her fingers now frantically rubbing her clit. Her breath was coming in short gasps as she fought to hold back her own orgasm.

"Your cock feels so good in me, Mark. So hard... so big. It fills me up, stretches me, makes me wet. I want you to fuck me harder, Mark. Come for me, I want you to come inside me...."

Mark suddenly pulled her forward, bending his knees and bracing his feet on the bed, holding her to his chest. His hands ran almost frantically over her back and ass, trying to force his cock as far into her as he could, pushing her down as he rocked his hips up, thrusting into her pussy, moaning loudly with each thrust. Emily leaned down, her lips at his ear, gasping out words in time to his thrusts.

"Fuck me... Mark... come on... come for me... harder... I can feel your cock... harder..." Her words became incoherent moans and cries as her own orgasm began peaking.

Mark suddenly cried out, arching up with one massive thrust, his hands convulsively kneading her ass. Emily could feel his cock explode inside her, feel his hot cum flooding into her as he ground his hips up against her, almost crushing her against him as he held her. He held himself still then, every muscle straining, as his cock continued to throb and twitch inside her, pumping out what seemed like endless amounts of come.

She let go then, her orgasm ignited by the feel of his cock exploding inside her. She raised her ass slightly, holding it for the briefest moment and then slammed it down on Mark as her orgasm peaked, her juices squirting out onto both of them. She could hear noises coming from her mouth, garbled words and cries, could feel her body dissolve into a series of shudders and twitches as her orgasm took over her whole body. She felt Mark's arms around her, holding her, keeping her from sliding off of him as she continued violently shaking for what seemed like ages.

When Emily finally opened her eyes, she was lying next to Mark, who was holding her close to his chest, his cock now resting on her thigh, coated in their collective orgasmic fluids. Mark was looking down at her, an amused glint in his eyes.

"Welcome back to Earth, Emily. You okay?" Emily nodded her head, not sure her voice would work. "That was pretty incredible, for both of us. I don't think I've ever seen you have an orgasm quite so huge. You were speaking in tongues there for a while."

Emily smiled. "Yeah, well... you know what they say: Go big or go home. And since we're not going home, to Texas that is, I thought big would be the way to go."

Mark threw his head back, laughing. He

pulled Emily to his chest, kissing her forehead. "And I wouldn't have it any other way."